Praise for Brenda Novak

"This story should appeal to readers who like their romances with a sophisticated touch."
—*Library Journal* on *Snow Baby*

"Novak perfectly captures the feel of small-town life, and her powerful story of two lonely, fragile people who find another chance at love is a sweetly satisfying and richly rewarding romance."
—*Booklist* on *Stranger in Town*

Praise for Kathleen O'Brien

"If you're looking for a fabulous read, reach for a Kathleen O'Brien book. You can't go wrong."
Catherine Anderson, *New York Times* bestselling author

"[A] heartwarming tale about loss and learning to love again."
—*RT Book Reviews* on *Texas Trouble*

Praise for Karina Bliss

"It's a bit of a tearjerker toward the end, but the emotional aspects of it are well balanced with humor and strong dialogue. I can't recommend this book highly enough."
—*DearAuthor* on *What the Librarian Did*

"Bliss demonstrates a skill for snappy dialogue and clever plotting that will captivate readers."
—*RT Book Reviews* on *What the Librarian Did*

ABOUT THE AUTHORS

It was a shocking experience that jump-started **Brenda Novak**'s career as a bestselling author—she caught her day-care provider drugging her children to get them to sleep. That was when Brenda decided she needed to work from home. "When I first got the idea to become a novelist, it took me five years to teach myself the craft and finish my first book," Brenda says. But she sold that book almost immediately, and the rest is history. Her novels have received both critical acclaim and thousands of enthusiastic responses from readers. Brenda and her husband, Ted, live in Sacramento and are the proud parents of five children—three girls and two boys. When she's not spending time with her family or writing, Brenda is usually working on her annual fundraiser for diabetes research—an online auction held on her website (www.BrendaNovak.com) every May.

Kathleen O'Brien was a feature writer and a TV critic before marrying a fellow journalist. Motherhood, which followed soon after, was so marvelous she turned to writing novels, which could be done at home. She's an unapologetic sentimentalist, with an iPod full of corny music, a den full of three-hankie romances and an address book full of lifelong friends.

New Zealander **Karina Bliss** was the first Australasian to win one of the Romance Writers of America's coveted Golden Heart Awards for unpublished writers, and her 2006 Harlequin Superromance debut, *Mr. Imperfect,* won a Romantic Book of the Year award in Australia. It took this former journalist five years to get her first book contract—a process, she says, that helped put childbirth into perspective. She lives with her husband and son north of Auckland. Visit her on the web at www.KarinaBliss.com.

That Christmas Feeling

Brenda Novak
Kathleen O'Brien
Karina Bliss

TORONTO • NEW YORK • LONDON
AMSTERDAM • PARIS • SYDNEY • HAMBURG
STOCKHOLM • ATHENS • TOKYO • MILAN • MADRID
PRAGUE • WARSAW • BUDAPEST • AUCKLAND

ISBN-13: 978-0-373-78413-4

This edition published by arrangement with Harlequin Books S.A.

For questions and comments about the quality of this book please contact us at Customer_eCare@Harlequin.ca.

www.eHarlequin.com

Printed in U.S.A.

CONTENTS

Dear Reader,

Welcome back to Dundee! It's been a number of years since I've returned to this fictional place myself. But I've missed it. And I know many of you have, too. I receive a lot of requests from readers for more Dundee stories, so it was especially fun to write *A Dundee Christmas,* knowing many of you will be happy that I've added another story to the collection. I hope you enjoy seeing Kenny, who first appeared in *Stranger in Town,* as a grown man as much as I enjoyed providing the update.

I also write romantic-suspense novels. Three just came out—*White Heat, Body Heat* and *Killer Heat.* If you like this story and my other Harlequin Superromance books, you might want to give them a try.

I love to hear from my readers. Please feel free to contact me at www.brendanovak.com, where you can download free 3-D screen savers, view video trailers for my various romantic-suspense books, enter monthly prize drawings and check out other cool things. You can also sign up to participate in my next online auction for diabetes research. I hold this fundraiser every May in honor of my youngest son and the millions of others who suffer from this terrible disease. To date my auctions have raised over $1 million!

Merry Christmas,

Brenda Novak

A DUNDEE CHRISTMAS

Brenda Novak

To all those who have written to let me know how much they love my other Dundee stories:

1083—A BABY OF HER OWN
1130—A HUSBAND OF HER OWN
1195—A FAMILY OF HER OWN
1242—A HOME OF HER OWN
1278—STRANGER IN TOWN
1296—BIG GIRLS DON'T CRY
1344—THE OTHER WOMAN
1422—COULDA BEEN A COWBOY

CHAPTER ONE

WHEN THE RATTLETRAP truck crested the slight rise that showed Dundee, Idaho, looking stark and barren beneath several feet of snow, Cierra Romero nearly swore. She would have—those words were the easiest English to remember because she'd even heard them growing up in Guatemala—except she'd promised God that if He got her safely to this town, she'd leave all the bad habits she'd picked up behind. "Fu…dge! You gotta be freakin' kidding me!"

The farmer and his teenage son who'd brought her all the way from where her last ride had ended—a place called Boise—glanced at each other and started laughing.

Cierra lowered her eyelids but watched them as closely as she could without being obvious. She'd heard that expression a lot since coming to the States. Had she said it wrong? Or was it merely that they had never heard those words spoken with a Spanish accent?

She didn't know, but now that they were making fun of her, she was glad she hadn't bothered to listen when they'd given their names. Cierra made it a habit not to grow too familiar with people if she could help it. Especially white people. These men would drop her off in Dundee and go to whatever place they'd mentioned—the name had been unintelligible to her—and she'd never see them again.

It was better not to get attached. To anything. She'd even had to find a new home for the kitten Charlie had bought her when she arrived in Las Vegas—because all her dreams had died when he did, including her ability to take care of anyone or anything she loved. Maybe she'd never been fond of her American fiancé. She hadn't gotten to know him well enough for that. Almost fifty years her senior, he'd chosen her from a bride website, and although he'd brought her to the U.S. more than two months ago, he'd spent most of that time in his office, running his business.

Still, she mourned him. Maybe he was as perverted as some people—those who disapproved—claimed he was for wanting to marry someone so much younger. But he'd been kind to her and, with the money he'd sent, generous to the three younger sisters who were living on their own in a squalid flat back home, counting on her to provide for them. Too bad he'd had a stroke and died the day before the wedding. If he hadn't encountered some complications with finishing up his divorce, they would've been married right after she arrived, and she wouldn't be floating around America on an expired visa, hoping to find a way out of her desperate circumstances.

"Dundee ain't what you expected?" the farmer said.

Hadn't she already made that clear?

Remembering that she didn't want to upset anyone, that she was living in this country only by the grace of God and would be sent back to utter hopelessness if anyone turned her in, she averted her eyes to hide her flare of temper. She might be as feisty as any Latina princess—at least, that was what her parents used to tell her before malaria took them to their graves. But she knew she had to appear somewhat docile if she wanted to get along as a foreigner in such a small community. "It will be fine."

"But you don't even have a suitcase."

Because she'd had to leave it when she caught the man who'd given her a ride to Salt Lake City hiding behind the building the moment they stopped for gas, using his cell phone when he said he'd be in the restroom. Afraid he was calling to report her, she'd run off, abandoning her clothes, toiletrics and extra money, which were still locked in his trunk.

"Someone waits for me," she said, and desperately hoped that was true. Arlene, Charlie's ex-wife, hadn't been the nicest person in the world. She'd stepped in to handle the funeral arrangements and had eventually taken enough pity on Cierra to send her to work for some brother she hadn't seen in years, a brother who lived near this town of Dundee. But Arlene had been the most vocal about her objections to Charlie's plans—and the most unfriendly when Cierra first got to Las Vegas. Cierra had overheard her telling Charlie's neighbor that it wasn't fair he'd toss her out like an old shirt after she'd been with him for so long, just to indulge his pedophiliac fantasies. She said he was too old to father the baby he wanted, the baby she herself had never been able to give him, and that he didn't need to bring in such a young girl to do that, anyway. She said he was *marrying* a baby.

"Good. I'm glad you have someplace to go because

it's awfully cold," the farmer said. "You wouldn't want to spend much time in the snow. Skinny little thing like you would freeze right quick. This area's experiencing record lows, just in time for Christmas."

Christmas… She'd been expecting a ring, a cake, a warm, dry place to live—for the next few years, at least. It was supposed to be her best Christmas ever. She'd believed that for once in her life she'd have the money to buy presents.

But maybe what had happened served her right for being so reluctant, in her heart, to marry an old man, even for the sake of her sisters.

"What day is it?" she asked. She no longer knew. The days were beginning to blur together. It was difficult to think when she was so hungry….

"December 16," the farmer's son supplied.

The sixteenth? Really? That meant it was Los Posadas, the first of the nine days of candlelight processions in her country, where children and adults alike carried the statues of saints through the streets to reenact the Holy Family's quest for lodging in Bethlehem.

The farmer brought them to a shuddering stop in front of a drugstore. "This okay?"

Since she didn't yet know how to find Arlene's brother, one corner was as good as another, wasn't it?

"Fine. *Gracias, señor.*" Bracing for the cold, she offered them a polite smile and got out. But as she reached into her purse to retrieve the slip of paper Charlie's ex-wife had passed along to her, she realized that what she was doing wasn't so different from the reenactments going on at home. She had nothing but this address and a stranger's promise that she'd be given shelter. What she found when she actually arrived was anyone's guess.

"SOMEONE'S AT THE DOOR," Brent said. "I'd get it, but... I'm a little tied up here."

Ken Holbrook lifted his head. They were working in the area off the kitchen, which was next to the living room, but he hadn't heard anything. "I don't think so."

"You might want to check. Maybe Mom and Gabe came up, even though we told them to let us get the cabin out of mothballs first."

"No, they had other plans." If anyone was at the door, it was more likely their real father. Since Ken had returned to Dundee, Russ had been dogging his every step, doing his damnedest to talk him into yet another loan, which he called "an infusion of working capital," for whatever business he was starting next. "No one's here," Ken said, hoping it was true. "There's a storm watch on."

Scooting over to get to his toolbox, Brent dug around blind since he was lying on his back and still had his head partway inside the furnace. He retrieved his wrench, then froze at the sound of a light tap. "There it is again. I'm pretty sure that's a knock."

This time Ken heard it, too. Had Brent invited Russ to the cabin? It'd be like him. Brent didn't feel the same resentment toward their father that Ken did. He'd been in elementary school when Russ was busy screwing up their lives, which had somehow imbued him with more forgiveness. But Ken didn't ask Brent, didn't want to talk about Russ, because he knew it would lead to an argument. Russ was the only thing they ever argued about.

With the wind kicking up, Ken still held out hope that it wasn't a visitor, especially their father. "I'll see what's going on. Just get the damn furnace fixed."

Leaving the cardboard box he'd been unpacking, Ken strode into the living room and peered through the peephole Gabe had drilled in the front door when their mother married him and they came to stay in this cabin that first summer. They didn't have any heat, so Ken didn't plan on opening it if he didn't have to. It was already cold enough to see his breath. But the moment he saw a petite woman with long dark hair standing on the porch without a hat, boots or much of a coat, he yanked the door wide—and gaped at the zip-up sweatshirt she wore with blue jeans and snow-covered tennis shoes.

They had a visitor, all right. But it wasn't their father….

Angling his head, he scanned the drive for a vehicle.

Other than his own Land Rover, which he'd parked outside because there wasn't room in the garage, he couldn't see one. How had she gotten so far into the mountains without a car, and dressed like *that*? "Can I help you?" he said uncertainly.

Chocolate-dark eyes, framed with the longest lashes he'd ever seen, appealed to him from a café au lait face. She was somewhere in her mid-twenties, and she was pretty. *Really* pretty. It was like finding Salma Hayek on his doorstep. But he was fairly confident the lack of color in her lips wasn't a good thing.

"I—I'm Cierra," she said, rolling the *r*'s, and reached out to give him a piece of paper that'd been crushed in one hand. Before he could accept it, however, she swayed and would've fallen had he not let it go and caught her instead.

"Brent!"

A clang, and subsequent cursing, indicated that Brent had dropped his wrench. A few seconds later, Ken could hear his younger brother jogging toward him. Nothing Brent did was ever very subtle. He was only twenty-one and still in college, but he was bigger than Ken, although, at six feet two inches and two hundred and ten pounds, Ken had never been considered small—except, maybe, when analysts compared him to the front line in football.

While he held her, Cierra's eyelashes fluttered as though she was fighting for consciousness but, a second later, she lost that battle and her eyes drifted shut.

"What is it?" Brent asked, coming up from behind.

Ken turned to show him, and watched his brother's mouth fall open.

"Wow!" he breathed. "That's exactly what I wanted for Christmas. How'd you know?"

There was no time to acknowledge his joke. "Grab the purse she just dropped and fix a place to put her. I think she's suffering from hypothermia."

Brent dashed inside, just ahead of Ken, straight to the master bedroom, where Ken had left his bags when they arrived a few hours earlier, and peeled the plastic cover off the mattress. The cabin had been closed up for so long it had a musty odor, but that would go away once they aired out the place. At least covering the furniture had kept it from getting too dusty.

"That's good enough for now," Ken said so Brent wouldn't waste time trying to put on the sheets. "Take off her shoes."

"What about her jacket?"

"No, that's okay. It hasn't started snowing again, so just her feet are wet."

Brent removed her sneakers so Ken could put her on the bed. She was coming around. Moving her head from side to side, she muttered in Spanish. Then her eyes opened, and she gazed up at them with a sort of mute resignation that unsettled Ken. Wouldn't most women be frightened if they woke to the sight of two large men—total strangers—while sequestered in a remote cabin?

This girl didn't seem to be scared. But if heading back outside into the weather was her only other option, he could understand that. Or maybe she was even closer to death than he'd thought.

"We've got to get her warm." He grabbed the blankets they'd dumped at the foot of the bed and waved for Brent to lie down on one side of her while he lay down on the other. Sandwiching her between them with the bedding piled on top was the quickest way he could think of to raise her body temperature. At least her clothes were pretty dry. Otherwise, she probably wouldn't have lasted this long.

She didn't fight their proximity. Her eyes closed again and she remained perfectly still, cold as marble but malleable as a doll.

"She going to be okay?" Brent whispered after several minutes had passed and she hadn't spoken or moved.

Ken pressed two fingers to the side of her throat. "Heart's beating."

"That's good." Brent pulled back just enough to get a better look at her face. "Where do you think she came from?"

"Mexico."

"Quit being a smart-ass. I mean today."

"How should I know?" Ken responded with a chuckle. Because of the age difference between them, they'd never been especially close but that was changing. Ken couldn't wait until Brent graduated from Boise State. Already, they were talking about teaming up to run a series of football camps for kids in the summer.

After a short pause, Brent spoke again. "This seems a little weird."

Ken raised his head. "Having a beautiful woman appear out of nowhere?"

"Sleeping three to a bed…with *you*."

Ken might've laughed, but he couldn't. He was too busy gasping as their visitor not only moved but slipped her frozen fingers under his shirt and right up against his skin. Her teeth chattered as she attempted to burrow so close he got the impression she'd climb *inside* his skin if she could.

Brent arched his eyebrows, obviously demanding an explanation.

"I'd say she's doing better," Ken said when he could bring his voice down an octave.

This met with no small amount of suspicion on his brother's part. "*How* much better?"

"Don't get excited. She's figured out how, uh, to maximize the heat I'm offering, that's all."

Brent sounded sulky when he answered. "I'm offering heat, too."

Because she'd pulled away at his initial reaction, Ken covered her hands with his to let her know it was fine to take what she needed. He'd survived worse. "Yeah, but I'm always the lucky one."

"You're not supposed to get lucky. What about Isolde?" Brent challenged.

Fascinated by the number of women who congregated around professional athletes, his brother always asked about his love life. Brent had been cut from the college team and would never experience the NFL for himself, so Ken usually indulged him. But he didn't like talking about his former girlfriend. "I broke it off before I moved back here, and you know it."

"It's for good, then?"

Although Ken had spent two years with Isolde, even brought her to Dundee last Christmas, he'd given her up when he rejected the New York Jets' offer to renew his contract. She dreamed of a life in the Big Apple and had aspirations in fashion design; he dreamed of raising a family while owning several businesses in his hometown, including a dude ranch in the mountains he loved. He was even toying with the idea of helping their stepfather coach football at the high school he'd attended, which would feed into his summer camps with Brent. "It's over for good."

"No second thoughts?" Brent pressed.

Ken had a million of them. Not just about Isolde but about football. He preferred to leave the game while he was still at his best, to go out on top and with both knees functioning properly. But every once in a while, he wondered if he'd acted prematurely. Did he have another year or two left in him?

He'd watched quarterback Roger Liggett writhe on the field a year ago while the medics came running from the sidelines, only to learn Roger would never be able to play ball again. Maybe he'd let that spook him into quitting too soon.

"No second thoughts," he lied.

CHAPTER TWO

CIERRA'S FINGERS BURNED. So did her toes. When she was first carried into the cabin, she hadn't cared what happened to her as long as she was able to get warm. But once her body temperature began to rise, so did her ability to think. Now she realized she'd put herself in a very tenuous, and potentially dangerous, situation. There didn't seem to be anyone at the cabin except these two men….

"*Gracias*, I— We can get up now. I am…better," she said, but *better* was a relative term. She'd walked for hours in the cold, following the ribbon of road that was supposed to lead to the address on that paper. And she hadn't eaten since yesterday morning. Arlene had said her brother would provide work but Cierra had to make her own way to Dundee. She'd done that; in the process, she'd lost the little she had left of what Charlie had given her before his death and was down to…nothing.

The men shifted and sat up, allowing her to do the same. Hoping they might recognize the address she'd been looking for, so she could beat the worse of the storm that was already starting to batter the cabin walls, she dug through her pockets for the slip of paper that'd brought her this far. But she couldn't find it.

"*Mi papel*…my paper. Is gone!"

The older of the two, the man with brown hair and brown eyes, reminded Cierra of a cowboy she'd seen in a western Charlie had played for her one night. But not because of his clothes. Dressed in a sweatshirt and tattered blue jeans, he wasn't wearing cowboy boots or a hat. It was the way his hair lifted off his forehead and fell to the side, long on top but short everywhere else, and the contours of his lean face and body that suggested he could've stepped right out of *High Noon*—at least, she thought that was the name of the film. The movies she'd seen since coming to the States were beginning to run together. Charlie had played lots of them for her. He'd said they'd help with her English, reinforce what the tutor taught her during the day. But she knew he resorted to his movie collection when he didn't want the burden of entertaining her.

"That's what you tried to hand me, isn't it?" he said, and climbed off the bed as if he knew where it was and planned to get it.

Seemingly eager to reassure her, the man who remained in the bedroom smiled. "Where you from?"

Afraid to reveal the truth for fear it would result in a trip to the closest immigration office, she stuck with what she'd been telling everyone who'd given her a ride. "Las Vegas."

"That's pretty far from here," he said with a whistle. "How'd you get all the way to Idaho?"

"It is a...very long story. You do not want to hear," she added with a dismissive air meant to imply that it would only bore him.

He opened his mouth to argue, but she interrupted him with a question of her own. "You two—" she waved to indicate the man who'd left the room "—you are brothers, yes?"

"That's right. I'm Brent. He's Ken. What's your name?"

With strawberry blond hair and hazel eyes, Brent wasn't quite as handsome as his darker sibling. But since she rarely saw light-colored hair in Guatemala, she liked it a lot. "Cierra Romero."

The man he'd called Ken returned with the corners of his mouth tugged into a frown, but the memory of the tautly muscled stomach and chest she'd touched as she warmed her hands made Cierra feel a bit jittery inside—a sensation she'd never experienced before. Perhaps it was the hunger and the cold.

"I'm sorry. I can't find it," he said. "It must've blown away when you fainted."

But...she'd put all her faith in that note, which included a personal note for her new employer, as well as the address where she was to go.

In an effort to sustain this latest blow with some dignity, she covered her face but was simply too hungry and exhausted to stem the tears.

An uneasy silence fell as she cried. She understood that these Americans had no idea how to react to so much negative emotion. The poorest person she'd met in this country would've been rich as a king in her village, so she felt quite confident that these two men had never been through anything remotely similar to what she had. They'd never been unwanted visitors in a foreign country, had never slept in the street or begged ride after ride with strangers. And they certainly had no idea what it was like to go without food for days at a time. They probably thought she was crazy. Or a lowly beggar, trying to swindle them by playing on their sympathy.

But everything that had gone wrong since her parents died was her brother's fault. If he'd kept the family in Todos Santos, where they'd been raised, they might have had a chance of subsisting off the land, like everyone else. But no... He'd believed he could get rich by moving to the city.

Instead, he'd gotten into trouble and been sent to prison.

She wasn't her brother. So why was she humiliating herself in front of these Americans? Where was her pride? She would not represent her country or her family this way!

Wiping her cheeks, she blinked to keep more tears from spilling over her lashes and looked up at their stricken faces. "I—I apologize for interrupting your afternoon." She formed the words as precisely as she could, and got off the bed so she could put on her soaking shoes.

The two brothers exchanged a glance that seemed to say, *What do we do now?* Then the older one, the one she found attractive, came toward her. "What was so important about that note?"

"Nothing. Please, do not worry. I— It was my fault." If she hadn't gotten lost, this never would've happened. The last person she'd asked for directions had said to take a right at the fork in the road, but she'd never come across a fork, and she'd been walking all day. She must have missed it and needed to go back.

"A storm's moving in," Brent said as she tied her

shoes. "I don't think you want to go back out, not without warmer clothes. How did you get here?"

Wasn't it obvious? "I walked."

"From where?"

She looked up at him. "Dundee."

"No kidding? That's a *hike!*"

"If you could tell us where you're trying to go, we could take you," Ken volunteered. "I've got a four-wheel drive."

Of course he did. He had everything. Like every other American.

But that was her brother and his anger talking. Cierra didn't want to let Ricardo poison her mind, too. She was just so…scared. Since her parents died, nothing had been right.

"That was on the note," she said with a wry smile.

The one called Ken blew out a sigh and scratched his neck. "I see. And you can't remember the address?"

She told them as much as she could recall, but it didn't help.

"That fork you mentioned—that could be anywhere between here and Dundee," Ken said. "We'd need more information in order to find it."

Cierra couldn't give them more information. She remembered some of the numbers on the note but not the words. They were too foreign to her. The English tutor Charlie had hired had focused on teaching her to speak. Writing was supposed to come later.

No one knew there'd never be a later….

"Do you have any other options?" Brent asked.

Other *options?* She wasn't familiar with that particular word but the context helped her understand. She'd been right about these two. They had no sense of what it was like to live with no safety net. She was tempted to tell them her only other "option" was to go back to Guatemala City and sell herself on the streets. But she wasn't sure they'd believe her. And if they did, they'd pity her—or think she was a whore they could use themselves. Maybe she was breaking the law by staying in this country, but she'd come here legally. She hadn't *wanted* Charlie to die.

She had a right to survival, didn't she? She also had the right to protect her sisters from what they'd become if she couldn't send money….

Even if she didn't have that right, she would answer to God. Or the immigration office, if they caught her. Not these strangers who, by virtue of where they'd been born, were so much luckier than she.

"Yes, I do have another…option," she lied. "Thank you. I will go."

Ken and Brent followed her out of the room. "Can't we take you?" Ken asked.

She didn't have the strength to walk back to Dundee. And yet it was her best hope of finding an alternative position. Maybe she could be a maid, or a dishwasher, or a cook for one of the businesses she'd seen. Despite all the anti-immigration sentiment, Americans still hired illegals because they worked so cheap. And no one could cook as well as she could. Her brother had told her that a million times. "Yes, *por favor.* If you would be so kind. I will go to Dundee."

The good looking one, Ken, seemed vastly relieved that they'd found a solution. "No problem. Take this."

Grabbing a heavy coat from where it had been tossed over a stack of boxes, he shoved it at her.

She hesitated. "This belongs to you, no?"

"Yes, but I'm fine. I won't need it."

When she still made no move to accept the coat, he took her hand and insisted she grab hold. "We're not leaving until you put it on."

Thinking she could give it back when she got out of the truck, she did as he said. It hung on her, came almost to her knees, but she was so grateful for the added warmth she ducked her head to zip it up just so they wouldn't see the depth of her relief.

"Let's go before the storm gets any worse," Brent said, and she hitched her purse over one shoulder as Ken led them out through a garage that, like the cabin, was stuffed with boxes.

"You are moving away?" If so, he had a lot of belongings. What could possibly be inside so many boxes?

"Moving *in*. I just bought this place from my stepfather," Ken explained. "I'll be staying here until I decide where I really want to live."

"It is nice," she said, but her response was absent-minded. She was no longer thinking about the cabin or the boxes. She was thinking about Ken's scent on the coat and how it made her pulse race. But that was childish. He wasn't the movie star from *High Noon* she admired so much. He lived in a completely different world and, after he dropped her off, wouldn't give her a second thought. He didn't matter. The only thing that mattered was what she'd find once she reached Dundee.

It was getting late, almost dinnertime. The valley was already buried in snow. And—she looked up in the sky—more was on the way….

CHAPTER THREE

WITH SO MUCH SNOW hurtling down, it wasn't easy to get off the mountain, even in an SUV. Had Cierra attempted her walk from Dundee any later in the day, she would've frozen to death—and wouldn't have been found until the snow began to melt. Ken couldn't believe she'd survived so long as it was.

While he drove, she sat rigidly in the passenger seat.

Sensing his attention when he glanced at her, she offered him another of her formal smiles, the kind that hid every thought behind it. He and Brent had both tried to talk to her, but she either pretended not to understand the question or she answered in vague terms. After an hour in the car, time spent creeping around each hairpin turn, they knew no more about her than they had at the cabin.

"Where do you want me to drop you off?" he asked as they finally rolled into town. He'd decided he wouldn't worry about her. He had his hands full with Russ and the changes going on in his own life. And she wasn't his problem. They didn't even know her.

Nibbling at her lip, she eyed the buildings they passed until she noticed the drugstore. When she pointed half-heartedly, he had the impression that she'd picked a totally random location, which was crazy. Something or someone had brought her, or coaxed her, to Dundee. Surely she couldn't be as friendless and destitute as she seemed. As soon as her friend, or whoever she'd been hoping to see, realized she hadn't shown up, they'd come looking for her, and all would end well, right?

"Here?" He pulled to the curb.

"Sí. Gracias."

When she unzipped his coat, apparently to return it, he caught her arm. "No. Keep it. I insist."

"But…I have no…" Blushing furiously, she raised her hands as if to say she couldn't compensate him for it, but no way would he let her take off that coat. He wouldn't be able to sleep at night if he did.

"I don't want it. Really. It's extra. I was going to throw it away."

She stared at him. *"In the garbage?"*

The shock in her voice told him how wasteful she found that, but if it made her accept the damn coat, he didn't care about her opinion of him. "Right, in the garbage. You might as well take it."

With a brief nod, and a determined tilt of her chin, she got out and waved. When he didn't drive off as she expected, she lost some of her false confidence and stepped into the drugstore.

"What do you think?" Brent asked above the steady swish of the windshield wipers.

Letting the engine idle, Ken watched the entrance to the drugstore. "I don't think she knows a soul at the store or anywhere else in town."

"I don't, either. She's trying to make us believe she belongs here, but she doesn't. What's going on?"

Ken shoved a hand through his hair. "I wish I knew."

"Should we have offered her some money?"

He'd already considered that. "She wouldn't take it. She's nothing if not proud. Didn't you see how she reacted when I gave her the coat? She didn't even want to *borrow* it, let alone keep it."

Brent got out and climbed into the passenger seat. "So what can we do? It's not like we can tell her we were about to throw away our boots."

The thought of her feet in those wet shoes bothered Ken. So did the memory of that brief moment when she'd slipped her hands up his shirt and burrowed into him. She'd only been hoping for a few minutes of warmth, but a woman didn't take that kind of liberty with a strange man unless she was too young or naive to know better—or too desperate to care. And Cierra wasn't naive. Although he doubted she was quite as old as he was, she'd seen a lot of hard living. That much showed in her large, stunning eyes.

"There's nothing we can do," he said, trying to convince himself.

"And if we don't leave now, the roads could become impassable," Brent reminded him.

Giving the Land Rover some gas, he eased into the street. But he didn't get very far before his conscience dictated that he go back and do some more research.

When he drove around the block instead of heading up the canyon, Brent glanced over at him. "What are you doing?"

"I just want to see what she does next." Parking the

Land Rover where she wouldn't be able to spot it should she emerge from the store, he got out.

Brent climbed out, too, and jogged to catch up with him.

With Christmas lights adorning almost every building in town, from city hall to the bowling alley to Jerry's Diner, and a Salvation Army bell ringer outside Finley's Grocery down the street, Dundee hadn't changed much over the thirty Christmases Ken had been alive. His ex-girlfriend had found his hometown the epitome of dull and boring. She hated the close-knit community, hated the feeling that everyone was a little too eager to get involved in their business. But Dundee's Norman Rockwell charm appealed to Ken. This was home to him. He wanted to raise his children where they could see his mother, stepfather and brother. His real father wasn't as much of a draw but, with his heavy drinking, Russ would need someone to look out for him in a few years. He was already having liver problems. Ken figured that, as the eldest, caring for Russ would fall to him.

Before reaching the entrance to the drugstore, he grabbed Brent's arm and peered through the window.

Cierra stood in the candy aisle holding something she obviously hoped to purchase—a Snickers bar?—while counting out change in the palm of her hand. But she didn't seem to have enough money. She searched her purse, checked every pocket, even the pockets of his coat and the floor, but eventually put the candy bar back.

"Oh, God," he muttered.

"What's the matter?" Brent asked.

"Why didn't we feed her?"

"She's hungry?"

"Of course she's hungry." But he'd been too worried about getting her wherever she needed to go to think about food. Efficiency had taken precedence over humanity.

"It's not as if we have bags of groceries at the cabin," Brent was saying. "Just those steaks we were planning to grill tonight. Feeding her would've meant asking her to stay for dinner."

And, had they waited, the storm could've made leaving impossible. But…he hated knowing she couldn't buy *food*. How long was it since she'd eaten? Walking from Dundee to his cabin would take all day. Unless she'd carried a sack lunch, she hadn't eaten since early morning, if she'd eaten then.

"So…she's broke?" Brent said.

"That's my guess."

Cierra wandered around the aisles, probably hoping they'd be gone by the time she came out. Staying inside, where it was warm, beat wandering the streets, in any case. It wasn't as if she seemed to have anywhere to go….

Suddenly, her head jerked up and she looked over at the cash register. The clerk must have asked if there was anything he could help her find, and that was enough to drive her into the cold. She gave the candy section one final glance, pulled the hood of Ken's coat over her head and started for the exit.

"What are we going to do?" Brent asked.

"Feed her," Ken said, and left the window.

When she stepped outside and saw them coming

toward her, she turned the other direction. And when they followed her, she began to walk faster and faster until she broke into a run.

Afraid they were frightening her by chasing her down, Ken slowed and motioned for Brent to do the same. "Cierra!"

She turned. "Did you…did you want your coat?" she yelled above the wind as if she couldn't imagine any other reason they'd be following her. If he'd been wearing a jacket, she probably would've continued to hurry away.

Ken blinked the snowflakes out of his eyes. "No. We were…heading over to the diner to…get a bite to eat and thought…you might like to join us." He'd certainly never lacked for female companionship, but thanks to his football career, he'd always had the cards stacked in his favor. He couldn't remember meeting anyone, at least in Dundee, who didn't appreciate his background. So he wasn't sure how to handle this woman, who was so prickly and suspicious and unlikely to be impressed with what he'd achieved in professional sports.

"It has really good food," Brent added to entice her.

She was tempted. Ken could tell. But just when it seemed she'd agree to join them, she threw back her shoulders. "I am not a prostitute. I will no trade sex for money. Or…or food. Or coat."

"Oh, we don't expect that!" Brent said. "We only want to make sure you—"

Ken cut him off before he could put his foot in his mouth. Brent didn't understand that their help couldn't come across as a handout any more than it could come across as an attempt to get laid. "We're not asking for sexual favors. We were actually, ah, wondering if…" What could he have her do that she'd find acceptable? "If you could clean the cabin so I could get settled in." Now that they'd lost so much time driving her to town, they really could use an extra pair of hands. And it would be a fair trade. She'd work for what he gave her, which would keep her dignity intact. And she'd have food and shelter until he could figure out where the hell she was supposed to go, which would appease his conscience. "What do you say?" he asked.

"You are offering work for me?" she clarified.

The hope in her face put a guilty knot in his stomach. Even when his mother was primarily raising him and Brent on her own, with their father making life a lot more difficult than it needed to be, he'd never lacked the necessities. "Yes. In exchange for food and shelter."

"I clean. You will see no one speck of dirt," she assured him.

He managed a smile. He had no doubt she'd take as much pride in her work as everything else. "Great. That's what I'm looking for. Do we have a deal?"

When her gaze strayed to the diner down the street, he felt a fresh pang of remorse for not giving her a bite to eat at the cabin.

"*Sí.* A deal," she said. Then she thrust out her hand to shake on it.

CHAPTER FOUR

TWO WOMEN WHO ARRIVED after they were seated kept staring at the three of them while they ate, but Cierra didn't care. She was too hungry to be distracted. She'd never had a meal, not in America, that tasted better than the meat loaf and mashed potatoes she'd been served. And just when she'd finished everything on her plate, Ken decided he couldn't eat all his steak. He'd said it would go to waste if she couldn't eat it for him, so she'd polished that off, too.

His actions proved how spoiled he was. Who ordered an expensive entrée and ate only a few bites of it? Brent had no trouble downing his lasagna. Like her, he seemed to be hungry.

But she didn't mind saving Ken's meal from the trash. She could've eaten *five* steaks. Or...maybe not *five*. By the time she'd swallowed the last bite, she actually felt full, but was able to make room for the banana cream pie Ken ordered for dessert.

It wasn't until Cierra had scraped every delicious crumb off her plate that she realized she'd eaten her pie even faster than Brent had eaten his. Self-conscious again, she lifted her gaze to find Ken watching her, his fork dangling halfway between his mouth and his plate, only a small portion of his pie gone.

"What? It is no good for you?" she said to cover her breach in etiquette. Throughout dinner she'd been careful to eat slowly and calmly, as a lady should, but when the pie arrived she'd grown sleepy and relaxed and wound up embarrassing herself.

"No." He pushed it toward her. "Go ahead."

She picked up her fork—then imagined how she must've looked shoveling that pie into her mouth a moment earlier. "I am…satisfied. Thank you." Pushing it away, she put her fork back on the table with a determined *clink*.

"It'll go to waste if you don't eat it," he threatened.

He said that about everything, and she was beginning to understand why. "Like the steak?"

"Like the steak."

"And the coat?"

He shrugged.

"Do you always throw away good clothes and food?"

"Easy come, easy go," he mumbled.

She probably would've given in, despite her fear of looking like a pig, but Brent spoke up before she could respond. "I'll eat it," he said, then yelped. Cierra guessed his brother had just kicked him under the table.

"Or…actually, no," he said. "I'm stuffed. You have it."

Cierra studied Ken, then Brent. Brent reminded her of the dog she'd had as a child. He was big and kindhearted, but a little goofy and oblivious to nuance. He had nothing to fear, no reason to be wary, because the world had always been a safe place for him. That was probably true of Ken, too, and yet…Ken noticed things.

He'd given her his coat because she needed it, just as he'd had her eat his meal because he knew she was still hungry.

She'd have to be careful around him, watch her every word, every move, or he'd soon know far too much about her business.

"Please, let him eat," she said, deferring to Brent.

"Fine," Ken responded, and she smiled as she moved the pie over to Brent, who ate it with the same gusto with which he'd eaten everything else. Meanwhile, Ken took a plastic card from his wallet and reached for the bill.

"How much?" Cierra asked.

His eyebrows slid up in question.

"Dinero?" She held one hand to her chest. "For me?"

"Doesn't matter. You'll work it off, remember? I've got it."

"I just…need to know." How could she make sure she kept her end of the bargain if she didn't know how much she owed him?

He waved away her concern. "Don't worry about it."

She was about to insist he tell her when the two women she'd noticed earlier walked over. One, a blonde at least five inches taller than Cierra, was the prettiest white woman she'd ever seen. The other, a curvy brunette much closer to her own five foot three, was almost as pretty.

"Ken, it's so great to see you again," the blonde crooned as they embraced.

"It's been a long time," he responded. "How've you been, Tiff?"

"Fine. Busy with my new flower shop. And you?"

"I'm in transition right now, but…hanging in."

Eyes filled with avid curiosity, "Tiff" looked at Cierra, then flashed a brief smile at Brent before returning her attention to Ken. "Are you home for the holidays or…"

"I'm home for good."

"Really? When did that happen?"

Cierra was so taken with this woman's light eyes and hair, she didn't immediately notice that Brent seemed equally impressed with her beauty. He couldn't stop fidgeting. He put his hands in his pockets, took them out again, shifted his weight from one foot to the other, tugged on the bottom of his shirt….

"Just this week."

Cierra knew that these women found Ken as attractive as she did. *Any* woman would. Again, she remembered the feel of his smooth skin against her cold hands, the solidity of his body, and felt an uncharacteristic twinge of jealousy…

"Where've you been staying?" she asked.

"My parents' house."

A crease marred her otherwise smooth forehead. "Not Russ's…"

"No, he and Roxanne have split up again. I've been at Mom and Gabe's. But I'm moving into Gabe's old cabin today."

She gestured at the snow coming down outside. "If you plan on going up the canyon, I hope you have four-wheel drive."

This woman was obviously quite familiar with Ken and his family. Was she his girlfriend? She couldn't be, or she would've known he was coming back to town. But they had *some* history. Cierra could sense it.

"I've got a Land Rover," Ken was saying. "Hopefully, we'll make it."

"Tiff" finally bestowed a polite smile on her, but Cierra got the feeling she'd been leading up to her next question the whole time. "And who is this?"

After Ken cleared his throat, he made a formal introduction. "This is Cierra. Cierra, Tiffany Wheeler and Stephanie Jernigan."

Stephanie nodded and smiled but it was Tiffany who continued to speak. "Cierra what?"

Assuming Ken had forgotten her last name—she didn't even know his—Cierra filled in the blank. "Romero." Then, feeling woefully inadequate and homely by comparison to these sparkling creatures, especially in her damp and dirty clothes, she added, "It is a pleasure to meet you," in formal English, just as she'd rehearsed with her tutor.

The crease in Tiffany's forehead deepened. Cierra's response had somehow confused her. "Likewise," she said. "So…where are you from?"

The question elicited a pang of homesickness, probably because Cierra couldn't even say her village's name. She had to call the place where she'd been living with Charlie Spanos *home*—a sprawling metropolis she considered brown and ugly by comparison. The colorful lights that glittered at night served as its only redeeming feature. She'd liked it when Charlie drove her down what he'd called "the Strip." "Las Vegas."

Tiffany turned to Ken. "Is that where you met?"

Cierra became conscious of the fact that she was wearing Ken's coat. Because it hung past her fingers and went down to her knees, and Brent was wearing his own coat, Tiffany would be unlikely to mistake its real owner. Cierra almost removed it and handed it back. She suddenly felt she was in the way of something happening, something she didn't understand, and didn't want to be. But it was too late. Returning Ken's coat would only make wearing it seem more significant.

"No," Ken said. "I…I have a friend who…recommended her to me, as a housekeeper."

Cierra wasn't sure why he'd lied, but she was grateful he hadn't embarrassed her by telling these women that she'd fainted on his doorstep.

"I see." Tiffany leaned toward her and lowered her voice conspiratorially. "Well…good luck with that. I hope he picks up after himself better than he did in high school." Straightening, she gave them all a charming smile. "I've got to get back to the shop. Brent, you're looking good, as always. Ken, call me when you get the chance."

"Sure," he said. "Nice seeing you."

They basked in the wake of her perfume for several seconds after she'd left. Then Brent seemed to snap out of his earlier hypnosis. "Man, she's gorgeous! Are you going to ask her out again or what?"

That flicker of jealousy bothered Cierra again—inexplicably—but Ken didn't answer. He walked over to the cash register and paid their bill. Then he waved them out ahead of him. But Brent kept talking. "I'm still not sure why you two ever broke up," he said. "You were so in love with her. Even Mom thought you were perfect for each other."

Ken pressed some button that unlocked the Land Rover. "I wasn't ready for marriage, and it didn't seem right to string her along if we weren't going to make the big commitment."

"She's had plenty of opportunities to get married since then and she hasn't," Brent said. "Word is she's been waiting for you."

"You're not the first person to tell me that," he said. "Get in."

They were climbing in when a big red truck stopped beside them.

"It's Gabe," Brent said.

Ken lowered his window and so did the driver of the truck. Although older, in his fifties, Gabe was a startlingly handsome man. Other than a touch of gray at the temples, he had hair that was even darker than Cierra's—black—but his eyes were as blue as Tiffany's.

"What's up?" Ken had to shout over the wind and the engine noise of both vehicles.

"Your mother sent me to the store," Gabe hollered back. "She didn't want to come out in this mess."

"Sure is ugly," Ken acknowledged.

Gabe shielded his face with one hand. "I thought you were at the cabin, getting moved in. What are you doing in town?"

"Errands."

Cierra saw a wheelchair fastened to the side of the truck but was distracted when she realized Gabe had spotted her—and was looking at her curiously.

"Where's Brent?" he asked.

Ken jerked a thumb over his shoulder. "In back."

"Here, Gabe," Brent called, and stuck his arm between the seats to wave.

"Hey." Gabe waved in response, but the way he used the handholds above him to adjust his position afterward suggested he was crippled, as Cierra had begun to suspect.

"Then, who is..."

Ken leaned back to accommodate his stepfather's attempt to get a better look at her. "Dad, meet my housekeeper, Cierra Romero."

Gabe's eyebrows shot up. "Did you say *housekeeper?*"

"Yep."

"I see. But...you've never mentioned a housekeeper. She from around here?"

"At this point, we're not sure where she's from, how she got here or where she belongs," he called back.

Cierra hadn't been expecting that. "I am from Las Vegas," she piped up, but she doubted Gabe could hear her and Ken didn't pass the information along.

Slinging an arm over the steering wheel, Ken eyed her skeptically. "Is that right?"

"Sí." She nodded. "Like I told you."

He suddenly seemed more interested in her than in Gabe. "And what state is Las Vegas in, Cierra?"

His question took her by surprise. "You...don't know?"

"I'm wondering if you can tell me."

No one had ever asked her that before. Everyone knew what she meant when she said Las Vegas. Sometimes they even dropped the "Las." *How did you like*

Vegas...? There's no place like Vegas.... What happens in Vegas stays in Vegas, huh?

"Ken..." Brent started to say, as if he'd help her, but Ken motioned for him to remain silent. "You know what *state* means, don't you?"

"Sí." States were similar to "departments" in her country, weren't they? But she'd never heard the city Charlie lived in connected with any other name. So maybe Ken was trying to trick her. "Vegas is in...Vegas," she said.

"That's the state as well as the city?"

Her answer sounded plausible, and not too different from Guatemala City, Guatemala, where her sisters were living and waiting for her to send more money. "Yes."

Rolling his eyes, he turned back to his stepfather. "See what I mean?"

"What did you say?" Gabe shouted. The storm was too loud. He'd missed it all.

"She doesn't quite have her story straight," Ken said. "But we'll figure out where she belongs."

CHAPTER FIVE

SEE WHAT I MEAN?

She'd answered wrong, given herself away. The fear that mistake created hung over every move Cierra made for the rest of the evening and the whole of the next day. But she kept a running tally of her debts to her new employer. By midafternoon, she owed Ken Holbrook—he'd finally told her his last name—for three meals, the coat, shelter from the storm and a bed. She also owed him for the toothbrush, toothpaste, shampoo and soap he'd had Brent deliver to her bathroom last night.

It felt so good to have a few simple belongings, to be able to bathe and wash her clothes and brush her teeth. She was deeply grateful and determined to be fair. She'd stay and work, as promised, until he got settled in but no longer. At that point, he wouldn't have enough chores for her to do. And as soon as he tired of her, he'd call the INS, if only because he didn't know what else to do, and she'd be sent back to Guatemala, where she and her sisters would be turned in to the street.

Fortunately Cierra managed not to think about that too much, especially since every thought she had seemed to revolve around the way Ken looked or smelled or laughed. She knew she had no chance of attracting him—she was so different from those women they'd met at the diner—but she was equally certain that she was quickly becoming infatuated with him. *Stupido!* He'd barely acknowledged her today. She needed to be thinking about how she was going to care for Chantico, Nelli and Xoco instead of daydreaming about the minutes she'd been pressed up against him on that bed yesterday. Her problems would not solve themselves. Even her brother hadn't been able to provide for the family, not until he'd started augmenting his income with drug money. And without a man to work in the fields, there was no going back to Todos Santos. So, legal or not, she had to make her immigration to America succeed, had to earn money wherever it was possible to earn money and send some of her wages to Guatemala. A little went a long way there. If she could stop mooning over this handsome American, get on her feet and find steady work, they should all be able to survive—

"Something wrong?"

She blinked. Ken had come to the door of the kitchen and caught her staring off into space. After the past few weeks of grabbing sleep and food whenever and wherever she could, and often going without one or both, her strength wasn't what it used to be. But she went back to polishing the hardwood floor so he wouldn't think she was lazy. "No, *nada*."

Wearing a pair of faded jeans that rode low on his hips and a T-shirt that stretched across his broad chest, he seemed even taller than usual from her vantage point on the floor. Although he'd been working for much of the day, moving boxes around, unpacking, building shelves in the garage, he'd recently showered. Damp tendrils of hair fell against his forehead, and he smelled like the wood he'd used to start a fire. Brent had fixed the furnace, but they'd decided to light a fire for the effect. Cierra liked it, thought it made the place cozier.

"Cierra," he said as he came toward her.

She rocked back on her haunches. Today, he'd ignored her or had Brent deal with her. Ever since she hadn't been able to name the state that went with Las Vegas, she'd gotten the impression he didn't like her. So why was he suddenly showing interest? Did he think she was slacking or doing the floor wrong? "Yes?"

"It's time to stop."

"Stop?" She couldn't stop; she wasn't finished yet.

"Right. Except for a few hours' sleep, you've been working every minute since we got home last night. This place is coming together in record time. It looks good. That's enough for one day, okay? Take a break."

Was he getting impatient for dinner? She'd asked Brent to buy a few things at the store so she could make empanadas, and he'd left for town. But, as far as she knew, he wasn't back.

"*Sí. Un momento.* I am almost finish."

When she resumed polishing, he squatted next to her. "*Finish tomorrow.* Got it?"

"Brent, he is here?" She couldn't figure out any other reason that letting her continue her work would bother him.

"Not yet."

"Then…why can I not clean?"

He touched her hand. "Because I want to watch a game, and you're making me feel guilty. So…go to your room and…relax. Do something else. Get in the Jacuzzi. Read a book. Whatever."

She set her rag aside, as if she planned to do as he asked, but the moment he walked out and the television went on, she returned to her work. She thought he'd be completely engrossed, that he'd forget about her, the way Charlie used to. But he was back a few minutes later.

"What are you doing?" he demanded.

This time she couldn't meet his eyes. She'd flagrantly disobeyed his orders, and now he was angry.

"Cierra?"

Jumping to her feet, she grabbed her rag and the polish and tried to squeeze past him to go to her room, as he'd requested, but he stepped in front of her, blocking the way.

Assuming he expected an apology or an explanation, she scrambled to offer one. "I—I am sorry. I just want…perfect." She gave him a hopeful smile. "You *comprende?*"

He stared at her until her smile wilted and her cheeks began to burn. She'd used a pencil to put up her hair so she could keep it out of her way while she worked. Maybe he thought she'd been presumptuous in taking it from his kitchen drawer without asking.

Pulling it from her hair, she held it out to him. "Is this it? Is this why you are angry?"

"I'm not angry. And why would I care about a pencil?"

When she had no answer, he shook his head and his gaze lowered to her clothes.

Painfully aware that they didn't fit her very well, especially since she'd lost weight, Cierra bent to dust the dirt off her knees. "I will wash up," she promised.

Taking her hand, he put back the pencil and closed

her fingers around it. "You deserve better," he said gruffly, and walked to the living room.

THE CABIN SMELLED FANTASTIC, so fantastic Ken couldn't concentrate on the game. Tony Romo was launching a pretty convincing attack against his former teammates, and yet he cared more about what was going on in the kitchen. And Brent seemed just as restless.

"Hey, can you quit it?" Ken asked. "I'm trying to watch the game."

Looking at the football he'd been tossing back and forth as if he hadn't even realized he was doing it, Brent threw it aside and Ken tried once again to focus on the drive the Cowboys were putting together. They'd already marched down the field to the thirty-yard line; a field goal could win the game. But it was no use. Inevitably, his thoughts wandered back to Cierra.

"Do you think she's okay in there?" Clearly Brent was preoccupied with the same thing. It'd taken Cierra all of twenty-four hours to win his undying loyalty. But Brent was an easy sell. He always had been. He was Russ's biggest champion, wasn't he? The only person Russ hadn't chased away over the years.

"She's fine," Ken said. And it was true—at least while she was here. But how long could he look out for her? She wasn't like a stray dog. He couldn't keep her forever. What would happen when he ran out of work for her to do? And how come she was wandering around the mountains of Idaho, penniless and homeless, in the first place?

She was proud, beautiful, capable. It didn't make sense that a woman like that couldn't provide for herself…

somehow, even if she was an illegal alien. Heck, she could find a man to take care of her if she wanted. What had brought her to America on her own? Had she gotten involved in drugs and wound up homeless? Been tossed out on the street by an abusive husband or father who'd enticed her here? Been kidnapped in Mexico, smuggled into the States and sold into sexual slavery, from which she'd recently escaped?

He recalled her bold assertion that she was no prostitute. He couldn't imagine a former sex slave coming up with that. But she didn't seem the type to do drugs—or smuggle them, either.

The wind whistled through the eaves. Brent must've heard it, too, because he gazed toward the picture window, which looked out onto the front porch. "Another storm's coming in."

"I can hear it." The impatience in his tone surprised him. But he didn't want to talk about the weather. He didn't want to talk at all. "Are you watching this game with me or what?"

Obviously offended by the sharpness of his words, Brent glared at him. "I'm sitting here with you, aren't I?"

That hardly answered his question, but he had no right to take his bad mood out on his little brother. He wasn't even sure what had made him so irritable.

Blowing out a sigh, Ken got to his feet. "Right. Yeah. Forget it. I'm just pissed that the Jets are losing. Want a beer?"

Reluctant to forgive him that easily, Brent shrugged. "I guess."

"I'll grab one," he said, and escaped to the kitchen.

Cierra had stopped cleaning, but she was cooking. She'd nearly died from hypothermia yesterday, yet he couldn't get her to rest. She insisted that she "owed" him so many hours, as if it'd cost him a huge amount to give her a few meals and a place to stay.

She had her back to him when he entered the room. Apparently, she hadn't heard his approach, which gave him a second to watch her. She was tired, as he'd guessed. She'd dragged a chair over to the stove so she could sit in between stirring whatever she'd put on the burner, and she kept rubbing her temples as if she had a headache.

The floor creaked beneath his weight and she tried to hide her fatigue by jumping to her feet and shoving the chair back under the table. "You are hungry, yes? It is almost finish." She spoke with more cheer than she could possibly feel, considering her fatigue and the headache.

He walked over to peek into the frying pan, which contained ground beef mixed with onions, eggs and other things he didn't immediately recognize. "Smells good."

"Empanadas. You have tried?"

"No."

"You will like. Soon you will eat."

Going to the cabinet, where he'd lined up his vitamins, supplements and protein powder only a few hours earlier, he found the Tylenol and shook a couple of tablets into his hand. Following a particularly rough football game, he took four to help with the aches and pains. But she weighed half of what he did.

Together with a glass of water, he handed them to her. "Swallow these. They'll stop your headache."

"Oh. *Sí.* Ouch." She tapped her skull with one finger and smiled to let him know she understood and appreciated the kindness. *"Gracias."*

He'd come in to ask her to level with him, to tell him exactly where she was from and what had brought her to Dundee. But knowing her situation would create a commitment of sorts, which was why he hadn't insisted on the truth so far. Why get any more involved than he already was? If she was an illegal alien, as he suspected, he'd have a duty to report her. But he didn't want to do that. It was Christmastime, for crying out loud. And maybe there was a good reason she'd left her own country. He didn't want to judge.

"Better," she said, even though the painkiller couldn't have worked yet, and put the glass in the dishwasher.

"Right. Everything's fine with you, perfect." If she could convince him of that maybe he wouldn't ask questions. Was that what she thought?

He knew she'd correctly interpreted his tone when a hint of wariness entered her eyes. But that only heightened his curiosity. Why was she so cautious, so secretive about her past? What was she afraid of? Deportation? Or was it something worse? He couldn't say, but she definitely didn't believe she could trust anyone—including him. "*Sí.* I am fine," she said stiffly.

This was getting him nowhere. He couldn't even decide how hard he should push her, which added to his frustration.

Heading to the fridge, he got the cold beer he'd promised Brent, but didn't return to the living room. His new housekeeper wasn't someone life had chewed up and spit out. No doubt she'd hit a rough patch, but she didn't fit the drug addict/sex slave scenarios he'd concocted. She wasn't crazy or emotionally broken or undesirable. Just the opposite seemed true. So *why* was she in her current predicament?

"Cierra?"

No answer. She'd gone back to stirring the food as if it required all of her attention.

"*Cierra,*" he repeated.

She didn't face him, but at least she responded. "Yes?"

"Look at me."

Setting the lid on the pan, she turned but there was no mistaking her reluctance to confront him. "Soon, you will eat."

Another attempt at diversion. She knew he hadn't been about to ask for dinner. "Someone, somewhere, must be looking for you," he said.

Her knuckles whitened on the spatula in her hand but she shook her head. "No. No one."

"That can't be true."

"Why not?"

He stepped closer, couldn't help testing her. She'd certainly kept to herself and out of his way so far. But she seemed to understand that he was challenging her and stood resolute, almost defiant, as she stared up at him. It was that fearless quality, along with her stubborn pride and her work ethic, that made him admire her, although she had nothing other than her beauty, not even a decent set of clothes, to suggest she should be admired.

"A woman like you…she doesn't get forgotten, doesn't go unnoticed."

"A woman like me?"

"A woman as beautiful as you."

She wasn't flattered; she knew he was merely stating a fact. Her only reaction seemed to be worry. "I will leave. Soon."

"I'm not asking you to leave. I just want to know who's looking for you."

"No one." She threw her spatula aside. "The man who wanted to marry me is dead, okay?"

Ken was doing exactly what he'd told himself not to do—digging into her past—but what she'd revealed demanded a follow-up. The man who'd wanted to marry her was dead? "When?"

"It has been three weeks."

Then why did she show so little emotion? Hadn't she cared for him? "Where? In Vegas?"

"Sí."

"How'd he die?"

"A…stroke?"

Ken had expected an accident or a gang shooting, the type of death more common to younger men. He couldn't remember the last time he'd heard of someone under thirty dying of a stroke. "Was it some…rare disease that caused it?"

"He had a bad heart, and—" she struggled to remember the word "—diabetes?"

"I'm sorry to hear that. How old was he?"

"Seventy-four."

Ken made no effort to conceal his surprise or his disgust. "No…"

Her eyes flashed with anger. *"Sí."*

"You were going to marry a seventy-four-year-old man? What are you, *twenty-five?* That's sick!"

Moving toward him instead of away, she lost the demure expression she'd adopted the past twenty-four hours—that of a housekeeper staying in the background, doing her work—and pounded a finger into his chest as if she was every bit his equal. "It is easy to judge when you have always had everything, is it not?" she snapped, and presented her back to him as she once again resumed cooking.

CHAPTER SIX

"WHAT DID YOU DO to her?"

Ken looked over at his brother. They'd eaten dinner and were back in front of the TV, but since the game was over, they were channel-surfing, looking for a movie or some other show to entertain them. "Who?"

"Cierra."

"I don't know what you're talking about," he said, but he did. During dinner, Cierra had been far friendlier to Brent and had positively beamed when he complimented her cooking. But, other than to set a plate in front of Ken, she'd barely acknowledged him.

"I think she's mad," Brent explained.

Reclining his chair, Ken crossed his feet at the ankles. "She's tired. And too proud for her own good."

Brent punctuated his response with a laugh. "And you're not?"

Ken clicked to a different station. "It's not the same thing."

"Sure it is. And maybe pride is all she has. Did you ever think of that? Why else would she guard it so fiercely?"

For once in his life, Brent had made a profound statement. Ken knew that comments like this stemmed from his little brother's sympathy for Russ, and his bitterness over the fact that Ken didn't share that sympathy. But just because he expected people to eventually get control of their lives didn't mean he had no empathy for their struggles. He was tired of being disappointed, that was all. How many chances did a person deserve? How many had Russ already wasted?

"She'll be fine in the morning." Tossing his brother the remote, he got out of his chair. "I'm ready for bed."

"What are you going to do about her?" Brent asked before he could leave the room.

Ken hesitated. "What do you mean?"

"She needs help."

"I know she needs help. What do you think I'm doing? I don't typically have the average homeless person move in with me, even at Christmas."

Lowering his eyes, Brent fidgeted with the remote. "But…this might not be a quick fix. I'm worried that you'll run out of patience. You're always so big on getting everyone to quit enabling others. And it's not like *I* can do anything for her. I'm just a starving student. I'll be heading back to school after the holidays."

They weren't really talking about Cierra, or not entirely. They were back to Russ again, the one subject they needed to avoid. So how did he respond? Most of his life he'd spent trying to figure out where caring and helping crossed the line to become detrimental to the recipient—and he still didn't have all the answers. "Dundee's fairly small," he said. "We've got to be able to find the place she was supposed to go. Now that I've gotten settled, I'll head to town in the morning and get it sorted out. Want to come along?"

Brent frowned. "I do. But I've already arranged with Gabe to paint that extra room in Mom's photography studio. It's a surprise for Christmas. Do you think you can handle it alone? Or maybe wait another day?"

Ken didn't want to wait. There was something about this woman that threatened him in a way he couldn't define. Maybe it was fear that he'd become even more responsible for her than he already felt. Or that he'd be tempted to enjoy more than her cooking and cleaning… "No, it's fine."

Brent stopped him again. "Ken?"

What now? Sometimes, Ken didn't like seeing himself through his younger brother's eyes. Brent perceived him as an authority figure, someone who was too old for his years, too disciplined, too unyielding. But Ken had had to be tough to survive, to be what their mother had needed him to be before she met Gabe. Brent had needed him then, too, although he didn't fully understand the dynamic that had created the differences between them. "What?"

"What if it isn't possible? What if you can't find where she belongs?"

"I will." Russ was enough of a challenge. With any luck Cierra would be staying somewhere else by tomorrow night.

HE FOUND WHAT HE WAS looking for so easily Ken almost couldn't believe it. Assuming he'd have a long day ahead of him, he'd left Cierra at the cabin where it was warm before dropping Brent off in town, but the search had taken only two hours. For one, thanks to the steepness of the mountain, there hadn't been as many turnoffs as he'd expected. He'd tried two or three, the ones closet to town, and eventually found the fork in the road someone had mentioned to her. Than, *bam,* the numbers she'd recited to him were there, affixed to a battered mailbox dangling from a wooden post.

Snow covered the driveway, left so long it'd hardened. Ice crunched beneath his boots as he made his way to the front door. But just because the walks hadn't been shoveled recently—maybe never?—didn't mean anything. The cabin was more of a shack, in poor repair, but that could be the very reason the owner needed to hire help. Perhaps he or she planned to clean it up….

Or…maybe this wasn't the right place, after all.

It fit all the parameters he'd been given, but Ken hoped there was another house in the mountains surrounding Dundee with 11384 in the address because it didn't appear that anyone was living here. A small, one-car garage leaned into the cabin. Assembled out of various building materials from bricks to corrugated metal to fencing material, it looked like a junkyard creation, a haphazard afterthought. And, judging by the snow piled against it, the door hadn't been lifted in some time.

Heavy drapes, closed tightly over the windows, made the cabin itself seem dark and empty. There were no Christmas lights, no decorations at all. But it was a remote location, a small outpost built on the same mountain as the property he'd just bought from Gabe. It didn't really make sense to decorate when there wasn't anyone around to see the result. *He* didn't have any lights up, did he?

As soon as Ken raised his hand to knock, the curtain moved, telling him someone was home. Whoever it was had peeked out at him. But that same someone seemed reluctant to open the door.

Trying to be polite, he waited a minute or two before knocking again. Then he called out, “Hey, I know you’re in there. I’m not here to bother you or cause any trouble. I just need to talk to you about a young Latina woman who’s been looking for this place.”

“What’s her name?” a male voice responded.

Whether or not he’d be admitted seemed to depend on his answer. “Cierra Romero.”

There were several thumps and other noises. When the door eventually opened, Ken realized it’d taken so long because the gaunt, fifty-something man staring out at him had been busy shoving stacks of junk out of the way so he could reach the entry.

What kind of person barricaded himself inside his own house? Ken wondered. Then it dawned on him that he’d met this man before—many times, although he hadn’t paid much attention back then. Mr. Baker had been the janitor when he attended Dundee High School. According to town gossip, he’d been fired several years ago for cornering a female student in the bathroom and trying to feel her up.

Was that true? The question itself was enough to give Ken pause.

“My sister called me, said she was coming.” Deep-set, bloodshot eyes peered out of a skeletal face as Baker craned his neck, searching for Cierra in Ken’s SUV. When he didn’t see her, he did what he could to smooth down his hair, which was standing up as if he’d just rolled out of bed. “Where is she? It’s a cold winter. I could use the company.”

Company… The scents emanating from the cabin threatened to turn Ken's stomach. Alcohol. Urine. And cats. Lots of cats. "She, um, she—" Somehow Ken couldn't bring himself to divulge Cierra's location. Not yet. He had too many questions that needed answering. "You mentioned your sister," he said, changing gears midsentence. "Where does she live?"

"Vegas. Her ex was going to marry this girl. Brought her all the way from Guatemala. But he croaked the night before the wedding, and then nobody knew what to do with her, so I said I'd take her."

How magnanimous of you. But what did it mean? She wasn't a piece of secondhand furniture. "You…you were thinking of…*marrying* her?" Envisioning Cierra stuck in this cabin with this man created mental pictures Ken did not want to see. Someone so young and beautiful couldn't possibly be happy here, especially if she had to service this disgusting person.

"Arlene didn't say that was part of the deal."

"Arlene?"

"That's my sister. Charlie's ex-wife."

"And Charlie is…"

"The man who was going to marry this girl, then died."

"Why was someone so old planning to marry someone so young?" Ken asked.

"Are you kidding? What man wouldn't love that?" he said with an appreciative laugh.

His response made Ken's skin crawl. "So you plan to…what?"

"Maybe I'll marry her," he responded with a shrug. "If we hit it off, eh?"

Stuart Baker would never bother with marriage. Why would he? That would require a trip to town, and it looked as if he avoided public settings at all costs.

Or maybe he *would* go to the trouble. As his wife, Cierra would have even less chance of escaping him.

"I see."

"So…where is she?" he asked again.

Ken masked his inner turmoil with a pleasant smile. "I'm afraid I have some bad news. She wanted me to make sure you received word that she won't be coming."

"*What?* Why not?" He sounded indignant.

"She, uh, she changed her mind. Decided to go home."

"To Guatemala."

"Yeah."

Baker's eyes narrowed suspiciously. "What about her sisters?"

Oh, God—there was more? "What about them?"

"Arlene told me they'd starve if she went back. Her parents are dead. Her brother's in prison. There's no way for her to support what's left of her family."

And it gets worse. "You were going to help her do that?"

"Me? You kidding? I don't have the money to support a whole family, but I can make sure she has a place to stay and gets a meal now and then. At least she won't starve with them."

Ken wondered if Baker had made his demands, and his limitations, clear from the beginning. Cierra had come a long way in hopes of reaching this location. She wouldn't have done it if she hadn't believed she could find legitimate work *and* save her sisters. After only two days in her company Ken knew that much. "Fortunately, you don't have to worry about her." He rubbed his hands together to warm them. "She's taken care of."

Baker leaned close. "You went to a lot of effort to tell me she's gone."

Ken met his gaze. "She asked if I'd pass the word."

"Because you two are friends?"

"We bumped into each other in town."

"Sure you did." His eyes swept down to Ken's boots and back up again. "You'd think a handsome football star like yourself could get enough women in bed without taking from the rest of us."

Ken hadn't necessarily expected Baker to recognize him, but he wasn't surprised. Even the folks in Dundee who didn't know him personally knew *of* him. Around here, being a professional athlete made him something of a celebrity. But he wasn't pleased by the implication. *"What did you say?"*

He noticed that two teeth were missing as Stuart stretched his lips into the approximation of a smile. "No offense, Slick. Just keep me in mind when you're done with her, huh? I'm not going anywhere."

Ken's hands curled into fists, but he couldn't say what came so readily to his lips. If he threatened Baker, told him to stay away from Cierra, the INS, now called ICE, which stood for Immigration and Customs Enforcement, would likely show up at his door. Then she'd be on the next flight to Guatemala. His coming here had obviously betrayed her presence. "Sorry but we're both missing out. *Since she's gone.*"

"Right. She only came north to go south again."

"Apparently."

"Just keep me in mind, like I said." And he shut the door.

CHAPTER SEVEN

WHAT NOW?

Ken drove up and down Main Street while trying to decide. He couldn't turn Cierra over to ICE, not after hearing about her situation. If she and her sisters couldn't survive in Guatemala, sending her back there wasn't an option. And no way in hell would he ever allow Stuart to be around her. He had more of a conscience than that.

But he couldn't let her stay, either. She was too close to his age, too attractive, and that meant, as a single man, he couldn't have her living with him. Last night he'd lain awake thinking about what it might feel like to touch her, to kiss her. And that wouldn't do. Not if he was planning to see Tiffany again. After having dated for so long in high school and college, they'd always expected to end up together. Now that it was time to settle down and start a family, he needed to get serious about finding a wife—not have a wild fling with some Latin American beauty. Especially when he knew that wouldn't help Cierra at all.

Someone honked. Blinking, Ken focused on the traffic around him and realized his father had just spotted him.

Shit... Bumping into Russ was the last thing he wanted.

Ken waved, hoping that would suffice, but his father motioned for him to pull over and Ken couldn't ignore him. He felt too much of an obligation toward Russ, who'd alienated everyone else in his life; all he had left were his sons.

After parking in front of the hardware store, Ken got out and slogged through the slush as Russ rolled down the window of his old Camaro. This Camaro didn't have any heat, so Ken had bought Russ a new truck last Christmas, but he must've sold it or given it to someone he owed money because Ken hadn't seen it since he'd unveiled the big surprise.

"Hey, what are you doing in town?" Russ asked. "Your mother told me you were at the cabin getting settled in."

Feeling guilty for not having returned his father's call a few days ago, Ken shoved his hands in his pockets. A pale blue sky stretched in all directions, but the air was bitterly cold, and he hadn't yet replaced the coat he'd given to Cierra. "I had to pick up a few things," he explained. "It's just a quick trip. I'm heading right back."

"That's too bad. I was hoping we could grab lunch."

"Not today. I've got a lot to do. But...soon," he promised.

"Let's set a date. I have a business opportunity that'll blow your socks off. Now that you're not playing ball, you gotta start looking at investments, you know? That money you earned won't last forever."

Ken already had investments that were performing quite well. He owned a video-game store in town and the dude ranch and didn't want to squander any more money on his father's latest network marketing scheme. It wasn't as if giving Russ an infusion of cash ever really improved his situation. After he lost whatever amount Ken had provided, he simply came up with a new business idea and asked for yet another "loan."

But Ken didn't want to get into an argument on the street. "Maybe we can talk about it after the holidays."

"When?"

"I don't know. January sometime."

"Give me a date, and I'll call up this guy I want you to meet." As usual, Russ pretended to be oblivious to his reluctance and kept pushing.

"After the holidays," he said again.

"Right. But we'll get together before then?"

"Of course."

"Hey, did you see the Jets get their asses handed to them by the Cowboys last night?" Russ chortled. "I tried to call you, but it went straight to voice mail."

Ken hadn't checked that message yet, or any others. He'd been too preoccupied. But he wasn't surprised the game had triggered another call. The Dallas Cowboys had always been his father's favorite team. It still grated on Ken to hear him talk about them. The entire time Ken had played for New York, Russ had badgered him to see if he couldn't arrange to be traded. "My boys had a bad night," he admitted.

"Bad night," Russ repeated, laughing. "Now that you're not there, the Cowboys could beat them *any* night."

Ken could've brought up their record against Dallas, which wasn't as one-sided as Russ suggested, but he knew that wouldn't help. His father wouldn't drop it no matter what. He'd just talk about rushing yardage or passing yardage or some other statistic where the Cowboys reigned supreme.

"I still can't believe you quit ball before playing for Dallas," he lamented.

Other than not being good enough to play himself, this was his father's greatest disappointment. But Ken had a few disappointments where Russ was concerned, too. His alcohol addiction was one of them. "Yeah, well, they'll be fine without me."

"You sure you don't have time for lunch?" he asked, and as Ken stared into the banged-up Camaro, with its torn seats and missing door handle on the passenger side, he knew he couldn't refuse. Difficult though his father could be, he was still his father.

"I guess I could squeeze it in."

AS THE HOURS PASSED, Cierra grew so nervous it was hard to continue working at her usual pace. She hadn't heard a word from Ken or Brent since they'd left after she'd made breakfast. Had they found the address on that paper she'd had in her pocket? Would she have a permanent place to stay, a good job, a chance to make everything that was wrong in her life right?

She prayed she would. Finding a job without some kind of introduction or sponsor would be practically impossible in Dundee, which seemed so…white. She stood out here. She'd probably have to move to a bigger city, where it was easier to blend in. But that would require time and the money to survive until she found work, and she had *no* resources. Her sisters had to be getting low on money, too. It'd been three weeks since she'd sent them anything. If she didn't land a paying job soon, they could lose their home despite her efforts.

The minute she heard the grind of the motor that raised the garage door—now that they'd cleaned out so many of the boxes, Ken could park inside—she hurried to the living room to greet him.

"So?" she asked as soon as he came in. "What did you find?"

Both arms full of sacks, he brushed past her on his way to the kitchen. "Nothing. I searched and searched but—" he put what he carried on the counter "—I finally had to give up. It's a waste of time. We don't have enough of the address."

She tried not to reveal the despair that settled over her. "I see. Of course. You did…all you could. *Gracias.* You were…good to look so hard."

The way he immediately turned his attention to the items he'd bought made her wonder if he was upset. "I don't want you to worry," he said tersely. "We'll figure out…something."

But she didn't want to be a burden on anyone. Especially a man she found as appealing as Ken. "Where's Brent?"

"Working on a project for my mother. He'll be staying in town for a few days."

"Oh."

He looked up at her. "I said not to worry, okay? You'll be fine."

"But my work here is almost done—"

"No, it's not. I still need your help."

"For what?" She waved around them. "Already I dust

and vacuum and straighten cupboards. And I—I clean your room. Iron all your clothes."

"You did?"

"Sí."

"Even my jeans?"

She nodded. *"Sí."*

He didn't act as if that was normal, but he didn't complain. "There's the Jacuzzi room and the gym. But you can do that later. It's time to get started on this." He gestured at the bags.

He'd bought tons of Christmas decorations—glittery rope, tinsel, red and gold balls and other ornaments, fresh pine boughs, lights. "You want me to...put this up?"

"That's right." He pulled a nativity set from one of the bags. "Christmas is in less than a week."

She'd been in the States long enough to know that most Americans decorated for Christmas. A lot of people in her country did, too. Guatemalans had Christmas trees and *nacimiento*—nativity sets—and presents under the tree. Although they focused more on Christ than Santa Claus, and the adults exchanged gifts on New Year's, their traditions weren't too different. But, other than buying presents for his family, she hadn't expected Ken to bother with any of the usual Christmas trappings. Was his family coming for dinner? "Is it company?"

"Company?" he repeated.

"Company...it is coming?"

The nativity set he'd bought looked expensive. She liked the sight of his large hands removing the fragile porcelain figurines from the packaging, which had *Lladró* written on the side.

"No."

"And yet you spend…so much money?" That seemed completely impractical to her. After getting to know him, at least as well as she had the past two days, she couldn't imagine that he was truly concerned about Christmas decorations.

He set the porcelain manger on the counter with the rest of the stuff. "Why not? Women like this sort of thing, don't they? Look, it's pretty. You like it, don't you?"

It *was* pretty. But as far as she knew, she was the only woman who'd see it. Had he bought all of this for her sake? To cheer her up because he'd known she'd be sad that he hadn't been able to find where she belonged?

Although he'd deny it, she suspected that might be the case. Christmas decorations, no matter how beautiful or expensive, didn't solve her problems, but the gesture was so thoughtful she didn't want him to feel he hadn't pleased her. Especially because it *did* please her.

"*Sí.* Of course." She fingered the Christ child that would remain absent from the *nacimiento* of her fellow Guatemalans until placed there on Christmas Eve. "This is…pretty, as you say."

"Cierra…" A serious expression claimed his face.

"Yes?"

He hesitated as if he didn't know how to say what was on his mind. Instead of trying, he ran a finger down the side of her cheek. "I'm sorry."

At his touch, her disappointment vanished beneath a giddy excitement the likes of which she'd never experienced before. She couldn't breathe. At first, she'd tried to tell herself that she preferred Brent to his more complex brother, but it wasn't true. Brent just seemed safer. And he probably was—because she wasn't attracted to Brent in the same way. "You—you have nothing to be sorry for," she managed to say. "You have been very…generous to me."

When his finger reached her chin, his gaze dropped to her lips. "You're shaking," he murmured. "Are you afraid of me?"

"No." But she was afraid of how he made her feel. She couldn't fall for a man with whom she had a far better chance of getting pregnant than getting married. In her situation, she had to make sacrifices, had to trade her youth, beauty and sexual favors for marriage, money and citizenship. Maybe what she had to do was too mercenary for most Americans to understand, but that was her reality. And there was no way that deal would hold any interest for Ken, who could have any woman, even the gorgeous blonde from the diner. Marrying another man like Charlie was the best Cierra could hope for. She had to be practical, understand her limitations. Her sisters were counting on her.

"I think maybe I'm a little afraid of you," he said.

She would've laughed, except she was pretty sure it wasn't a joke. "Do not worry," she said. "I will be gone soon. I promise."

CHAPTER EIGHT

KEN DIDN'T UNDERSTAND what had come over him in the kitchen. All the while he'd had lunch with Russ, picked out the tree, which he'd strapped to the top of his Land Rover, and shopped for the decorations, he'd been cursing whatever had led Cierra to *his* doorstep. And yet he would've kissed her a few minutes ago if she hadn't backed away.

He should get on the phone, see if he could find someone else who might be able to hire her as a cook or a housekeeper. Maybe one of his married football buddies needed a nanny for his kids—except he couldn't imagine any wife being pleased about living with another woman as attractive as Cierra. There was a reason that men having affairs with their nannies had become a cliché. Also, because she wasn't a citizen yet, he'd have to be discreet in his inquiries, which would take time, and it was spending time with her that worried him. When he'd told her he hadn't been able to find the address she seemed to think would be her salvation, she'd tried so hard to bear up under the disappointment, to show her gratitude for the little he'd done, that he'd wanted to pull her into his arms.

He would've assumed that reaction came largely from a desire to protect and console the less fortunate, except that whenever he imagined holding her, they were both naked. That was the part that shocked him. He'd pointed a finger at Mr. Baker for having a prurient interest. He certainly didn't want to be guilty of the same thing.

"Can I ask you a question?" He'd already dragged in the tree and wrestled it into its stand. Now they were putting on the lights. So far, they'd worked mostly in silence, probably because Ken hadn't been able to think of anything except the softness of Cierra's cheek and the way she'd looked up at him when he'd touched her, which wasn't something he wanted to talk about. Her rapt expression had sent a charge of sexual awareness through him, and he was still fighting its effects. He was pretty sure she knew that—and understood that getting involved with him would not be good for her. Every time they accidentally brushed hands or stood too close, she moved out of reach.

"Cierra?" he prompted when she didn't respond.

Her expression remained guarded. "You may ask, *sí*."

"Will you answer?"

"Maybe yes." She gave him a tentative smile. "Maybe no."

He'd tried convincing himself that her personal life, especially her sex life, was none of his business. But ever since she'd mentioned her seventy-something-year-old fiancé, he'd been burning with curiosity. "Did you sleep with him?"

She didn't bother pretending she didn't know who he was talking about. "Why do you ask, Señor Holbrook?"

It was too intrusive a question. He'd been aware of

that. "Well, *señorita*—" he winked as she grinned at his response "—my mind keeps going back to it."

"Because…"

Because he was a man and any man would wonder. Because he was turned on by her. And because he didn't like what she'd been through.

In the interests of keeping things simple, however, he chose Answer Number Three. "Allowing the old men of one country to exploit the young women of another because of economic need is…*wrong*."

"But I was grateful to Charlie," she explained. "Without him…I had no hope for…so many things."

Now that Charlie was gone, was that hope lost? It had to be, right? Her situation had grown even worse. And yet Ken couldn't help being glad that old Charlie had kicked the bucket. Picturing someone fifty years her senior pawing at her made him cringe.

She continued to talk, picking her words slowly, carefully. "He offered me…a fair offer, one I…say yes. *I* make the choice."

But she'd had no choice. Not really. Not with her sisters' well-being on the line. "That doesn't answer my question," he said.

No longer willing to meet his gaze, she insisted they finish winding the lights around the tree. "We were engaged. And I was living with him."

"Only the two of you were there?"

"Sí."

"For how long?"

"Two months."

"But you knew his ex-wife."

"She was angry, bitter. She come over to argue with him about divorce all the time."

"Did he have kids?"

"No. He said that was what he wanted from me. A baby."

"So that's a yes? You slept with him?"

A grimace twisted her lips. "He said we were married…in our promise to each other, *sí?* And I was afraid…I was afraid he think I no keep my word."

She'd feared he wouldn't help her sisters if she refused. That was the real story, and it was exactly the type of thing Ken had been afraid of. "That's *definitely* a yes."

She didn't confirm it, but she didn't deny it, either.

Stuart Baker cornering a young woman in the high school lavatory didn't seem a whole lot different. Cierra had felt cornered, too, or she never would've agreed to marry this Charlie, let alone allow him to touch her. If he'd really wanted to help someone in a third-world country, why hadn't he donated to the Red Cross?

Because he wanted to help himself, first and foremost. It was the self-interest driving this "buy a bride" scheme that bothered Ken. That and the inequitable distribution of power in such an arrangement. "And?"

The question surprised her. "And?" she repeated as they finished with the lights and added garland.

"Was it as bad as I'm imagining?"

Lines formed on her forehead. "I no want to talk about it."

Ken interrupted her as she reached into a box of ornaments. "He didn't hurt you, did he?"

She stared at the angel she'd grabbed. "No."

Could he believe her? Maybe. Maybe not. But he had one other concern. "Is there any chance you could be pregnant?" In his view, that was the only way her situation could get worse.

"No."

He released her. "You're sure?"

"Positive."

"*How* positive?"

"Stop! I know because…he could not…could not…" She sighed in frustration as she struggled to find the right words. "Father a child. You understand?"

"You mean he was sterile? Or impotent?"

"I don't know the meaning of those words."

"He couldn't get it up, couldn't get hard?"

Face flushing crimson, she whirled around to hang her angel ornament on the tree.

"That's right, isn't it?" he pressed.

"Sí." Her answer was muffled, but he heard it.

"So how could he expect to father a child?"

"He said a doctor would help."

"So how did he have sex with you."

She waved him off. "Stop!"

"Okay." He waited until she finally looked up at him. "Just tell me one more thing."

"What?" she asked suspiciously.

"How'd you get through it?"

Climbing the short ladder he'd brought in, she began hanging ornaments on the upper branches. "I close my eyes."

"And pretended he was someone else?"

She didn't respond but a guilty smile gave her away.

"Who?" he pressed. "An old boyfriend?"

"No."

He handed her another box of ornaments. *"Who?"*

Rolling her eyes in exasperation, she attached several snowflakes to the tree. "I can no tell you!"

"Why?"

"You will laugh."

She tried to return the empty box, but he wouldn't take it. "Now you have me *really* curious."

"The cowboy lawman in…a movie, okay?"

"What movie?"

"It was called…*High Noon?*" She scratched her head as if puzzling out whether or not she'd named the correct one. "*Sí,* that is right. *High Noon.* May I have more snowflakes?"

He *did* laugh. "Where did you see that old show?"

"Charlie played it for me after I arrive."

Accepting the empty box, he passed her some icicles. "So you think Gary Cooper was handsome?"

"Sí."

"I'm sure my mother, and her mother, would agree with you."

Her hair caught in the tree, and Ken got up on the ladder to free it. "How did it feel when Gary Cooper made love to you?" he murmured as they stood there together, only inches apart.

He thought she'd refuse to answer this, too. It was more inappropriate than anything he'd asked so far. But she surprised him.

"Like it should, I think."

"You've never been with anyone else?" he asked.

"No. My father, he was…very strict." She made a fist

to show "strict." "A woman who is not a virgin is no worth much."

She wasn't a virgin now. But that didn't matter to Ken. "Your father planned to sell you?"

"*Sell* me? No! Make a contract."

Wasn't it the same thing? In a situation like that, how was a marriage license any more than a piece of paper? "That's what you call it?"

"He had heard of others…doing the same. But he no want to do it. Only if…if things get bad…really bad."

"Desperate."

"*Sí.* Why else would he send me away?"

Learning that even her father planned to use her upset him enough to curb the arousal playing havoc with his thoughts and emotions. He wouldn't take advantage of her. He wanted to help her without making her feel she had to perform any "services" for him. Granted, Ken was tired of Russ creating his own problems and then flailing around, looking for someone to rescue him. But Cierra wasn't like that. Cierra was a victim of circumstance.

Stepping off the ladder, he plugged in the lights. "What do you think?"

"Beautiful," she whispered.

"That's what I think, too," he said, but he wasn't talking about the tree.

CHAPTER NINE

THAT NIGHT, CIERRA LAY in bed awake, staring up at the ceiling and breathing in the scent of pine, which pervaded the whole cabin since Ken had brought the Christmas tree inside. After they were done decorating, he'd lit a fire while she grilled the steaks he'd taken out of the freezer and they'd eaten together.

Being with him was completely different without Brent. It was far more intimate and, because of that, more unsettling. Every once in a while, she'd glance up to find him watching her. She knew what he wanted. She was pretty sure she wanted the same thing. She'd never made love to a man of her own choosing, a man as virile as the lawman she'd always fantasized Charlie to be.

Ken had reminded her of that lawman from the beginning. Perhaps she'd never have another chance to be with someone she found even more handsome than Gary Cooper. She'd soon leave this place and, she hoped, get work until she could secure another husband via the website. Who knew how old the next guy would be?

But everyone she met in America was temporary—white faces that would soon pass out of her life. Someday, she'd be able to go home. And she didn't plan on taking an illegitimate baby back with her.

The floor in the hall creaked. She could tell that Ken was as restless as she was. At first she thought he might come to her room like Charlie used to. Although she'd allowed him into her bed, she'd insisted on having her own room until the wedding. But then she remembered the moment she'd been standing on the ladder with Ken, when he'd made the decision not to touch her, and how determined and resolute he'd acted since. He'd laughed and teased her, shown her a romantic movie and given her a T-shirt to wear to bed, but he'd kept his hands to himself.

"How did I end up here?" she whispered into the silence. She could never have imagined a place like Dundee, or a man like Ken, while living in Todos Santos. Maybe she should be grateful to have shelter, but it was torture being in the same house with him. She craved the pleasure Charlie's fumbling hands had on rare occasions hinted was possible, knew Ken could deliver what Charlie had been unable to. But she doubted they'd be having this problem if Brent had stayed at the cabin. Without him, they had too much privacy to explore what they were feeling.

Earlier, Ken had offered to let her use the Jacuzzi. He'd said it would help her sleep. She hadn't taken him up on it because she didn't have a swimsuit. But she was interested now.

She waited until she was almost certain he'd gone back to bed, then found her way to the gym mostly by touch. The Jacuzzi was located to one side of it, enclosed in glass. Except for patches of moonlight that filtered through the pine trees outside, the room remained cloaked in darkness that felt as thick as the steam rising from the water.

She liked this place, with its smell of chlorine, its wooden pegs draped with fluffy white towels and the moon and stars reflecting off the snow outside. Wondering what the people of her village would make of a glass room that looked out on a snowy mountain, she smiled wistfully as she dipped her foot in the water.

Hot. Just as she'd hoped…

She pulled off Ken's T-shirt as well as her panties, since they were the only pair she owned, and stepped into the water. The inky blackness made her feel safe despite her lack of clothing—until she came up against a man's leg. She could feel swim trunks, but it still surprised her. She gasped and might've screamed if Ken hadn't spoken when he did.

"It's only me."

Only? "I—I did not realize you were here. I am sorry to interrupt you…your Jacuzzi bath. I will leave."

He caught her wrist. He didn't tug her toward him, but he didn't release her, either. She got the impression he was waiting to see how she'd react.

"Ken?"

"Are you sure you want to go?"

"I should." That didn't really explain what she was thinking and feeling, but he seemed to understand.

"Yes, you should." He dropped her wrist, but still she couldn't bring herself to get out.

"Cierra?"

"Yes?"

"You're still here."

"Sí."

"Why?"

"I do not know."

She heard the water sluice off him as he stood.

"My heart, it's pounding," she whispered.

"So is mine. See?" Taking her hand, he placed it on his chest.

She wasn't sure she could feel *his* heartbeat, but she felt warm skin covering hard sinew. Mesmerized, she let her fingers slide curiously over it, then up his neck to hold his face between her palms. Just touching him made her feel as if she was being consumed by liquid fire.

"Kiss me," he murmured.

Don't think. Let go. Just once. Rising up on tiptoe, she touched her lips to his and heard him growl deep in his throat. He liked the contact—and so did she. She felt him coaxing her to deepen the kiss and was soon thrusting her tongue as eagerly into his mouth as he was hers.

She wasn't sure if he realized she was naked. He hadn't touched her except to lightly settle his hands at her waist, which meant it wasn't too late to slip away so that he'd never learn. As far as he knew, she could be in her bra and underwear, right? But she didn't want to go. She allowed him to guide her between his legs as he sat down. Then he held her in place as his mouth moved to her breast.

He knew she was naked, all right. Despite the darkness, he must've seen her undress. Or maybe he'd heard the soft plop of her clothes when they hit the cement.

Instinctively, her hands moved to his head. She intended to push him away, to put an end to this before it went too far. But she'd overestimated her willpower. Instead of insisting he stop, she moaned at the sensations he brought to life and anchored him against her.

His mouth traveled up, licking the water from her neck along the way. Then he eased her down on his lap and, although it was covered by fabric, she could feel the part of a man that had no longer worked for Charlie.

Obviously, Ken didn't have the same problem.

KEN WAS DOING EVERYTHING he could to hold himself in check. He'd thought he could pleasure Cierra without getting too carried away. What was the harm in some skinny-dipping? Kissing? Maybe even a little exploring? None—except he couldn't seem to stop.

"Maybe we should think about this," he said.

"No!" she gasped.

Laughing at her emphatic response, he lowered his head to look at her face. He had condoms in his room. Should he bring her there to finish what they'd started?

He was still trying to decide if his conscience would agree to it when she kissed him again. It wasn't the most artful kiss he'd ever received but the simple sweetness of it seared him to the bone. With kisses like that, he doubted they'd make it to the bedroom. He already had one hand on her breast while the other searched for even more sensitive territory.

He'd just reached his goal when someone called his name. Cierra heard it, too, and went rigid. "Brent!"

"I'll take care of it." Setting her away from him, he whispered that she should stay there. Then he got out of the Jacuzzi and wrapped a towel around his waist before his brother could come looking for him.

"Brent?" he hollered as he walked out.

By now his brother was halfway across the gym. "I thought you might be in the tub."

"I was just getting out." Putting a hand on Brent's shoulder, he steered him back toward the kitchen. "What are you doing here? I didn't expect you for a day or two."

"I told Mom about Cierra. She wanted to send some clothes for her, insisted I bring them right away."

"Clothes from where?"

"From the store. Where else? She spent the entire afternoon shopping and loved every minute of it."

"But…how did Mom know Cierra's size?"

"I told her she was small."

Ken knew how small. If he closed his eyes, he could still feel her beneath his hands.

"If these don't fit, we can take them back and get others," Brent was saying. "Where is she?"

"She went to bed a while ago." Which was true. Ken just didn't mention that she'd slipped out.

"Good thing I didn't knock on her door." Brent pointed at the decorated tree. "She do all this?"

No way was Ken going to admit he'd helped. Brent would find it a little too amusing. "Yeah."

"Looks nice. Where'd she get the stuff?"

"I brought it back when I went to town earlier."

"Really?"

Ken scowled. "What's the big deal?"

"I didn't think you'd decorate for Christmas, that's all."

"It's not like I'm Scrooge."

"No, not Scrooge. Just…I don't know if *I* would've done it."

"I thought Cierra could use the distraction."

"Good idea." He sounded impressed. "You locate the address you were looking for this morning?"

Figuring it was best to tell everyone the same story, Ken shook his head. "Nope. No luck."

His brother clicked his tongue. "What are we going to do about her?"

If Brent hadn't shown up so unexpectedly, Ken would be making love to her. He couldn't seem to focus on anything except the feel and taste of her. "I don't know. I guess I'll hire her until we arrange something better, huh?"

Brent frowned at the floor. "You didn't dry off very well. You're getting water everywhere."

"What? You're Mom now?" He punched his brother in the arm. "I'm beat. See you in the morning." He went to his room and stayed there until he heard the television go on and knew Brent was occupied with a movie. Then he crept back across the gym to get Cierra. Now that he'd had time to clear his head, he realized it'd been a mistake to touch her as intimately as he had. He couldn't start dating again if he was sleeping with his housekeeper. What kind of a lecher would *that* make him?

As he opened the door to the Jacuzzi and smelled that first blast of chlorine, he was trying to decide how he was going to apologize and tell her about his change of heart.

But he didn't have to say anything. Apparently, she'd already come to the same conclusion. When he got there, she was gone.

CHAPTER TEN

CIERRA BURROWED BENEATH the covers of her bed, seeking refuge and comfort. So much had changed in the past few months; *she'd* changed. She hardly recognized herself anymore. She'd come to America to get married. Instead, her fiancé had died and now she was staying in a remote cabin with the reincarnation of the handsome movie star she'd fantasized about for the past three months. But that didn't mean she was suddenly going to live a fairy-tale life. She had to protect her heart, keep herself together and do whatever was necessary to survive. Her determination was all she had.

Her door opened slightly. "Cierra?" It was Ken, speaking in a low voice so Brent wouldn't overhear.

Was it too soon to pretend she was asleep? She knew it was, and yet she didn't want to discuss what had happened. She preferred to forget it, chalk it up to the general insanity and misfortune she'd encountered since her parents died. "Yes?"

"Are you okay?"

"*Sí*. I am fine." Would he come in, expect to be welcomed into her bed, despite Brent's presence?

She hoped not, and yet she had mixed feelings when he didn't even try. "I'm sorry. I got carried away. It—it won't happen again," he said, and the door clicked shut.

A KNOCK AT THE FRONT door woke Cierra the next morning. She assumed Ken or Brent would get it but, when they didn't, she began to wonder if, as their housekeeper, that was her job.

Climbing out of bed, she rubbed her eyes and checked the alarm clock on her nightstand. It was barely eight. Who would drive up to the cabin so early?

She put on her only pair of jeans, smoothed down Ken's T-shirt, which she'd worn to bed, and ran her fingers through her hair to make herself as presentable as she could in ten seconds. Then she hurried to the living room. She was just reaching for the door handle when she heard Ken behind her.

"Who is it?" he asked with a yawn.

"I don't know." She stepped back in case he wanted to answer it, but he stayed in the hall and motioned for her to go ahead.

A second later, she was facing Tiffany Wheeler, who was doused in the same perfume she'd had on at the diner. Her hair, makeup and clothing were as perfect as ever, too.

"Hi." Tiffany's smile faltered when she saw that Cierra was, once again, wearing Ken's clothes, especially when she spotted Ken and he wasn't wearing a shirt.

Cierra knew that, at first glance, it looked as if they'd been in the same bed. But she shouldn't have worried that Tiffany might suspect any such thing. A second later, Ken's ex-girlfriend shrugged and broadened her smile as if this couldn't *possibly* be what it looked like. Ken would never be interested in someone like Cierra. Cierra had nothing to compete with.

"You're getting all settled in, huh?" She spoke to Ken as though Cierra wasn't standing there and held up the plate she carried so he could see it. "I made you some homemade cinnamon rolls for breakfast."

"Come on in. You caught me sleeping but I'll grab a shirt."

Cierra dutifully took the rolls and closed the door behind her.

"Place looks great," Tiffany said while Ken was gone. "Did you do all this yourself?"

Cierra and Ken had done it together, but she didn't think he'd want her to mention that. He hadn't told Brent last night. She'd heard him say she'd done it all. *"Sí."*

As Cierra put the rolls on the dining table, Tiffany noticed the *nacimiento* displayed between the couches and Ken's chair and crossed over to it. "Oh! I saw this at Gerdy's Boutique and wanted it myself," she said, her eyes wide. "Isn't it gorgeous?"

Maybe she'd get it someday. She wanted Ken, too, didn't she? *"Sí."*

Tiffany studied her for a moment. "You know, you have really pretty eyes. If you'd like to come over sometime, I'll help you put on a little makeup. It wouldn't take much. Your skin is already flawless. A bit of mascara on those lashes and you'd be stunning."

Stunning. Cierra didn't feel she could ever be *stunning*. Not compared to Tiffany. But she had to give Ken's ex-girlfriend credit for trying to be nice. Or was Tiffany merely making it clear that she didn't view Cierra as any kind of threat?

Mom thought you were perfect for each other. Brent had said that about Tiffany and Ken. And they probably were. They even looked like they belonged together. So what would one half of that equation want with a blue-collar illegal immigrant from Guatemala who had three sisters to feed?

Ken reappeared, looking as good as if he'd taken the time to shower. He hadn't. He'd merely put on a pair of jeans with a sweater and house shoes, and combed his hair. But he didn't need to do much. With his rugged face and muscular body, he was attractive no matter what. "How about one of those rolls?" he said.

"I will make coffee." Cierra ducked out of the room as soon as she felt it was safe to do so without appearing rude. But the kitchen opened onto the living room and, even though they'd lowered their voices, she could hear Tiffany and Ken talking about her after she'd left.

"Your housekeeper is so sweet, Ken. How old is she?"

"I haven't asked, but I'm guessing she's about twenty-five."

"How long have you had her? Was she with you in New York?"

"No. We met when I flew in to Boise."

Cierra peered out through the crack in the door. Tiffany stood close to Ken, and touched his arm at every opportunity. "You're lucky to have someone like her. It's got to be nice having help. Does she cook?"

"She does. She hasn't made a lot yet, but what she's served has been terrific."

"Mexican food?"

"Guatemalan."

"You'll have to ask her if she'll teach me a dish or two."

"I'm sure she wouldn't mind."

"Awesome! That would be fun!"

"Hi, Tiff!" When Brent joined them, Cierra returned to the stove to prepare eggs and bacon. She wasn't certain whether additional food was expected with cinnamon rolls, but she preferred to keep busy. That made it easier not to obsess about Tiffany.

"You drove all the way up here just to bring my bum brother some rolls?" Brent's voice carried back to Cierra, but she knew Tiffany's response wouldn't be as loud. Wanting to hear it, Cierra tiptoed over to the door.

"Actually, I came here because I wanted to ask him a question." She seemed a little nervous despite her usual confidence.

"What is it?" Ken's face was filled with curiosity.

Tiffany glanced from Ken to Brent and back again. "Some of my friends, three different couples, are going skiing at Silver Mountain Resort tomorrow, then staying over at a cabin. I was hoping you'd be my date."

Ken's mouth dropped open. "Uh, that sounds good, but I'm not quite settled in—"

"I'll be around to take care of what's left," Brent said. "Me and Cierra. Go, have a great time."

Hands in his pockets, Ken cleared his throat. "Right, it's the holidays, after all. So…sure, I'll come."

"Thank you!" Tiffany threw her arms around him, then hugged Brent. "Can you pick me up at my place first thing in the morning? Around six?"

"Sure."

"Because of the storms, I think we should take your Land Rover, if that's okay."

"No problem."

"I'm glad you can come," she said, and started for the door.

"You're not staying for breakfast?" Brent asked.

"No, I've got a lot to do today so I can be away from the flower shop. But enjoy the rolls. Smells like the coffee's ready."

"Thanks." Ken showed her out, then turned back to his brother. "That came out of nowhere, didn't it?"

"Are you kidding?" Brent replied. "You know Tiffany's been waiting for you to come home for years. How can you be surprised?"

Ken didn't respond.

"You're going to have a blast," Brent added.

"Yeah, should be fun," Ken muttered.

Cierra hurried to the stove but could still hear Brent's booming voice. "This is the beginning of the end for you, bro. You're going to make the big commitment soon. I can feel it."

Again, Ken didn't reply, but Cierra agreed with Brent. Why wouldn't Ken want Tiffany? What was there not to like?

Nothing. Tiffany had everything a man could want.

KEN COULDN'T HELP wondering what Cierra had thought of Tiffany's visit. She wouldn't look at him as she served breakfast, so he knew she'd heard their conversation. Was she mad?

She must think it was weird that, after saying he wanted to make love to her, he'd accept an overnight invitation from another woman. He knew it made him seem shallow and insincere, as if he'd attempted to use her, and he hated that. He wanted to explain that he'd only accepted Tiffany's invitation because he didn't want to embarrass her by refusing. The whole community had expectations for them that made him feel obligated. But maybe it was better to forget what had happened last night rather than address what had happened today.

Of course it was. Cierra didn't expect anything from him. So why did it bother him so much that she might be upset? What was it about this dark-skinned beauty in her ill-fitting clothes that affected him on such a gut level? Was it just that she was different, unique, a challenge because of that damn pride? If so, he couldn't be sure the attraction would last. He'd never met a woman he couldn't forget with a little time. And Tiffany was… Tiffany was the woman everyone had always thought he'd marry.

"What's going on around here?" Brent broke the silence.

Ken peered at his brother over the rim of his coffee cup. "Excuse me?"

"You're both so quiet." He motioned to Cierra, who had her back to them as she loaded the dishwasher.

"I think we're all tired." Predictably, Cierra said nothing. She was blending into the background again. But Ken knew her feelings weren't as neutral as she pretended.

Brent slapped the table. "You should be jazzed, man!"

Ken couldn't bring himself to agree, because he wasn't. "It'll be okay," he said with a shrug.

"Why are you acting so weird?" Brent asked.

A knock interrupted them, relieving Ken of the need to reply. Someone else was at the door.

"Hey, if that's one of Tiffany's friends coming to invite me, I'm in," Brent said, and jumped up to answer it.

Ken followed him into the living room. But it wasn't one of Tiffany's friends. It was Russ.

What could their father possibly want *now?* Ken had already caved in and given him some money just to get him to stop asking.

"What's up, Dad?" Brent asked.

"Not much." Taking off his baseball cap, Russ shook the snow from it onto the mat. "I just came up to meet the new housekeeper."

Ken thought he must've misunderstood. Had Russ just mentioned the housekeeper? How did their father know about Cierra? Ken certainly hadn't talked about her. He'd figured the fewer people who knew, the better, at least until he could decide what to do. "Did Gabe say something?" he asked in confusion.

His father pulled his cap back on. "No. Stuart Baker showed up at the bar last night complaining to everyone who'd listen that you'd stolen his future wife." Russ laughed as he said it, but Ken didn't find it funny.

"He *what?*"

"Who's Stuart Baker?" Brent asked.

No one answered him.

"He was pretty pissed about it," Russ went on. "When he wouldn't quit bitching about you, we nearly went at it. I told him I'd know if you had a woman up here. But he was so adamant, I began to wonder. Especially when he said you should learn to keep your pants zipped or someday you'd run into someone who'd make you sorry you didn't."

Ken felt his muscles tense. "Baker isn't pretending to be that guy, is he?"

"He hinted that he'd like to do what he could. But that was the alcohol talking. He wouldn't even fight *me*," his father added with another chuckle.

Ken was tired of his father's barroom brawls and was glad this one had been avoided, even if Baker deserved a beating. Ken didn't need anyone to stick up for him.

"Keep his pants zipped!" Brent repeated. "Ken hasn't been sleeping with Cierra."

The image of Cierra standing naked in front of him flashed through Ken's mind. Did *almost* count? In the hours since the Jacuzzi, there were plenty of times he'd wished that Brent hadn't come home when he did. Now he was back to being glad.

"Baker had better shut up before I pay him *another* visit," he said. "Cierra doesn't need him running around, stirring up shit." Not if, as he suspected, her visa had expired.

Russ's eyebrows shot up. "That means it's true? You've got some Guatemalan woman living here?"

Afraid that Cierra had already overheard most of what had been said, Ken held up a hand. He wanted to send her off to clean the gym or something before they discussed this, so they could speak freely. But that didn't stop his clueless brother from calling after him.

"Wait a second! You found the address she was looking for? Why'd you say you didn't?"

Now it was too late to keep this quiet. He didn't know if Cierra was listening, but he felt he had to answer Brent in a way that everyone could hear and understand, just in case. "I didn't want her there," he said. "It wasn't a good place."

"But…you told me you didn't find it." Brent sounded confused.

"*Because it wasn't a good place,* like I told you. You should've seen it."

"Why would you lie about that?" Brent asked. "When you've been dying to get rid of her?"

Ken grabbed his brother's arm. *"Will you shut up?"*

"She's in the kitchen," Brent snapped. "She can't hear us."

His brother could be so obtuse. "Just shut up," Ken said again. Then he scooped his keys off the coffee table and stalked out. He didn't want to deal with his father right now. He didn't want to deal with Brent, either. And he most certainly didn't want to see Cierra's face if she'd heard one word of what they'd said.

"Where are you going?" his father called after him.

"I've got stuff to do." He slammed the door on his way out.

CHAPTER ELEVEN

WHILE KEN WAS GONE, Brent gave Cierra a whole pile of new clothes. He said they were a gift from his mother, that his mother expected nothing in return, and kept pushing her to try them on. But she didn't want to touch them. She wasn't happy about the clothes or anything else. She felt sick inside. For several reasons. For wanting to be with Ken so badly she'd humiliated herself by believing, even if she wouldn't acknowledge it to herself at the time, that he might be genuinely interested in her. For hoping the situation could be different. For burdening him when he wished to be rid of her…

"So what do you think? It's pretty, right?"

Forcing herself out of her thoughts, she refocused on Ken's brother. He was waiting for her reaction to the last item he'd taken from the bag—a sweater he laid on the couch.

"Beautiful," she breathed, and allowed herself to finger the soft knit. It *was* beautiful, one of the prettiest sweaters she'd ever seen. But that didn't change how she felt about accepting such an expensive gift.

"So try it on!" he said.

Realizing that he didn't understand her resistance and was disappointed as a result, she finally nodded and carried the clothing into her bedroom.

Almost every item fit. She'd come out to show it to Brent, so he could feel he'd accomplished what he'd set out to do. He'd tell her how wonderful she looked in it. Then she'd try on the next thing and thank him again. It was an agonizing process for her, but when it was all over he seemed satisfied and eventually left for town to finish some painting for his mother.

Once the sound of Brent's engine dimmed, Cierra donned her old clothes and sank onto the bed next to the pile he'd attempted to give her. These garments were so much better than anything she'd ever owned, so similar to what she'd seen Tiffany wear. She thought she might have a chance of capturing Ken's interest if she could look more…American. More…affluent.

But she couldn't pretend to be something she wasn't. New clothes didn't change who she was or remove her responsibilities.

Getting his T-shirt from where she'd put it in a drawer earlier, she folded everything into a neat stack and laid his coat across the top. She didn't want to take any of it. She preferred to leave knowing she'd worked for the food and shelter he'd provided and that he was no worse off for having met her.

The phone rang, but she ignored it. As of this moment, she no longer worked for Ken, so it wasn't her place to answer. She was on her way out—but just as she reached the front door, she saw the *nacimiento* he'd bought for her to enjoy and paused in regret.

Would it be so terrible to take a small token to remember him by?

No. He probably wouldn't even miss it. Christ wasn't supposed to be in the manger yet, anyway.

KEN RETURNED TO THE CABIN relieved and excited. He'd spent most of the morning at his mother's place, calling every associate he could think of, searching for a legitimate position Cierra could fill. And he'd found one. Lawrence Smith, a guy Ken had known in college, was living in Boise. Recently divorced, he had full custody of his three children and ran an import company that specialized in plywoods from Ecuador, the Philippines and Guatemala. His current nanny was getting married and moving to California the first of the year, which meant he needed a new one. And he didn't mind that, for the time being, Cierra wasn't a U.S. citizen.

The only hard part had been convincing Larry to hire Cierra instead of the woman he'd already interviewed, and to do it sight unseen. But Ken had vouched for her and promised to compensate Larry if she didn't work out. Fortunately, Larry had been mollified when he learned that Cierra spoke English as well as she did. He considered it a bonus that his caregiver would be able to communicate with his children *and* teach them Spanish, since he frequently traveled to Spanish-speaking countries.

Eager to tell Cierra the news, Ken had tried to call the cabin, but she hadn't picked up. And now that he was home, he couldn't get her to answer when he called her name. Where was she? In the Jacuzzi?

That would surprise him. She wasn't the type to relax in the middle of the day. It wasn't like her to hang out in her room, either, not when there were boxes that needed to be unpacked.

He checked her room—and saw some clothing stacked on her bed. Judging by the tags, all still attached, these were the clothes his mother had bought. And, of course, he recognized his shirt and coat.

"Cierra? Hey, you around?" He already knew she wasn't. That clothing told him as much. But he looked in the Jacuzzi room. And the gym. And the patio out back. He even unlocked the old workroom, where Gabe used to build his furniture. She wasn't anywhere.

It wasn't until he came back to the living room, however, that he realized she was gone for good. That was when he spotted the nativity set he'd bought, remembered how much she liked it and noticed that something was missing.

AT LEAST IT WASN'T snowing. And this time Cierra had a name; that would make the search easier. The slip of paper she'd brought from Vegas had probably held the same information, somewhere in that jumble of writing. If only Cierra had paid more attention to the details, she might've arrived at Baker's in the first place.

Almost as soon as she'd started walking, two older women, Darla and Deanna Channing, sisters in their early seventies, pulled over to see if she needed a ride. They were taking advantage of the break in the weather by heading to town for supplies. Apparently, they owned a cabin not far from Ken's.

Cierra had planned to start her search for Baker once she reached Dundee. She'd thought she'd have to go there to find someone who knew him well enough to give her directions. But when she mentioned his name, Deanna, the driver, said she used to be Baker's schoolteacher. Not only did she know him, she knew where he lived and offered to take Cierra there.

Certain her luck had finally improved, Cierra felt her spirits lift—until they got to his cabin. Then she wasn't sure what to do. The decrepit old shack looked as if a strong wind might blow it down the mountain. She knew Ken wasn't impressed with the place, but she hadn't expected it to be quite so bad.

"This is it?" she said, stalling.

"This is it. His mother used to be a good friend of mine, God rest her soul. She lived here, too, before she passed four years ago."

Darla, the sister, frowned. "Doesn't look as if he's done much to keep up the place."

Maybe he couldn't, Cierra thought. Maybe Baker was poor, like her. If that was the case, she didn't want to discriminate against him. She knew what it was like to be treated differently because of her economic status.

But there were the comments Ken's father had made about Baker. Ken's family didn't hold him in very high esteem….

Grasping the door handle, she paused. "Do you know much about your friend's son?"

"No." Deanna adjusted the wool hat she wore to keep her ears warm. "There were some allegations once—"

"Allegations?" she interrupted, asking for clarification.

"She doesn't understand that word," Darla cut in.

Deanna patted her hand. "Never mind, dear. It doesn't matter. His mother told me he had a boss who was out to get him, that he was falsely accused of some wrongdoing. But I'm not one to pass along gossip so we'll leave it there."

Gossip… Was that what Ken and his family had been reacting to? Cierra hoped that was all it was.

Thanking the sisters, she climbed out, but turned back when Deanna lowered her window. "Would you like us to wait for a few minutes?"

Relieved, Cierra nodded, then approached the front door and knocked twice.

No one answered.

"I don't think he is home," she called back.

The Channings briefly conferred. "Would you rather go to town?" Deanna asked.

Why would that help? She'd only been going to Dundee in order to find *this* location. "No. I will wait."

"You're sure? It's cold out, young lady."

"I am warm enough. And…the sky is clear today, yes?"

"For the moment," Deanna grumbled, as if it could change quickly. But she promised they'd stop on their way back to make sure Cierra wasn't still standing on the stoop, and pulled away.

Cierra knocked several more times, just because she had nothing better to do, and was surprised when she finally heard a noise from within.

"Hello? Is anyone at home?" she said loudly. "My name is Cierra Romero. I was…I was supposed to work for a Mr. Baker? His sister sent me."

She heard someone say, "Well, what do you know." Then the door opened and a man who hadn't shaved in some time squinted out at her as if the sun was far too bright an intrusion into his dark little home.

"Slick finished with you already, huh?"

"Slick?" She didn't know anyone by that name.

"The big NFL football stud. Ken Holbrook."

Clasping her hands in front of her, she resisted the urge to fidget. "I no work for him now."

"So…what kind of work did you do?"

Cierra wasn't sure she liked Baker's smile. There was…something about it. "I clean house. Unpack boxes."

"And then you cleaned his pipes, right?" he said with a laugh.

His joke made no sense to her. She hadn't cleaned any pipes…. "Pardon?"

"Never mind." He looked her over carefully. "You *are* pretty. Just like my sister said."

Cierra didn't respond. Her looks didn't have anything to do with their arrangement. She already knew she'd never marry *this* man. Maybe Charlie had been old, but he'd also been kind. He hadn't reeked of alcohol. And he'd had far more to offer than a filthy dump. She didn't want to be here. But one of the men with whom she'd hitchhiked had taught her a saying and it definitely fit: *Beggars can't be choosers.*

"Come on in." Stuart opened the door wider to make room for her, and Cierra swallowed hard as the smells drifting out of his cabin hit her nostrils. Was this really what she wanted to do?

She didn't budge. "What are you offering in return for my labor?"

"Ooh!" He laughed as if he thought she was funny. "You're a businesswoman, huh? Let's just say that I'll be happy as long as you give me what you gave Ken Holbrook."

"I charge the same for all," she said, but got the impression that she'd once again missed some nuance in the conversation.

He grew serious. "Here's the deal. You keep the place clean and you cook, and I won't call the INS. Simple enough?"

She didn't like that he'd mentioned immigration. "Dishes? Dusting? Vacuuming? Laundry?"

He gave her a slight bow. *"Sí."*

Was he mocking her? It was so difficult to tell. But she believed Charlie's ex wouldn't have sent her here if it wasn't safe. This was Arlene's brother. Maybe she hadn't been nice to begin with, but she hadn't sent Cierra back to Guatemala, either.

After Christmas, or in a few months, she'd learn of other opportunities and be able to find a better situation. Or she'd be able to post on that bride website again. "Then...I accept."

"I'm so glad I could measure up to Slick."

Measure up... Cierra was fairly certain no one could "measure up" to Ken. At least, she'd never met another man like him.

"I've always wanted to earn the approval of an illegal alien," he added with a wink.

"You are...being funny?" she asked, confused again.

"No, no. Just amusing myself. Come on in, like I said."

As he stepped back to admit her, she put her hand in her pocket and curled her fingers around the glossy porcelain Christ child she'd taken from Ken's. The memory of having known Ken would be enough to get her through the next few weeks. And, as soon as possible, she'd find a new place to live….

CHAPTER TWELVE

WHILE KEN PACED in the kitchen of his parents' house, Gabe sat nearby, in his wheelchair. Hannah stood at the table, wrapping presents.

"I don't know where else to look," he said. "I've already driven up and down the canyon three times but didn't see her. And she was on foot! She couldn't have gone far by the time I got home and realized she'd left."

"I've never seen you this worked up." Hannah took the piece of tape her husband held out. "Do you really think this woman is in danger?"

"She could be. But she's not the type to reach out for help. She's…maddeningly stubborn."

A curious expression lit Gabe's eyes, and he smiled. "That sounds like grudging respect to me."

He couldn't meet his stepfather's gaze, didn't want Gabe to misinterpret what he was feeling. It was guilt that had him worked up, nothing more. "I *do* admire her. I've never met anyone with her character. Someone who's been tested to such a degree and still won't bend. But enough is enough, you know? I get that she's decent and willful and independent. I get that she feels responsible for her sisters and will do anything to help them. I even get that she wants to support herself and not be some charity case. What I *don't* get is the fact that she's walking around wearing a thin sweatshirt when she could be wearing a heavy coat, a coat I'd never miss. And I don't like that she doesn't have a dime to her name, even though I would've happily given her some cash, if only she'd take it." He pivoted at the stove and headed back toward them. "You should've seen how hungry she was when I first found her. I don't think she'd eaten in days. And you know what she did? As soon as the bill came for our dinner, she asked how much she owed me so she could be sure she worked it off. She was determined not to short me a cent."

"Sounds rare and admirable," Gabe said.

"She is rare and admirable. But..." Grabbing the extra roll of Christmas paper his mother motioned for, he handed it to her. "She didn't take those clothes you bought her, Mom."

Hannah glanced up from her work. "I spent a lot of time picking those out. Didn't they fit?"

"Brent said they fit perfectly, but they qualified as a handout, and she won't accept a handout. That's what I've been trying to tell you."

Gabe leaned back in his wheelchair. "So where do you think she's gone?"

"Baker's, I assume. But I've been by his place twice, and I can't get anyone to answer the door."

Adding a bow to the gift she'd been wrapping, Hannah pushed it aside and finally gave him her full attention. "Maybe no one's home."

"Stu Baker is a freak," Ken responded. "He rarely leaves the house. Unless it's to go to the bar."

Hannah sank into a chair. She wasn't wearing any

makeup, but Ken thought his mother was more beautiful than most women who were perfectly made up. She had a natural glow about her, an easy smile. He used to hate being compared to her—everyone said they looked so much alike—but ever since he'd grown up, he felt a great deal of pride when someone told him they resembled each other.

"So what do you want to do?" his mother asked.

"I want to find her so I can tell her I have another job for her. I want to take her to Boise and know she's safe."

Gabe scowled. "I don't understand why you feel so responsible for this woman, Kenny. You offered to help her—you *did* help her—and now she's moved on."

"I'm not taking responsibility for her. I just… I don't want her to be with Baker. *He's* not in it to help her."

"Then why is he in it?" his mother asked.

"To use her, and the thought of that turns my stomach."

Both his parents stared at him.

"She's not that type," he explained, trying to counter the level of emotion with which he'd responded. "She won't sleep with him if she has a choice, but…I'm afraid he won't give her one. So, you see? She could be in danger."

Gabe and his mother exchanged a knowing look. "That's what I thought," his stepfather said.

Ken looked from one to the other. *"What?"*

"You've got it bad."

"I have no idea what you're talking about."

"That fear gnawing at your gut?"

"That has nothing to do with…with what you're inferring," Ken snapped.

His stepfather smiled. "It doesn't?"

"No!" he said. But then he remembered how it had felt to touch Cierra in the Jacuzzi and how panic-stricken he'd been since finding her gone. "I feel guilty that Brent made her think I didn't want her around," he said, but he knew Gabe wasn't buying his denials. Neither was his mother.

"Sure you do," Hannah said with a laugh. Then she stood. "Come on. Let's head back to Stu's. I'll go to the door this time. It won't be as intimidating to open up to a woman. I'm less likely to break his face for stealing my girl."

"Stop it," Ken grumbled, but he couldn't deny that he felt relief at the prospect of finally being able to talk to Cierra.

FROM WHERE HE SAT, parked down the road and out of direct view of the windows, Ken watched his mother approach Baker's door. She knocked, waited, knocked again. Then she turned to face them and shrugged as if to say she wasn't having any luck.

A third knock brought no better result. Finally, she started back.

"Shit," Ken grumbled, and got out before she could reach the Land Rover.

"What are you doing?" she asked as he stalked toward her.

"I'm going in."

She tried to bar his path. "You can't do that! You could go to jail for breaking and entering."

"Then I'll go to jail."

"Gabe?" she called, glancing past him to her husband.

Gabe had opened his car door when Ken got out. "Let him go," he advised. "Maybe he's right about this girl's safety."

"I'm worried about *his* safety," she muttered, but stepped out of the way, "Be careful," she added.

"I'll be fine," he told her. "Stay with Gabe."

Fortunately, she seemed to understand that he didn't need anything more to worry about and did as he asked.

Stu Baker's house looked as empty as it had on his previous visits. The only thing different was the tire tracks. Two lines cut through the snow on the drive—evidence that he'd left last night and possibly today.

Ken didn't bother with the front door. That was a waste of time. Instead, he went around to the back and checked every window. He was hoping to see inside, to get some idea of whether or not Cierra was there, but the windows were covered so completely they might as well have been blacked out.

With its low-ceiling and tacked-on look, the room at the back was more like a shed or a storage area. But this door was warped and far flimsier than the one in front. Ken felt he'd have a greater chance of forcing it open.

Lowering his shoulder, he rammed it, and wasn't too surprised when the lock popped. He'd spent years in football perfecting his ability to hit. He was good at it. But it hurt a lot less with pads.

"Baker!" He stood in the open doorway, rubbing his shoulder.

No response.

"Hey, *Baker?*" He'd been right about the room. It had a dirt floor, black plastic covering the windows and smelled like a cellar. Maybe there was a door to a cellar in here somewhere but, if so, Ken couldn't see it. Stacks of magazines and newspapers, empty soda bottles and beer cans, old clothing, cat hair and God knew what else covered the floor and various, worn-out furniture.

"Cierra?" Wading through the mess, Ken headed for the next room. An accordion-style partition led into the regular part of the house. When he opened it and peered through, he could see light in the front and moved toward it—until he heard a noise from one of the side rooms he'd already passed. Whirling around, he dodged a blow that probably would've cracked his skull.

As he feinted to his left, the lamp Baker held came down on a wooden chair, shattering the glass middle section. *"What are you doing in my house?"* he screamed. *"What do you want from me? How dare you come in here without permission!"*

As Baker raised the lamp again, Ken prepared to take further evasive action. "I'm looking for Cierra. Did she come here?"

"No! Get out!"

Hoping to forestall another swing, or give himself more room to maneuver, Ken backed up. But he wasn't leaving, not until he had Cierra. "I'm talking about Cierra Romero. The woman from Guatemala you were expecting. She left my cabin this morning. I think she was on her way here."

"If she was, she never showed up. Now get out."

Ken wasn't sure whether to believe him. But she didn't seem to be here now, and that made him wonder if he'd jumped to the wrong conclusion. "You'd tell me if she did, right? Because if I find out you're lying, I'll be the one taking the swings."

"Are you threatening me?"

Ken didn't bother denying it. "Damn right."

"You don't see her, do you?" A scrawny cat wandered into the room to see what all the fuss was about. Baker moved it to one side with his foot—a none-too-gentle motion—but he seemed to be calming down and he'd lowered the hand with the lamp. "Because she's *not* here. I don't even know what she looks like."

What did that mean? Had she already left the area? Hitchhiked out? Possibly. She'd hitchhiked here to begin with, hadn't she? But the idea of her alone on the road again upset Ken. It was so dangerous. And how would he ever find her? "Shit!"

"Sorry to disappoint you." The smugness in Baker's voice irritated Ken but at least the idiot had put his broken lamp on the table. "Now, will you go? I shouldn't have to point out that you're trespassing."

"Sorry." Suddenly Ken felt foolish for strong-arming his way in without proof that Cierra was here. "I'll pay to replace your back door. The lamp's on you. If you'd answered when I knocked, this could've been avoided."

"I don't have to answer your knock if I don't want to. There's no law that says I can't ignore you. But I can fix the door myself," Baker grumbled. "Just get out and leave me alone."

"Fine." Shoving a hand through his hair, Ken headed back the way he'd come in. But he had enough reservations about what Baker had told him that when he passed the kitchen, he snapped on a light.

"What are you doing?" Baker snarled.

"I can't see," he said. But he'd really been thinking about all the time Cierra had spent in his kitchen. He knew that if she was here that was the first thing she'd clean.

Unfortunately, the kitchen was as filthy as the rest of the house.

Convinced at last, he was about to turn off the light when he stepped on something—something so small he wouldn't have noticed it otherwise. But when he glanced down to see what it was, he was awfully glad he'd put his foot where he had.

Baker was lying.

CHAPTER THIRTEEN

KEN LEFT BAKER'S HOUSE with the knuckles of his right hand scraped and bleeding.

His mother and Gabe both opened their doors when they saw him. "What happened?" Hannah called. Gabe said nothing. He simply waited until Ken climbed behind the wheel for an explanation.

"The bastard told me she never came here," he said, smacking the steering wheel.

Two thuds sounded as they shut their doors. "You don't believe him?" Hannah asked.

Straightening his leg so he could reach inside his pocket, he pulled out the porcelain Christ child he'd found on the floor and handed it to his mother in the passenger seat. "This proves she did."

She studied it. "This is her figurine?"

He didn't explain that it was actually his. He didn't care about the decorations; he'd bought them for her. "Yes."

Hannah motioned toward Baker's shack. "So what happened in there?"

Ken shook the pain from his hand, then started the car. "Nothing much. One punch and Baker was ready to tell the truth."

Hannah put the Christ child in the tray on the console. "And that is?"

"She was here, but now she's gone." Making a U-turn, he drove toward the main highway.

"You're sure she's gone?" Gabe asked.

Ken sighed as he drove. "I searched the whole place. Baker said she came for a couple of hours but decided not to stay."

"Why wouldn't he tell you that from the beginning?"

"That's what has me worried. I'm guessing he doesn't want me to find her, doesn't want me to talk to her. Maybe I won't be happy about what I hear."

Hannah turned on the heat. "So where did she go?"

"Who knows?" he replied. "Supposedly, she left with two old women. But that's probably a lie, too. She doesn't know anyone else."

"Did you ask Baker for any names?"

"I did. He said he didn't get a close enough look to recognize who it was."

His mother frowned. "What were they driving?"

"A red '57 Chevy. But I've never seen a truck like that in Dundee."

"I have," Gabe said. "It belongs to Deanna and Darla Channing."

The pain in Ken's hand suddenly vanished. *"Who?"*

Gabe smiled. "Two old women. They live up the canyon from my place—your place now."

They'd reached the main road, but Ken didn't turn. Letting the engine idle, he used the rearview mirror to look at his stepfather. "You're positive about that? There aren't a lot of those trucks on the streets anymore. I would've noticed it had I seen it around here."

"You haven't been home long enough. They just inherited it from their father, who lived in Boise. They haven't had it more than six months."

Feeling a resurgence of hope, of purpose, Ken glanced at the Christ child Cierra had taken and lost. "How do I get to their place?"

"Just head on up the hill. I'll give you directions from there."

KEN HAD EXPECTED *finding* Cierra to be the most difficult part of his day; he hadn't expected her to refuse to see him once he did.

"She's here, but…she won't come down." Deanna shrugged apologetically when she returned to the living room, where he and his parents were waiting.

Ken blinked in surprise. "Why not?"

Deanna moved closer. "She's pretty upset," she whispered. "She was running down the street when we came upon her, with Stu Baker chasing her. She won't say what happened but…judging by the bruise on her cheek, there was a tussle."

"A *tussle?*" Ken repeated.

"That's how it appears. We didn't get to hear Stuart's side. As soon as he saw her get in the truck with us, he took off for the house."

No wonder Baker wouldn't open his door and had tried to hit him with a lamp. He'd probably assumed Ken knew Cierra had been hurt and had come for retribution.

The look on his face must've revealed his rage,

because Deanna lifted her hands in a placating gesture. "From what I can tell, it didn't go too far. Cierra's strong, determined. She got away before anything...*serious* could occur. But...she's understandably rattled."

Attacking her wasn't serious? "I want to see her," Ken said.

"I can't *force* her to come down," Deanna responded. "Maybe if you give her some time, come back in the morning—"

"I'm not leaving. I have a job for her, a position in Boise, with someone I know and trust. Unless you can offer her as much, tell her to come down."

Deanna's older sister walked into the room. Ken had the impression she'd been listening while working in the kitchen. "You should have her go with him," she murmured to her sister. "The way things are now she'll only run away the minute we're not looking. You heard her when we got her in the truck. She kept saying Baker was going to call the immigration people, that she had to leave town right away."

Ken's mother got to her feet. "Do you think he really called them?"

Gabe wheeled his chair forward until he drew even with her. "He'd better not have."

"I wouldn't put it past him," Ken said. "We need to get her out of here."

With a nod of agreement, Deanna went back upstairs and eventually returned with Cierra, whose sweatshirt was stretched out, as if someone had been yanking on it. The deep scratch on her neck and the bruise on her cheek made Ken wish he'd done a lot more damage to Stu Baker than he had. "You okay?" he asked.

As usual, she raised her chin, daring the world to bring her to her knees. *"Sí."*

Although Ken was dying to know the details—so he could hold Baker accountable for what he'd done—he didn't ask about her ordeal. Cierra was a private person and the situation at Baker's had no doubt embarrassed her. She wouldn't want to talk about it in front of anyone else. Instead, he introduced his parents, whom Cierra met with as much polite reserve and dignity as if they were royalty.

"Ken has some good news for you," his mother announced.

"I found you a job," he said. "A good job."

Cierra lifted a hand. "I know you…are trying to be nice. You have been kind to me, and I am…grateful, *sí?* But I will go my own way now."

"Just hear me out," he said. "It's in Boise, which is an hour and a half from here. Even if Baker called ICE, they won't find you. Not if we leave right away. And my friend really needs you."

It was obvious she hadn't planned to let him sway her, but when she heard that his friend *needed* her, she hesitated, and Ken realized how important it was to her that the need be legitimate. "It's true," he continued. "This is no favor. His wife, the mother of his three children, left them last year to pursue a modeling career. He's a busy man, trying to run his import company, and he could use a housekeeper and caregiver for his children. Since many of his imports come from South America, he's very excited that you speak Spanish."

"The children…their mother *left* them for a career? She could no do both?" From Cierra's expression, it was clear that she couldn't conceive of making such a choice. "Who is watching the children now?"

"A nanny who's getting married and moving away." Ken was getting through to her, he could tell. "So what do you say? Will you at least give it a try? I know you'll like Larry. He's a good guy who's been through a lot and could really use a break. And he's offering room and board and fifteen hundred dollars a month."

It was a fair offer. Ken hoped her pride wouldn't keep her from accepting it.

"But your friend has not even met me," she said.

Forever the skeptic. "I told him how wonderful you are."

She blushed at the compliment, and her eyes shifted to his parents before returning to his face. "I will help him. Of course I will help."

Relieved, Ken smiled and felt his heart skip a beat when she smiled back. "Good. Let's go."

THE HOUSE WAS BEAUTIFUL, a mansion. Cierra had never seen anything like it. At five foot seven and at least two hundred and fifty pounds, Larry wasn't nearly as handsome as Ken, but he was nice. She immediately felt safe around him and, as far as she was concerned, the children—three girls ages eight, six and four—were a bonus. They had to take her to the Christmas tree first thing to point out all the brightly wrapped packages that waited there for them.

Their innocence settled on her like new-fallen snow, helping her slough off the memories of Baker—what he'd said, what he'd done and what he'd attempted to do. The hours spent dealing with him, the fight that had erupted when she refused to disrobe, didn't matter anymore. He hadn't got what he wanted. And she already felt like someone else, someone stronger and better than the poverty-stricken immigrant she'd seen through his eyes.

Maybe that was partly because she now wore one of the dresses Ken's mother had given her. Hannah had said Cierra could pay her back out of her first check if she wanted to, but that she should look presentable for her job, and she'd been right. Cierra liked the way the dress floated around her knees, the stylish tights that went underneath and the ankle-high boots Ken had insisted they buy. She hadn't felt so pretty in a long time.

Glancing up from where she sat on the floor, admiring all the Christmas gifts with the girls, she found Ken watching her and couldn't help grinning back at him. On the drive, he'd told her he'd come to Boise often to see her. But she didn't believe him. He'd probably get together with Tiffany as his family expected. Then he'd forget all about her. But she was glad to have known him for the week she had. She'd always treasure the memory of their kiss in the Jacuzzi. That was the best Christmas present she could think of.

He surprised her by staying longer than she'd thought he would—for dinner and a movie. She guessed he was trying to help her make the transition, to be sure she felt safe and happy, and that made her love him all the more.

When the movie ended, Larry said his goodbyes to Ken. Then he went in search of the children's current nanny, who'd been on the phone with her fiancé most of the night, so she could get the children to bed.

"What happened with Baker?" Ken asked as Cierra walked him to the door.

"I don't want to talk about it."

He lowered his voice. "Did he attack you?"

"Ken..."

"I'm calling the police."

"No! He told me I cannot...press charges? Is that the right words?" When he nodded she went on. "They will send me back to Guatemala if I try."

"Then I'll handle it on my own."

"By fighting? You will go to jail, and I already have a brother in prison. It is not worth it. I am fine now."

"Only because—"

"Please...let it go," she broke in. "He did not hurt me. You see I am fine."

He blew out a sigh. "I'll think about it."

She tilted her head. "Please?"

Finally, he jammed his hands in his pockets. "I'll try."

"Thank you."

"You like it here okay?"

"Yes. This is a good place, a good job. And I thank you for it. You have been very kind. I will send the money for this dress and these shoes and the other clothes. Please thank your mother, too."

He cupped her face. "This isn't goodbye, Cierra."

He said that now.... "*Sí,* but...even if it is, I want you to know that...I understand. There is no—how do you say—obligation? It is okay if you do not come back. Just...be happy. Always."

The wind had picked up. When she shivered, he pulled her into his arms to warm her, and she felt his lips brush her temple. "You know what would make me happy?"

Unable to resist, she rested her cheek against his chest. "What?"

"Knowing you'll be here waiting, excited to see me when I return."

She angled her face up. "You think I should wait? For how long?" she teased.

"You don't believe I'll come."

"I am sure you mean to. But…who knows what will happen on the ski trip? You might change your mind, eh?"

He touched the tip of her nose. "I'm not going on the ski trip."

"Why not?"

"Because I asked Brent to take my place, and Tiffany agreed. I'm not interested in her." Chills traveled down her spine as he pulled her even closer and his lips moved against the rim of her ear. "I'm interested in *you*."

Was he making fun of her? If so, it was cruel. "An illegal immigrant from Guatemala?" she said doubtfully.

"I might be a dumb jock but I know when I've found someone special," he said, then he kissed her like he meant it. "When I'm with you I don't miss football. I don't miss other women. I don't miss anything. I feel… content. I'm coming to take you to Dundee for Christmas, Cierra, so be ready."

As he left her standing on the stoop, even the chill wind couldn't diminish the warmth that radiated from somewhere deep inside her. He was coming back. She could trust him. But she wasn't sure she *really* believed that until he turned around.

"Oh, you dropped this." Reaching into his pocket, he held something out to her.

Curious, she met him halfway down the walk to see what he could possibly mean.

Tears filled her eyes when he set the Christ child in her palm and closed her fingers around it. "We'll need that for the manger, so don't lose it."

"I won't," she breathed, and she didn't. She kept it safe in a drawer in her new bedroom until he returned for her on Christmas Eve. Just like he promised.

* * * * *

Dear Reader,

I grew up on a street famous for its Christmas Card Lane. Every year the city created dozens of gigantic "cards" and displayed them for miles along the bay walk, complete with lights and music. Hundreds of cars rolled down the street each night, curly-topped heads thrust out the windows to get a closer look.

It was sheer magic. Or so I thought at the time. I was too young to ask how the cards were created, much less how they were trucked out and erected and electrified, taken down, stored or paid for.

Later, when I had my own home and saw how vexing even a few icicle lights could be, I looked back on Christmas Card Lane with new eyes. I understood that real people gave up their holiday time to create that wonderland for us. And the idea for this story was born.

Old Duke Araby's Christmas Joyland is beloved by all in his little Virginia town—all but his own two grandsons, who always hated the festival that cheated them of the attention they craved.

Nate has been estranged from Duke for twelve years. When he hears Annie Browning's radio SOS for help at Joyland, he returns to the ranch to check things out. He's not looking for reconciliation, and he certainly isn't looking for love. But, as we all know, you can't ever tell what you'll get for Christmas.

I hope you enjoy their story. And I hope your Christmas is full of love and unexpected gifts of joy.

Warmly,

Kathleen O'Brien

P.S. I love to hear from readers! Visit me at www.KOBrienonline.com, or write me at P.O. Box 947633, Maitland, FL 32794.

WE NEED A LITTLE CHRISTMAS

Kathleen O'Brien

To my father and mother,
who taught me the magic of words,
of Christmas and of love.

CHAPTER ONE

THAT COLD, MID-DECEMBER DAY at the Araby Ranch started out so well.

At dawn, the first snow of the season began to fall, and it kept coming down in big, puffy flakes. It filled the branches of the firs and trimmed the roofs of the house, barns and stables in glistening vanilla icing.

Annie Browning had finished her first cup of coffee just as the sun climbed over the eastern ridge. She was already outside and up near the chimney of the big house changing burnt-out bulbs when the first flakes drifted onto her lashes.

She put out her tongue and caught one. Though it melted instantly, she imagined it tasted like Christmas. Like cinnamon and pumpkin pie and candy canes and the chocolate Santas that fit neatly in the toe of her stocking.

Her helper, Jasper Smits, one of the longtime Araby ranch hands, held out a hand and let the snow tickle his fingertips. "Duke always said an early snow was a good omen."

"Says," Annie corrected firmly, pushing down the flicker of panic at the past tense. *Damn it.* Why did everyone assume that Duke was doomed? She knew that, for an eighty-nine-year-old man, two broken hips

and double pneumonia was pretty darn scary. But Duke could beat all of that, and more. Duke was the toughest man Annie had ever met.

"I hope he's right about the snow, though," she added with a softer tone, aware that Jasper, too, had blanched at his accidental slip. "We could use a little luck here at Joyland this year."

Jasper nodded and went back to unscrewing burnt-out bulbs and inserting new ones. He didn't repeat the obvious, that, given the magnitude of the task, luck might not be enough.

Joyland was more than just a little Christmas festival. It was a phenomenon. For forty years now, the people of Hallam Fork, Virginia—and much of the state, for that matter—had flocked to the twenty-acre Araby Ranch. From the day after Thanksgiving to the moment the bells tolled midnight on Christmas Eve, every square inch of the ranch transformed into a wonderland of lights and toys, candy and angels, songs and sleighs and stars.

Even under Duke's experienced guidance, it required months of preparation, and dozens of people. This year, with Duke in the hospital, it was going to take a miracle.

Still, if miracles could be bought with hard work, Annie was ready to pay the price. While they'd been riding in the ambulance to the hospital, she'd held Duke's hand and promised him she'd keep Joyland open, just like always.

By God, she was going to make good on that promise. The old man's family had abandoned him years ago, and Joyland was all he had left. It meant everything to him.

And Duke meant everything to Annie.

Jasper watched the ladder for her as she climbed down from the roof, all the bulbs gleaming colorfully now in the early-morning chill. The staff at Araby were hyper-conscious of safety these days, mostly because of Duke, but also because if even one employee had to take a sick day, they were sunk.

Unfortunately, the good luck of the snowfall didn't last long. Half the workers, both paid and volunteer, didn't show up for one reason or another. Annie had to scramble to fill the posts—the "reindeer" trots in the snowy paddocks, the sleigh rides through Lollipop Land in the east pastures, the Santa Singers in the barn, the Gingerbread Village behind the big house.

None of the scheduled groups arrived on time, either, so the logistics of moving them through the stations became a nightmare.

She had almost no time to work on anything except damage control. Someone had to start getting the Christmas Eve finale ready, though, so she dispatched Jasper to dig the lumber and set pieces out of the storeroom.

If things would settle down, maybe she and Jasper, with the help of a couple of ranch hands, could construct the set over the next two or three days. As long as nothing else went wrong...

As she walked through the snow to the old barn, where the Gray Horse, the small antique shop she'd inherited from her foster mother, was housed, she tried to think what she'd say when she saw Duke tonight. She never shared anything disturbing, though he was in a coma now that pneumonia had set in, and maybe wasn't even aware of her presence. Just in case, though, she'd make it sound as if everything was going smoothly. She'd tell him about the great weather, about the happy faces of the children who didn't care if there was a long line to sit on Santa's lap, or that the photographer didn't really know much about taking pictures.

She had hoped she might find a few minutes to work on her origami angels, one of the visual surprises planned for the finale, but she had just entered the craft room at the back of the store when Jasper showed up at the door, looking wet and dirty, red-faced and furious.

"It's ruined."

Annie paused in the act of pulling out a tray of silver paper. She tried not to overreact, but Jasper wasn't the type to exaggerate. "What's ruined?"

"The set. The lumber. Everything."

She felt her heart speed up. "Everything?"

Jasper slapped his dirty hand against his wet jeans. "Everything. The stage. The risers. The steps. The overhead frames. The pulleys."

"But..." She could hardly take in the magnitude of the problem. This stage, used only for the extravagant finale on Christmas Eve, was elaborate, the culmination of years of Duke's experiments with theatrical effects. It had been a marvel of layman's engineering, especially since it could be disassembled and stored efficiently until it was needed a year later.

She swallowed hard. "How?"

"The storeroom has a leak. Big one. It must have been raining in all year. I thought Duke had checked it. He usually does, sometime in the summer, to be sure. But I guess he..." Jasper clearly didn't want to finish the sentence. "I guess this year he didn't."

"Can anything be salvaged?"

"No. It's not safe. Warped, rotted, rusted, you name it. You've got kids this year, right, singing or dancing or something? If we cut corners, try to make do with any of the old stuff, someone could end up getting hurt."

She didn't argue. This year, the Foster Families Association had joined forces with the Donate a Dream Foundation to form a holiday children's choir—and there was no way Annie was going to mount their production on a dangerous stage.

In forty years, no one had ever been hurt at Joyland. No one had tumbled from a horse or a ladder. No one had choked on a gumdrop or slipped on unsalted ice.

Except Duke. She felt a burn of anguish in her chest, picturing the lanky, white haired old man, lying alone in that sterile room, tossing in his fevered nightmares, worrying about his beloved Joyland. He'd watched so carefully over everyone but himself.

But if she thought about that, she'd never be able to stay focused.

"It's all in the details," he'd said a million times. "Watch the details, and the big picture will take care of itself."

She set aside her origami paper. Much as she loved the project and the idea of the angels tumbling from the "sky" at the stroke of midnight, the effect was a frill. It could be eliminated if need be.

"We'll have to rebuild, then." She pulled out the calendar. "The choir comes to rehearse on the twenty-first.

That's five days, not counting today. How many men will you need to get it rebuilt by then?"

Jasper scowled, concentrating as he figured in his head. She could see him arrive at a number, then go back and recalculate, hoping to get a better answer.

"Four," he said finally, though he didn't look happy about it. "Five if you want the mechanical stuff, too. And you should know, Betty and Imogene went home early, running fevers. I don't know if they'll be back tomorrow or not."

She didn't bother articulating the obvious. Even without the threat of a flu thinning the ranks, she didn't have five workers to spare. She didn't have four.

She didn't have even one.

When Duke first had his accident three weeks ago, support had poured in. When that trickled off as people went back to their own lives, she'd hit up everyone she knew, from the guy who worked on her car to the cashier who sold her supplies at the craft store. She'd moved on to her customers at the antique shop, the neighboring ranchers, all Duke's friends, even the guys she'd dated once or twice through the years.

Most of them had said yes to some small chunk of time, either for her sake or for love of Duke. But most of them had, by now, also needed to return to their own jobs and families.

She scoured her mind, biting her lower lip till it stung. Out of the corners, she managed to dig up one or two more people to ask….

But they were long shots. And besides, it wasn't enough. Especially if people were falling ill.

Jasper watched her glumly, picking bits of sawdust

from his gray, grizzled hair. "We could cancel the finale," he said. His voice was graveled with misery. "Close a day early. Just one day—"

"No." She stood. "Not one minute. I promised Duke."

"But surely even Duke would understand—"

"No." She smiled at the earnest ranch hand, who loved his boss almost as much as Annie did. Failure wasn't an option. "I have an idea."

"You do?" He looked skeptical. He'd recruited everyone he knew, too. His son had been on the payroll for three weeks, and his elementary-school-aged grandkids were pitching in after class for free.

But she did, indeed, have an idea. It was a little bit crazy, and she wasn't at all sure Duke would approve. But it might work, and that was what mattered.

She pulled her coat and hat from the mahogany rack by the door.

"It's okay, Jasper," she said with all the conviction she could muster. "You start on the new stage, okay? One way or another, I'll get you those extra hands."

NATHANIEL ARABY NEEDED this vacation. He hadn't had three days off together since he bought the construction company from his boss five years ago.

But no...it had been a lot longer than that. He propped his elbow on the driver's side window and let his hand dangle across the wheel. Though Roanoke was miles behind them, the traffic on I-81 North was at a dead stop, so he had plenty of time to sort it out.

Tuning out the raucous laughter and silly vacation excitement of the four buddies squeezed into the car with him, he did the math in his head. He hadn't had time for goofing off during the seven years before he bought the company, either. During those years, he'd been breaking his back to earn a living, scrimping to accumulate a down payment and learning the construction business from the gritty ground up.

And he sure hadn't been on any trips during the six years before *that*, not since the day his mother had dropped him and Garth at the Araby Ranch in Hallam Fork, Virginia. The boys, used to the bustle of Washington, D.C., had been horrified. Hallam Fork was nineteen linear miles of pure nothing in northern Virginia. More tree stumps than horses, more horses than people.

It was just a visit, she'd said. A chance to get to know the dour and gloomy grandfather they'd rarely seen and didn't like.

She'd said they'd love it. Of course, she'd also said she'd be back soon, a few months at the most.

Nathaniel's fingers squeezed the wheel, as he remembered Garth's fury. At fifteen, Garth had been full of undisguised contempt. He'd especially hated the dirty work, and had accused Duke of buying the boys from their mom for slave labor. Nate, only twelve and less opinionated, had been luckier. He didn't mind hard work. He didn't even mind being sweaty and dirty.

The more bone tired he was at night, the easier it was to get to sleep without missing his mom.

Nate shook the memory away, and brought his thoughts back to the point. *Vacations.* Yeah. Add it all up, and it was nearly eighteen years of working 24/7.

He needed this one. Needed it bad.

The traffic inched, then stopped again. He stared at

the snow that danced around his windshield wipers and listened to his friends singing to some corny country song on the radio. All four of them were smart guys—a doctor, a lawyer, an architect and a wizard with computer code. But not one of them could carry a tune.

Not that he cared. He ought to be singing along.

But he wasn't. Instead, he was wrestling with this edgy feeling that taking a vacation right now was a mistake.

What in hell was wrong with him?

If this was the first real vacation he'd had since he was twelve years old, how come he wasn't looking forward to it more?

"Nate, buddy, lighten up!" Spencer, squeezed with two other guys into the backseat of the Mercedes, leaned forward and grabbed Nathaniel's shoulders, shaking them. "Repeat after me—skiing, schnapps, sex. Skiing, schnapps, sex." He grinned at Nathaniel in the rearview mirror. "Not necessarily in that order."

Al, on the far side, chuckled. "Maybe schnapps should go last, just to make sure you don't screw up the other two."

Jim, in the middle, agreed with a thumbs up, and Carson, who had drawn the long straw, and therefore got to sit up front where there was a little breathing room, nodded.

"Good thinking," Carson said, giving Nathaniel a curious once-over. "But Spence is right, Nate. You don't look like a guy who is about to have the time of his life."

"Sorry," Nathaniel said. He smiled. "Someone was

torturing a bunch of hyenas in the backseat, and I was trying to tune out the screech."

"Hey." Spencer kicked the seat. "I resent that. Did you know I was in the glee club in high school?"

Nathaniel met his grin in the mirror. "Spence, I wouldn't bet anything you even *went* to high school."

The others chuckled, enjoying the joke, because, though Spencer was a cardiologist, he did sometimes act like a buffoon. But even as Nathaniel laughed along he found himself wondering...

Was that why he wasn't looking forward to this vacation? Had he inherited his taciturn, workaholic grandfather's inability to let loose and enjoy himself? God knows, Melinda had thought so. She and Nathaniel had dated for six months, and he'd assumed she was as satisfied as he was, but apparently he'd been mistaken.

"You live for that construction company," she had said through her tears as she dumped him last month. "You don't love me. You don't love anything but your job."

She'd been right about that, anyhow. He didn't love her, and he'd never told her he did. He didn't love anyone, which seemed like a damned smart move, given what he knew about that emotion.

But she was wrong about his loving his job. He didn't.

Truth was, he didn't *love* anything. Love was for suckers. He liked being his own boss, but if he lost the company today, he'd find something else to do tomorrow.

All this time, he'd believed he had chosen his life philosophy. Chosen to be sensible. Self-protective. Rational.

Wouldn't it be a kick if it was genetic instead? If the buzz-kill gene, the selfish-bastard DNA, had simply shown itself at last, and he'd ended up like the old man?

"So, Miss Annie Browning, tell us a little bit about Joyland."

Nathaniel's attention jerked to the radio, which had begun to crackle, thanks to the weather. Had the interviewer really said *Joyland?* Or had Nathaniel's thoughts conjured the word, like some kind of emotional black magic?

He tried to remember exactly how far they'd traveled up I-81. They were probably…maybe twenty-five miles from Hallam Fork. Maybe they really had been talking about Araby.

Subtly pressing the steering wheel control button, he dialed up the volume. Though he knew that the others would be curious, and in fact they began peppering him with questions almost immediately, he didn't care.

He'd observed early that the guy in charge was the guy who didn't feel the need to explain himself to anyone.

Like his grandfather, the only male in the Araby household who hadn't cried when it became clear that Victoria Araby was not coming back to reclaim her sons.

The only one who didn't cry when Garth joined the army just to get away.

Or when they got the news that Garth, too, was never coming home.

So, yeah. Lesson learned. The guy with the power was the one who didn't give a crap.

"Shut up, guys," he said calmly. He turned the volume even higher. "I want to hear this."

They all listened, then, though only he understood why. In a few sentences, he knew he hadn't imagined the reference. The two people on the radio were really talking about Joyland, which this year apparently was in desperate need of volunteers.

And they were talking about Duke Araby. Nathaniel's grandfather.

"So, Annie, we all want to know. How is Duke? The hips were bad enough, but now we hear he's got pneumonia, too. How's the old boy holding up?"

The interviewer sounded chummy, as if he and his guest had progressed to a first-name basis in a big hurry—or already had been.

A young woman's voice, clear and musical, but with a hint more reserve, answered. "He's amazing," she said. "You know how tough Duke is."

A strange prickle skimmed across Nathaniel's hairline as he realized that, though she'd managed to remain upbeat and polite, Annie Browning sounded worried. And she hadn't really answered the question.

Broken hips…plural? And pneumonia.

Nathaniel understood what that might mean for a man of nearly ninety.

"Fantastic. Fantastic. Send him our love, next time you see him."

The interviewer was an idiot. He should have pressed this Annie Browning, whoever she was. He should have made her cough up more details.

"If you want to send cards, my friends, Duke's in County Memorial, room two-oh-two. But if you really want to help, head on over to Joyland. Ask for this little lady here, Miss Annie Browning, and she'll put you to work. Isn't that right, Annie?"

"Yes," the young woman responded, again with that undercurrent of anxiety that made Nathaniel feel strange. "I do so hope that some of you can spare the time to help out. Duke never likes to ask for assistance, but Joyland means so much to so many people. This year, we have more charitable groups participating than ever. But without Duke it's...difficult. As everyone knows, he's the heart and soul of Joyland."

"Oh, yes," the interviewer said. "I can't imagine Joyland without our beloved Grandpa Araby."

Nathaniel made a short, snorting noise. He caught himself quickly. He hoped no one else had heard.

But come on. "Beloved Grandpa Araby"? Some myths never died, did they?

Annie resumed her restrained plea. "The truth is, if we don't get more help, for the first time in forty years Joyland might actually have to close its doors."

Joyland might have to close? Nathaniel did laugh at the horrified gasp from the interviewer. Joyland, closed?

Would the earth stop rotating in its orbit?

Hardly. It was about time the citizens of Hallam Fork realized that Christmas came like clockwork every year, whether or not the Joyland bells were ringing.

"What the hell *is* this?" Spencer sounded annoyed. "Find some decent music. Nate needs another serenade."

"Shut up, Spence," Carson said, his eyes on Nathaniel, as if he realized something strange was happening, though of course he couldn't have any idea what.

Nathaniel's knuckles were white on the steering wheel. And the traffic had finally begun to move. He clicked the wipers up another notch to deal with the snow that suddenly seemed to be flinging itself insanely in all directions, and applied his foot to the gas.

He wanted to laugh at the whole thing….

And yet, something in Annie's voice stopped him. As she continued her plea, her dignified, yet vulnerable, voice tugged at him strangely.

She sounded too young, too fragile, to shoulder such a load. That was what bothered him. He knew the dimensions of the Joyland burden firsthand. Every year, it had taken ten full-time men to pull off the miracle, as well as every free moment he and Garth and about twenty different Hallam Fork charitable organizations could spare.

He wondered who was helping her this year. How many of the ranch hands were still hanging around? Surely, by now, with Duke nearly ninety, his ranch was on the decline. Nathaniel had been vaguely aware that Joyland still existed, but he ordinarily thought and read about it as little as possible.

He and Garth had despised the Christmas extravaganza. Garth, especially, had seen it as a showy exercise in hypocrisy. Sure, it was easy for their grandfather to stage a big production for the local disadvantaged children, making himself look like some kind of saint. It was a cinch to pretend to care about orphans and little kids in wheelchairs.

But where was that famed Araby patience, generosity and love when it came to his own two grandsons?

And yet, in spite of himself, as Annie went on describing the special events planned for this year, Nathaniel found himself picturing the mesmerized faces of the children who had paraded through every Christmas.

He wouldn't have thought he would remember them so clearly. But he did. And he suddenly saw Joyland through their eyes. For them, it wasn't hypocrisy, illusion and a cranky grandfather who wanted you to work like a dog. For them, it was magic. Perhaps the only magic they had ever seen in their difficult young lives.

And then, even more unwelcome, came the picture of his burly, bossy grandfather, flat on his back in a hospital bed, drifting in and out of consciousness. Perhaps even preparing to die.

Did Duke dream of Garth, or of Nathaniel?

Did he call out his dead son's name?

And, if he did, who answered? The nurse?

Or perhaps this overburdened, innocent Annie Browning?

Nathaniel glanced around the road, wondering how far away the exit was. His fingers twitched on the wheel. His hand moved toward the blinker.

Goddamn it.

This was wrong. This was more than wrong. It was borderline nuts.

And yet, bewildering even himself, Nathaniel put on his turn signal, maneuvered around three other cars, angled the Mercedes onto the exit ramp and eased off the highway.

When they realized what was going on, his passengers erupted into confused and laughing protests. But Nate ignored them. He drove until he saw a half-empty restaurant parking lot.

He nosed the car into a slot. Then, without killing the engine or the comfortable heater, he dug out his cell phone. If he put in a call to his main office now, Bill, his assistant, could get a rental car to him in half an hour.

Then Carson could take the Mercedes on up to New York, and the other three could still make their plane to Vermont.

Spencer leaned forward and caught a glimpse of the cell phone in Nathaniel's hand. "What the *hell,* Nate?"

"What, you've got a sudden hankering for crappy pancakes?" Al looked at the chain restaurant irritably. "You have to use the john? What's going on here?"

Carson waited in silence, clearly aware Nathaniel would answer when he wanted to, and not before.

"Sorry, guys," Nathaniel said, punching his first speed dial preset, Virginia Construction Company. That had always bugged Melinda, who apparently believed that the speed dial list was the totem pole of love.

As the phone rang, Nathaniel glanced over his shoulder to make eye contact with the others. "There's been a hitch. I'm sorry. I won't be able to join you on the slopes this year."

"Oh, man, Nate, no." Al and Jim sounded stricken.

"What? Is it Melinda?" Spencer bounced slightly in his seat, sounding for all the world like a kid badgering his parents to let him in on a grown-up secret. "Darn it, Nate! *What?*"

But Nathaniel had no intention of satisfying his friend's childish curiosity.

What could he say, anyhow?

He wasn't sure he'd ever be able to explain this completely, even to himself. Why was he giving up this much-needed, well-earned trip? Why didn't he find compelling the vision of pink-cheeked Nordic blondes in tight ski pants, blazing lodge fires, five-star hotel rooms and all the booze you needed to keep your blood warm on a cold Vermont night?

Why would he pass all that up?

In the end, he really had no idea. Not one that made sense, anyhow.

All he knew was that there was an old man in Hallam Fork who might be dying. A man who wasn't Annie Browning's responsibility.

All he knew was that, after twelve long years, it might be time to go home.

Even if it was only to say goodbye.

CHAPTER TWO

ANNIE HAD BEEN STANDING on the rafter for almost fifteen minutes, the origami angels carefully laid out before her. She had her hair dryer in hand, ready to whisk the complicated folds of paper off the beam as soon as someone was there to see them fall.

But no one came. As her arm began to get tingly, she stuck the hair dryer in the back of her jeans, like a cowboy's gun, and used her other hand to grab the upright. Why hadn't she brought her cell phone with her? Jasper must have forgotten he'd promised to stop by and help her after lunch.

Drat. She didn't want to climb down, then up again, not if she could help it. Her years of gymnastics had left her fairly sure-footed, even on this narrow beam, but she'd twisted her ankle this morning. Plus, she had programs to print. And she'd promised to run the Candy Cane Treasure Hunt at three, when Jimmy Torrey got here to cover the shop. After that, she would spend an hour taking photos at Santa's Workshop, filling in for Jane, who was the most recent volunteer to succumb to the flu.

And then Annie had to get to the hospital to see Duke.

She glanced at her watch. Ever since she was a kid, she'd always organized her life hour by hour. For a foster child who had so little power, control felt as important as air.

These days, her life was scheduled down to the minute. And she had only two minutes to spare before she had to scrap this experiment.

Hopefully, she scanned the quiet, cluttered antique store beneath her. Not a customer in the place. But she might get lucky. Jimmy might come early. He loved to look at the new merchandise.

Besides, her shop in the renovated barn was centrally located on the Araby ranch, and the people who flocked to Joyland often dropped in to look around her place.

She blew a damp curl of hair out of her face and stared at the door, willing it to open. All she needed was someone, anyone, to tell her if the angels looked okay as they tumbled, dangling from the fishing wire. She had a nagging suspicion she'd made some of them too small, and they looked more like sky dandruff than a host of heavenly silver seraphs.

To her delight, the door moved, setting off the chimes she'd programmed to play "Jingle Bells."

"Hi!" She bent her head as far as she could without toppling. "Up here! I'll be with you in a minute, but could you maybe do me a favor first?"

The customer was a man, unfortunately. Rotten luck. She didn't like to stereotype, but most men really didn't catch nuances of aesthetics. She had one customer who collected Civil War ephemera, and he didn't care about anything but price. If it was expensive, he wanted it.

"Up where?" The stranger's voice was deep, and its clipped tones sounded cautious. She spotted a pair of long legs in soft, expensive jeans—what she called "vacation denim," marking him as a tourist, not a local. The legs walked slowly in her direction and stopped by the cash register.

She tried to peek further. The legs looked strong and moved well, and she was curious to discover what face went with them. But from this angle, the painting she'd hung from the rafter hid everything beyond the man's torso. Which, for the record, was also nicely designed.

"Up here," she said again. "Can you stand right there a minute? I just need someone to watch while I blow the angels down." She chuckled, knowing how nuts that sentence sounded. "It's for the Christmas show. I need to know if the angels are big enough."

A moment's silence. Then a simple, "All right."

She flicked on the hair dryer and waved it over the rafter. Two dozen angels, each one unique, each made with a piece of gorgeous silver, white, blue, glittered or foiled paper, spilled over the edge, fluttering down, then floating gently at the end of their strands of fishing wire.

From up here it looked great. She could only hope the effect was as pleasing from below.

But if the sight had thrilled the stranger, he showed no signs of it. He didn't clap, or laugh, or gasp, or react in any way. Apparently if she wanted a compliment, she was going to have to ask for it.

"Well?" She stuffed the hair dryer into her jeans, unplugged it, and began descending the ladder. "What do you think? How did it look?"

"It looked fine."

Fine? She'd spent hours making the angels. She'd brought her papers over to Duke's place every night for months, so that after she made his dinner she could create while he watched TV. The rain of angels at midnight had been his idea, and she'd worked even harder since he got sick, as if following through on his wishes could magically make him well.

Of course, this stranger couldn't know that, so she tried not to take his lack of enthusiasm personally.

"Were they big enough? Could you tell they were angels, or did they just look like lint?"

"They looked fine."

She still had her back to him, coming down the tall ladder, so she indulged herself in an eye roll. Just her luck. She decided to christen her special effect, and she got the Grinch for an audience. Even Jasper would have said something nice.

"Okay," she said, giving up. She hit the ground and brushed her hands on her hips. "Well, thanks for helping, anyhow."

She turned around, hoping Jimmy would show up soon and wait on him, so that she could go do something more productive. Scrooges like this weren't likely to buy anything. He'd probably wander around finding fault with everything in the store.

Then she got a look at his face, and something she saw there made her feel…strange.

She knew this man.

Didn't she?

She couldn't quite place him, but she felt sure she'd seen him before. His face lived up to the promise of his body—rich brown hair, strong bones at the jawline and cheeks, and a straight-on gaze that kept his dark-chocolate, caramel-flecked eyes from being too pretty.

Overall, an interesting mix of elegant and earthy. A good haircut and expensive clothes, but no-nonsense muscles and big hands that looked accustomed to work.

Too bad he seemed to be allergic to smiling.

His gaze ran over her quickly, from her messy hair, which probably had cobwebs in it, to her jeans, which really should have been thrown away last year.

"Are you Annie Browning?"

She nodded, suddenly cautious. She still couldn't place him, but she had a strong feeling her associations weren't happy ones. Such an attractive man shouldn't make her feel so…

Sad.

"Yes. I'm Annie." She smiled, though she didn't overdo it. "Can I help you with something?"

"Is this your shop?"

She nodded again. Maybe that's where she knew him. Maybe he'd been one of her mother's customers, back when the Gray Horse had been located in town. "It was my mother's originally. I took it over and moved it here when she died a couple of years ago."

"Why here? Why right in the middle of Araby Ranch?"

She frowned. His questions weren't exactly rude, but they were curt, and they were odd. "Because Duke offered me a good deal. He renovated the old barn, and it made a great store, with living quarters behind—"

"You live here?" His eyebrows came together, as if he were displeased.

Suddenly *sort of* remembering him wasn't enough. Ordinarily, in a small town like Hallam Fork, everyone happily minded everyone else's business, but during the six weeks of Joyland the small town was overrun with outsiders.

Probably not brilliant to tell this total stranger where she slept at night.

"I'm sorry," she said instead of answering. "I feel as if we might have met, but I can't quite place…" She let it drift off.

He smiled. "No. I'm pretty sure we haven't met before. I haven't been to Hallam Fork in more than a decade. Long before your time. But I take it you're a friend of my grandfather's." He held out a hand. "Nathaniel Araby."

Her mouth fell open. She knew it must look moronic, but she didn't seem to have control of her jaw. Nathaniel? He was right. They hadn't met officially, but…

She had seen him once before—twelve years ago.

She hadn't recognized him because he'd been barely eighteen years old then, and besides, she'd seen mostly his back as he sneaked out the back door, glancing over his shoulder, shocked to see people huddled in the kitchen when he'd obviously assumed everyone was outside at the Joyland finale.

Of course, he didn't recognize her, either. But how could he? At the time she'd been fourteen, and pissed off, and crying into the cup of hot chocolate Duke had made for her. And she'd been merely one of those annoying foster kids the ungrateful Araby heir apparent had made no secret of hating.

Nathaniel had turned at the last minute and seen her staring at him. Eyes narrowing, he'd put his forefinger to his lips in a sign she couldn't mistake.

Be quiet.

Hey, no problem. She'd turned back to her hot chocolate, too miserable to give a damn what trouble some other teenager was cooking up. She'd been soaking up Duke's attention, and she wasn't interested in sharing it with anybody else.

Through the years, she'd often wondered—what would she have done if she'd known that was the last time Duke's grandson would be seen in Hallam Fork?

If she'd known that the boy disappearing through the back door would become the last in the long line of Arabys to break the old man's heart?

"You're really…Duke's grandson? I can't believe it."

"I take it there's not much family resemblance."

"No." She shook her head firmly. "None."

But she was fibbing, of course. The subtle similarities were there. The lanky height, the shoulders made for wood-splitting. And the unblinking intensity of the eyes.

But Nathaniel had walked away from his grandfather twelve years ago. She'd seen him do it. He didn't deserve to waltz back in and claim kinship this easily now.

Which brought to mind the central question. Why *had* he come back?

Suddenly the lightbulb flicked on. He admitted having heard her radio interview. Obviously, he thought Duke was dying. Had he come for a deathbed reunion, or a final confrontation? Or, even more cynically, an advance peek at the will?

Every suspicious, defensive nerve in her body stood at alert. She'd long ago appointed herself Duke's guardian, housekeeper, surrogate granddaughter and friend, and she wasn't going to stop now.

"No," she repeated dismissively. "No resemblance at all, I'm afraid."

He shrugged. "Well, I can't say that breaks my heart. The old man always was a fairly mean-looking buzzard."

Buzzard? She blinked, covering the urge to smack him. "Yes, I suppose Duke might appear that way to outsiders, people who don't know him very well."

Something flickered behind his eyes when she called him an outsider. She wondered whether it was pain or anger, and she didn't care. He didn't know Duke, not like she did. He'd picked the wrong time to come back, and if he thought she was going to let him hurt his grandfather again, he had another think coming.

She took a breath, tapping her fingers against a bookcase topped with a display of toy soldiers. "So. If you're not here out of concern for the old buzzard, may I ask why you bothered to come back at all?"

His smile, which hadn't been very deep to start with, twisted slightly.

"You can ask," he said. "But I'm not sure I can answer."

"Can't? Or won't?"

"Can't." He shrugged again. "Frankly, it beats the hell out of me. As I parked the car, I was entertaining the possibility that I might be insane."

She opened her mouth, but nothing immediately presented itself as an appropriate response. She didn't have much time to think, because "Jingle Bells" rang out again, and Jimmy came barreling through the door.

“I’m sorry I’m late.” The boy forced himself to stop on the mat, where he peeled off his jacket and stomped snow from his boots. He unwound his scarf, revealing his pale, freckled face. He clearly saw the customer, but in true Jimmy form he never stopped talking.

“I was ready, but Dad had to drop Carly off first. Oh, and he wants to talk to you. He’s parking. I’ll go get the broom and the Brasso. I’m okay here, so you can head on over to the candy cane hunt if you need to.”

She watched the skinny ten-year-old streak toward the storeroom. Polishing wasn’t first on her list, since yesterday’s customers had wrecked the Christmas corner, and that needed rearranging. But Jimmy prided himself on always having something to do without being told. She didn’t have the heart to squelch his enthusiasm.

She glanced at Nathaniel, who was scrutinizing her with an extra dose of curiosity.

“Your son?”

“No.” Good grief. She touched her hair, wondering how bad she must look today, if he believed she could possibly have a ten-year-old child. She was only twenty-six, for heaven’s sake. “Jimmy’s a friend. He helps out a few days a week after school. He’s been putting in more hours since Duke’s accident, of course. Everyone has.”

“Hey, Annie,” a diffident male voice broke in. “I know you’re busy, but have you got a minute?”

She looked over. Mick Torrey, Jimmy’s dad, had entered the store, obviously catching the door before the jingle chimes could reset themselves. He gripped a heart-shaped Christmas tin in his gloved hands.

“Elaine sent some cookies over for Duke. Oatmeal.

You know how he likes them." Mick's pleasant, beefy face looked sheepish. "I know it's a waste right now, but she was determined to send them anyhow. It's just killing her that she can't do anything else."

"I know, Mick," Annie said. She took the pretty poinsettia-decorated tin, from which a comforting wave of cinnamon and nutmeg rose. "Tell her thanks. I'll give them to the nurses, if Duke's…not able to eat them."

"Thanks." Mick slapped his cap against the palm of his gloved hand. He looked as if he might start crying, which was no wonder, with all he had to worry about. His wife was eight and a half months through a difficult pregnancy. Plus, his seven-year-old daughter, Carly, was struggling in school, and word was she might have to be put in a special-needs classroom.

"Jasper told me you've got to rebuild the main stage," he said. "I wish I could stay and help. You know I would, except with Elaine's having to be in bed so much—"

"It's fine, Mick. Don't even think about it."

"I know. It's just that—" He looked from Annie to Nathaniel, chewing on his lower lip. His face cleared. *"Nate?"*

He moved forward awkwardly. "Nate Araby? Oh, my gosh. Is that really you?"

Nathaniel looked bewildered. He tilted his head, as if he thought a different angle might make the man in front of him familiar. "Yes," he said. "I'm Nate."

Mick paused, his wind-burned cheeks reddening further as he realized the recognition was one-sided. "Oh, that's okay, you probably wouldn't remember me. I'm Mick Torrey. We were in high school together. Of course, I wasn't part of your crowd, not really. We were in a few classes together, but it was such a big deal when we heard you'd run off, and—"

He stopped, obviously stricken.

Oh, Mick. Annie wished she could have put her hand over his mouth. She turned to Nathaniel, wondering how he'd react. Mick was such a sweet, hapless guy. If Nathaniel smoked him, she'd run the arrogant jerk through with the Civil War sword she kept behind the counter.

But to her surprise, Nathaniel was still smiling. His eyes were cold, the way she sometimes saw Duke's eyes look, but probably Mick was too flustered to notice anything as subtle as that. The smile was what counted.

"Mick Torrey," Nathaniel repeated, putting out his hand. "Of course. Weren't you the defensive end our senior year? You saved the season single-handedly. Our quarterback wasn't worth a plug nickel, if I remember right."

Mick laughed, nodding agreement. "Fumblefingers Eckert. Twenty-two percent pass completion that year. He was the principal's son, though, so..." He shook Nathaniel's hand as if it were the handle of the water pump behind his barn. "Good to see you, Nate. Really. I guess you came home to visit Duke. He'll be so damn glad. You know, to see you again. Before..."

He swallowed, unable to go on. Annie put her hand on his forearm and squeezed bracingly. A couple of years ago Duke had loaned Mick money to prevent foreclosure on his farm, and he worshipped the old man, even more than most people around here.

She hoped he could hold back his tears, because if he started bawling, she might fall apart, too.

With a strangled sound, Mick put his beefy hand on Nathaniel's shoulder, and suddenly the three of them were one big circle, like a group therapy ice breaker. Annie felt discomfort and tension moving off Nathaniel in icy waves.

"He'll be so damn glad," Mick repeated, his voice swollen.

Nathaniel's cool gaze flicked from one to the other, then, with a smile, he stepped back gracefully, breaking contact with the others.

He fixed his eyes on Annie. "Do you think he'll be glad?"

She answered that glacial gaze steadily. No blinking. No sugarcoated platitudes. He might as well know that not everyone in Hallam Fork was as naive and forgiving as Mick. Some of them remembered what it had been like when Nathaniel disappeared that Christmas Day, and some of them held grudges.

"Well," she said without any particular inflection. "He'll certainly be surprised."

CHAPTER THREE

IT DIDN'T WORRY Nate a bit to know that, in spite of her call for help, Annie Browning was not happy to see him. Clearly, she would have vastly preferred for him to load his suitcase right back into his car and drive away. Far, far away.

Her instant rebuff had surprised him a little at first, even though merely driving onto Araby land had put him in a crappy mood, and he hardly entered with his Mr. Congeniality face on.

But he'd quickly realized the problem. Obviously Duke had painted an evil picture of his heartless grandson, and she had it framed in her head like the Wanted sign at the post office.

Fine. She didn't like him. So what? When it came to rejection, Annie was a novice. Nate was accustomed to feeling like an interloper at Araby. If she'd welcomed him with open arms, now, *that* would have felt weird.

Her emotions had played out fairly openly on her face, and he'd watched her start with shock, move to anger that he'd dare to show up unannounced and uninvited, and finally end in resignation. She couldn't send him away—she couldn't decide for Duke whether he wanted to see his grandson. She might be Duke's special friend and self-appointed guard dog, but Nate was kin.

He even saw the moment hope flickered across her face. Hope that maybe his arrival was a blessing in disguise. Maybe the two Araby men could be reconciled at the eleventh hour, bringing ease and forgiveness to Duke's dying days.

Or maybe Nate was imagining all that. Maybe she was being practical. He'd seen the skeleton staff they were using to run Joyland. She needed all the help she could get. Even his.

She'd seemed a little shocked that he wanted to stay at the ranch, but she'd handled that, too. She'd sent Jasper to open the house for him.

One whiff of the familiar wood-and-leather smell, and Nate questioned his sanity all over again. It was just for tonight, though, he promised himself. One night wouldn't kill him. If it was too oppressive, he'd look for a hotel room tomorrow.

He put his suitcase on the bed in the guest room, instinctively avoiding the larger room he'd shared with Garth and, of course, never once considering invading Duke's domain at the back of the house.

His leather bag looked out of place against the purple, green and brown country quilt, which was new since he'd been here last. This bed used to have a blue chenille spread. He could see it so clearly he almost touched the new quilt to be sure it was real.

But he didn't. He was good at compartmentalizing his emotions, and, as he stood at the foot of the bed, staring out the window at the snow, he made his mind go blank. As if it had a real door, he shut his brain against the memories he felt pressing there, shifting restlessly.

Memories of Garth. Of his mother with red-rimmed

eyes, dressed in yellow polka dots, waving goodbye through the station wagon window. Of the long days he watched the road till his eyes burned, waiting for the station wagon to turn the corner.

Arguments between Garth and Duke that shivered the pine walls, and muffled tears that soaked Nate's pillow. Beef stew eaten in stony silence, and whippings by the barn. Garth slipping through the window, saying, "Go to sleep, Nate. I'll be back in the morning. Unfortunately."

A rap on the door frame roused Nate now. To his shock, he realized the shadows stretched in long rectangles across the bed. He must have stood here, lost in his empty brain, for half an hour or more.

Annie waited at the threshold. Her hair, tossed and crazy earlier, now neatly pulled into a ponytail. She'd put on lipstick, black pants and a sweater, and a set of armor-plated poise.

It suited her. She'd been cute before, all blonde, blue and pink, and he suspected she'd always have an innocent, waifish quality. But suddenly he saw that, in her way, she was quite beautiful.

And that made him wonder. Why was she here? What was a smart, attractive woman like this doing, wasting her life on a dusty antique store and an equally dusty old coot like Duke?

Her black coat draped over her arm. She was wiggling her fingers into her gloves. She wasn't here to stay.

"Hello," he said politely.

"I'm going to the hospital now," she said, equally

polite. "I have to be there by seven if I intend to catch the doctor. I thought you might want to come."

He'd thought about this, naturally. Once he dropped off his friends, he'd had way too much time to consider all the ramifications of this visit.

What exactly was his goal? Was it to satisfy his curiosity about what he'd left behind?

Was it to ease Annie's unfair burden? Was it to check on the ranch and Joyland? Did he want to see if Duke had changed? To reconcile with him? Or simply say goodbye?

He'd gnawed on it all the way to Hallam Fork, and he still didn't have any good answers.

"I don't think I'll go tonight," he said. "I'll call the doctor in the morning, but for now I think I'll just settle in. Maybe I'll see if I can help with the festival. Does J-land still offer the candlelight carols?"

"Yes, but I think that's covered tonight. If you really want to help, we're short a couple of sleigh drivers. Think you could handle that?"

"Sure." He unzipped his suitcase, glad he hadn't been headed to a Hawaiian vacation. At least he had all his cold-weather gear. "I'll probably see you tomorrow, then?"

"Okay." She turned halfway, then stopped, looking at him over her shoulder. "Nathaniel," she said, her voice clear and frosty, "if you do decide to visit Duke, will you let me know first?"

He raised his eyebrows. "Why?"

"Because—" She took a deep breath and started over. "What I'm trying to say is, I hope you won't try to visit him alone. I don't know whether Duke is aware of things, of who's there or what's said around him, or any of that. But he might be, and I want to be sure you are...I want to be sure you don't..."

He waited, wondering how she'd finish. What did she think he might do? Lean over the bed rail and berate a dying man for sins committed a decade ago? What good would that do? If recriminations could bring Garth back, Nate would have shouted his lungs out years ago.

But, as if this house had drained him already, he didn't have the energy to explain himself—or the desire. You could explain how to lay a solid foundation, or why you were letting an employee go. But explaining emotions was like trying to catch fire.

"I'll keep your concerns in mind," he said.

She lifted her chin. She was too bright not to notice that he'd evaded her point. "Will you agree to check with me before you go?"

Damn it. They'd reached a fragile truce, and he hated to upset it, but he wasn't going to make promises he might not keep. It was quite likely he'd rather visit Duke alone. It might stir up feelings he had no intention of making public.

"Will you promise?"

"No."

Her fingers tightened on her coat. "No?"

"I'm sorry, Annie. I know you care about him, and I'm sure you're very important in his life. But I'm not going to wait around for your permission, if I decide I want to visit my own grandfather."

"I see." Her eyes narrowed, the blue as cold as ice. In fact, he thought with a wry, inner smile, her eyes looked more like Duke's than Nate's ever had.

"Well, I won't worry too much," she said. "It's been twelve years since the urge last came over you, so I'll assume we're not in any immediate danger."

ANNIE REGRETTED that comment all night.

She'd been way out of line. And it hadn't even been a reaction to anything Nathaniel had actually said or done, but rather a defensive reaction to her own fear. Fear that his arrival might somehow upset Duke.

And the bigger, deeper fear that being upset might make Duke more fragile.

Still, why had she let herself be such a harpy? Did that help Duke? As Duke himself loved to put it, nobody ever caught happy by loading their trap with nasty.

She shook her head, thinking of all the wisdom he'd shared with her through the years, and how little apparent good it had done. She had hoped she'd tamed that waspish tongue of hers long ago, but apparently it was only dormant, not dead.

The next morning, she decided to keep the antique store closed. She put the Back At sign out on the door, arranged the clock hands to 3:00 p.m., and headed for the horse arena, where they were slowly rebuilding the stage.

The snow crunched underfoot as she moved past the deserted candy cane fields, her palms wrapped around her coffee mug for warmth. It was only 6:00 a.m., and the sun hadn't made a dent yet in the temperature.

But that hadn't kept the troops from coming out in force. The large training oval was already teeming with workers. The finale wouldn't be canceled this year if these people had any say about it. Half-finished bleachers rose jaggedly in a semi-circle, and at the far end the new stage was beginning to take shape.

Out of the chaos, Jasper loped toward her. He wasn't smiling. He rarely smiled. But she could tell he was deeply pleased with something.

"Damn if we haven't hit the jackpot," Jasper said around the toothpick he always kept in his mouth. "This new guy knows what he's doing."

Annie looked behind him. "Duke's grandson?"

He nodded. "Yeah. I mean, *really* knows. He owns his own construction company. Can you believe the luck?" He held out a coil of frayed wire, which they must have stripped from the old stage. "Electricity, even. The rotating set is finally rotating again. He just may be the saving of us."

She nodded, wondering why her thoughts were so conflicted. That stage, which rotated to display a series of Christmas tableaux, complete with backdrops, special lighting and microphones for each, was one complex piece of engineering.

She should have been delighted to get expert help. She *was* delighted. But that the help should come in the form of Nate Araby…

Jasper hurried off to check on the horses. Though Duke had closed the training component of his ranch a couple of years ago, they still boarded several, and they'd taken in a few temporary horses to draw the Joyland sleighs.

Annie slowly made her way toward the stage, greeting friends as she went, consulting on problems and admiring progress. Nate seemed unaware of her arrival. He stood beside Paul Abernathy and his ten-year-old son, Vance. They seemed absorbed in testing the hinged rafters that would create the roof effects.

Her mission this morning was repainting some backdrops, so she stood at the side, pretending to fiddle with the brushes. But really she studied Nate, knowing she wouldn't have many opportunities to do so unnoticed.

His chiseled profile must take after his mother's side of the family, because he was more handsome than Duke could ever have dreamed of being. His brown hair drifted onto his high forehead in a way she found inappropriately sexy, given the circumstances. He had one long leg propped on a platform for stability, and he bent at the waist…showing off those broad shoulders and narrow hips.

One after the other, he deftly drilled screws into the hinged beams. She'd never seen manual labor look so graceful.

From this angle, as she watched him work, he looked worlds different from the boyish, angry-faced Nathaniel of her memories. For more than a decade, she'd been sore at that boy, the one who eased out the kitchen door and disappeared, leaving his life, his home, his family, behind.

His family. That was what had shocked and offended her the most. At fifteen, with two failed foster homes behind her and no sign of a third chance anywhere in sight, she would have given everything she owned to have a family.

And he threw his away like garbage.

It was going to take a while to change her mind about a guy like that. Didn't matter how clever he was at drilling and splicing, or that he'd pitched in without waiting to be asked.

She picked up a paintbrush and feathered it across her palm, testing to see if it was fresh enough to use.

It didn't even matter how good he looked in those jeans….

At that moment, he looked over and caught her watching him. She blushed, which made her furious with herself.

"Morning," he said with a raised eyebrow and a smile.

That brought Paul's attention her way, too, something she regretted. Paul was one of the guys she'd dredged up from her past when she was desperate for help. They'd dated two or three times last year, long enough for her to discover what a chauvinistic bully he was under his glossy exterior. No wonder his marriage to Vance's mother hadn't lasted.

After three rotten foster fathers, the last thing Annie wanted in her life was another bully, so Paul had been let down easy.

Too easy, maybe? He seemed ready to turn "helping" into "flirting," even right in front of his son. He sauntered over to Annie with his lightbulb smile.

"Wow, lady, when you cast your net, you bring in the big fish, don't you? I wouldn't have thought anything on earth could get Nate the Great back to Hallam Fork!"

She frowned. *Nate the Great?* How adolescent was that? She did the math, and realized that Paul must have gone to high school with Nate, too. And, unlike poor geeky Mick, Paul probably had been part of Nate's popular crowd.

In these dramas, Annie's sympathies were always with the outcasts and losers.

"I didn't reel him in, Paul," she said crisply. Her gaze drifted back to Nate, who was discussing the rotating set's mechanics with Vance. "I'm sure he's only here because of Duke's accident."

Paul laughed. "Don't be modest, Annie. You know you lure us all in with your siren song. He probably heard you on the radio and thought—"

She never heard the end of the sentence.

"Vance! No!" Annie's heart pounded as she saw Paul's son wedge himself into a corner and bend down to look curiously at the inner workings of the set. "Vance! Don't touch that!"

To her horror, the boy had just pressed the button that would, if the electricity actually had been connected, shift the set into its second position. Vance recognized the problem as soon as the motion started, but the exit was blocked, and he couldn't think fast enough to get free.

In about three seconds, the moving stage would crush Vance against the wall.

It all happened so fast. Vance was yelling, and everything began to blur. Then, somehow, Nate had reached across the corner, grabbed the boy and dragged him over the top of the stage.

As Vance tumbled safely onto the arena dirt, the wooden platform slid into its slot and clicked in place. Right where the boy had been standing.

Breathing heavily, Paul raced to his son's side and seized his upper arm with fingers as tight as talons. "Damn it, Vance! What kind of moron are you? Didn't

I tell you not to touch anything? I should have left you at home with your mother, where you couldn't get yourself killed."

Annie saw the man's dilated eyes, and she knew he was simply frightened, but she also knew that Vance was scared, too. Getting trapped wouldn't have killed him, but it could easily have broken his leg.

She opened her mouth to say something, but before she could speak, Nate broke in.

"It was my fault, Paul." Nate's voice was smoothly apologetic. He touched the other man's arm, as if to remind him that he was gripping the boy too hard.

"Are you kidding? The fool pushed the button and—"

"Yeah, but I told him to." Nate eased Paul's hand down, then turned to Vance. "Are you okay, son? I'm so sorry. I wasn't thinking about you being in the way."

The kid nodded mutely, staring at the ground, clearly unwilling to look either his dad or Nate in the eye. He still trembled slightly.

"I'm sorry, Paul," Nate said again. "There's a moron here, all right. But it's me, not Vance."

Annie heard Paul grumble, obviously reluctant to let go of his anger, but equally unwilling to seem upset with his buddy Nate.

Annie met Nate's innocent gaze over the boy's bowed head. She tried to keep her own expression blank. But her poker face wasn't as good as his, and she had a feeling he knew that she knew.

No question. Nate was lying.

Why? Why would he cover for Vance, someone he'd

met maybe half an hour ago, and a fairly disagreeable kid, at that?

Nate winked, or at least she imagined he did.

It was such a brief movement, over in a twinkling, and he turned away, picking up a pair of needle-nose pliers. But it was enough to leave her rooted to her spot, immobile and confused.

She'd imagined that Duke's vanished grandson was a seriously selfish son-of-a-gun, the kind of man who cared for no one and pleased himself at any cost.

Instead she'd found…what?

She couldn't quite get a fix on him, and that bothered her.

Who exactly was Nathaniel Araby?

CHAPTER FOUR

NATE'S CELL PHONE woke him from a sound sleep. He almost ignored it, then remembered he'd given his number to the nurse's station when he talked to the hospital earlier. Just in case.

Nate had been downright shocked to learn that his name was listed among the people with whom the doctors could discuss Duke's medical condition, but perhaps that list had been made years ago, before Nate even left Hallam Fork.

Whatever the reason, that list had definitely simplified getting information. But it also meant they'd probably call him if anything went wrong.

His fingers fumbled across the unfamiliar nightstand, found the phone and answered it.

"Nate, it's Annie. I just heard from Imogene, the head nurse. Duke's taken a turn for the worst."

She didn't actually ask the question, but he heard it anyhow. He didn't answer immediately. His gaze went to the window, where he saw a frenzied dance of snowflakes, illuminated by the cold, white moon. He cracked his neck, feeling the burn from lifting about a hundred rafter beams. He stared at his feet and realized he was too tall for this bed, which had probably been carved a hundred years ago.

"I'll drive," he said. "I'll meet you at the car."

She didn't talk on the way, which was fine with him. Bill had sent Nate the best rental car he could find on short notice, but the heater was crap. The roads were badly illuminated, and, given that it was three-thirty in the morning, he needed a cup of coffee in the worst way.

He considered letting Annie go up ahead of him, while he negotiated with the vending machine, which was trimmed in cheap blue and gold garland. But at the last minute he realized he would just get lukewarm panther piss out of the damn thing anyhow, and he joined Annie in the elevator.

When they reached the second floor, a middle-aged nurse bustled out from behind a station, around which colored lights had been awkwardly strung. If it was supposed to look festive, it failed.

The woman met them at the door to Duke's room, where a sprig of fake holly covered his name, leaving it to say "uke Araby."

"I hope I'm wrong," the woman—he assumed she was Imogene—said quietly. "But his breathing is much worse tonight. He has a definite rattle. So I thought… better safe than sorry, right?"

She looked curiously at Nate when she said this, and her inflection indicated it might be a real question.

"Sure," he said, because she seemed to expect it.

"Absolutely right," Annie said with extra warmth, as if to make up for his lack of it. "Thanks, Imogene. Is it okay for us to sit with him a while?"

"Of course." The nurse inched open the door with the tips of two fingers. "I'll be out here if you need me."

Though Annie made a beeline to Duke's bed, Nate

didn't know his way. He hung near the threshold, waiting for his eyes to adjust. The room seemed alive with shadows and stray light. Blue numbers blinked their mysterious messages on vaguely threatening monitors. A bag of tear-colored liquid hung from a silver pole, both glistening in the moonbeams.

The smell of alcohol and antiseptic and hospital soap was overpowering. And the sounds…what were those sounds? Nate took a minute to separate the slow, steady hiss of the oxygen from the rattle that emanated from Duke's lungs like the sound of water passing over pebbles.

"Hi, Duke," Annie said. She took the old man's hand and bent over the bed, her uncombed curls so delicate and golden, the smile on her face so serene, that if Duke woke now he'd probably think he was dead and being welcomed by an angel.

But as Nate's vision adjusted, he saw details more clearly. And he knew that the odds were mighty slim of Duke waking up tonight.

Or tomorrow. Or ever.

To his surprise, the thought came into his chest like a fist. Duke might really be going to die.

"I brought someone to see you," Annie said. She rubbed the old man's limp hand between her own, as if he were merely sleeping, and she could gently chafe him into consciousness. "You won't believe it, Duke. It's Nathaniel. He's come home."

He wondered whether she'd expected a Christmas miracle. Had she believed Duke would jerk to a sitting position, eyes wide, arms outstretched, galvanized by the thought of his beloved grandson?

Someday, Nate decided, he was going to have to explain to Annie what things had really been like back then on the Araby ranch. He'd come tonight of his own free will, though, and he didn't intend to lurk in the shadows.

"Hello, Duke," he said. He took his position on the other side of the bed and looked down at the man lying there.

For a minute he felt strangely disoriented, and he gripped the rail to steady himself. He had come prepared to hide his emotions. What he wasn't prepared for was…not to have any.

But what emotions would make sense here? The name on the door might be Duke's, but this body didn't belong to him. Not anymore.

In Nate's memory, his intimidating grandfather had been a sequoia, towering and powerful. This bony, felled form covered by a thin blanket might as well have been a pile of twigs.

The only feature that looked the same was the nose. Rising from high between the bushy silver eyebrows and extending long and hooked toward the thin lips, it was a nose that belonged to a hawk. Now that the old man's face had grown so gaunt, the nose jutted more prominently than ever.

Duke's eyes had always been a clear, cold blue, capable of piercing you like an ice dagger. What would they look like now, if he could open them? Could either age or sickness rob them of that terrifying, glittering intensity?

Nate felt Annie's gaze on him. When he looked up, she smiled. He had the feeling she knew his thoughts.

"He's lost a lot of weight since he's been sick," she said. "Hospital food. Wait till he gets back to my chili and chocolate cake dinners. I'll have him looking like himself in no time."

She cooked for Duke, too?

"You must be tired," he said. "Why don't you sit in the armchair?" He recognized the scarred brown leather. She clearly had brought it from the ranch.

"No, you take it." She wriggled onto the edge of the bed, careful not to dislodge the IV. "I usually sit here. There's plenty of room for me, but it might be a tight fit for you."

He almost laughed at that. A tight fit in more ways than one. But the armchair was comfortable, and they sat without speaking a few minutes, adjusting to the strange intimacy of the dark room.

Out in the hall, bells chimed randomly, and the rhythmic slap of soft-soled nurses' shoes moved back and forth, but no one entered to break the silence.

He watched Annie from his shadowy corner, marveling at the peace she seemed to project, though he knew she must be worried sick. Occasionally she brushed her fingertips across Duke's forehead, and then she'd tug gently on the edge of the sheet, settling it around his shoulders.

Obviously Nate needed to know more about the arrangement between these two. Since it was clear she wasn't leaving anytime soon, he might as well start finding out now.

"How did you meet Duke?"

She looked up. Her face was pale, all eyes in the moonlight. Her curls looked like snow-fire around her shoulders. "I was one of the foster kids who came to Joyland."

"Oh." He and Garth had hated those kids. Well, to be more exact, they'd hated the way Duke showered all that time and attention on them. Let one of those adoring little kids try living at Araby for a week, instead of just visiting for a day. Then they'd know the truth about sweet old Mr. Duke. "Did you love it?"

"I hated it," she said with a smile. "But then, I hated everything in those days. Especially things that seemed to be all sugary-fake fairy tale, you know?"

"Yeah." He smiled. That was exactly how he and Garth had seen it. "I know."

"I was only fourteen, and I was pretty unhappy. I'd been through two foster homes, and I'd been told it would be darned hard to find a third. When they took us to Joyland on Christmas Eve, I ditched the chaperone and ran off for a cigarette behind the barn." She refolded the edge of the sheet more neatly. "Duke found me there. It's probably not an exaggeration to say he more or less saved my life that night."

Nate was having trouble picturing any of this. Annie Browning incorrigible? Rejected by two separate foster families? And Duke finding a way to help her through all that? He wondered how old she was, exactly. How long ago had this been? She wasn't anywhere near thirty, which meant it had probably happened not long after Nate himself left Hallam Fork.

"How?" He shifted in the chair, sitting up a little straighter. "How did he save your life?"

She looked down at Duke. "I'm not sure I can explain. He didn't say much. He's a man of few words. Of course you know that even better than I do. I guess it was more the way he listened."

Stranger and stranger. In Nate's experience, Duke didn't listen. He gave orders and expected them to be obeyed. When they weren't, he brought out the belt.

"I honestly don't remember exactly what we said. I just know that, after we talked, I felt different. He made me see, somehow, that people can't love you unless you let them. If you go into a relationship with your heart closed, even if you're only trying to protect yourself, love can't get in."

She smiled. "It sounds very simple, even stupid, now. But I honestly hadn't ever thought about it that way before."

It did sound simple. Far too simple. Nate knew better. These decisions weren't always voluntary. Sometimes hearts closed all on their own, after a terrible loss, or a ruthless beating, and they simply lost the ability to open up.

"Anyhow, I did find another family. A wonderful woman who was a real mother to me. I didn't scare her off, and I was able to be myself. Duke and I have been friends ever since."

"And how long has that been?"

She hesitated. She glanced out the window, and he didn't know whether she was counting or stalling.

"It was twelve years ago," she said finally. "This Christmas Eve."

Twelve years ago.

He did the math. He sat, staring blankly at the silhouette of Duke's IV and his curly-haired bedside angel.

Twelve years ago, on Christmas Eve, Nate had carried

out the plan he'd been secretly perfecting for two years, ever since Garth's death. At the stroke of midnight that year, Nate had turned eighteen, and was legally free to get the hell out of Hallam Fork. He'd been waiting in his room, beyond ready, pacing with impatience, bare-minimum bag packed, forcing himself to hold off until Duke was immersed in the Joyland finale.

Naturally, the old hypocrite ate that part up—dressing as Santa, posing under the spotlights on his famous rotating stage and basking in the adulation of his public.

Somehow, though, Nate's calculations had gone dangerously awry, and he'd almost been caught. When he reached the kitchen, he'd been terrified and furious to see Duke sitting at the pine table, talking to a brat-faced kid with Goth clothes, dirty blond hair and angry eyes.

Blond hair…

No. Surely not. But…

He almost forgot he was in a hospital room. He almost laughed out loud.

"That was you?"

The angel nodded. He had a feeling she was laughing, too. "That was me. In all my fourteen-year-old glory. Now you see why I couldn't hang on to a foster family?"

"Not really. If families could send away every kid who dressed in black and copped an attitude, there wouldn't be any kids left."

"It was more than attitude, I promise you." She shook her head softly, as if remembering. He had a sudden wish that he could have known her then. He would have liked to see those blue eyes flashing with temper.

"I've always wondered about you, though," she said. "About why you left that night."

He didn't respond. Surely she didn't want him to recite his grievances against the old man now? Duke seemed to be floating in another world, far away from this room, but what if, somehow, he still could hear?

"I mean..." She shrugged. "I just wondered why you left like *that*. You were eighteen, weren't you? Duke couldn't have stopped you, if you really wanted to go."

He wondered whether it would have been possible to explain, even if they'd been alone, with time for detail and privacy for candor. It was complicated. His escape had been plotted out for two years, and yet, in some ways, it was as primitive and mindless as if he'd been an animal chewing his way out of a trap.

Clearly, he hadn't trusted himself to make an open break. The truth was, *eighteen* was only a number. Nate hadn't been a man anywhere except on paper. If he'd come face-to-face with his grandfather, he would have been twelve again in an instant, helpless and unsure.

But tonight, for the first time, he became aware of a new truth, a piece of the puzzle long repressed. He'd kept his flight secret because, somewhere deep inside, he'd known that running away was wrong. That it was cowardly and cruel.

He had fled because he couldn't survive in the place where he'd been abandoned, working and sleeping alongside the memory of his dead brother. But he had left his grandfather there alone, to live among the ghosts.

No matter how cold and hard the man had been, how unwilling and unloving a guardian, he probably had deserved better than that.

"It's complicated," Nate said, repeating that lame phrase even as he realized that this new pinch of guilt was here to stay.

He listened to his grandfather's slow, rattling breaths. "I think maybe the bottom line was...I didn't know how to say goodbye."

THOUGH ANNIE WOULDN'T HAVE THOUGHT it possible, they both slept. By the time dawn came, suffusing Duke's hospital room with a weak, lemony light, his breathing had evened out, and the nurse said she thought the real danger had passed.

Annie and Nate drove to the ranch in silence. She felt too stale and achy to be talkative, and luckily he seemed comfortable with simply sharing the space. She wondered briefly whether her questions had annoyed him last night, but he didn't seem grouchy. Just weary.

God knew she was exhausted, too, having tried to sleep sitting up on that sliver of plastic mattress, but she had no time for a nap. Workers continued to fall victim to the flu, and the Joyland curse seemed to have taken hold: whatever went wrong would require at least ten men to fix.

Good thing she'd had her will reinforced by the visit to Duke last night. Otherwise, she might have put up the white flag and closed Joyland's doors. She was tired of worrying about sickness, and safety, and whether the Christmas dreams of a thousand sad-eyed children would come true.

Perhaps, she thought, it was a blessing in disguise that she had to go off-property this afternoon. She'd bought an antique sleigh from the Patterson farm—the perfect prop for the pictures with Santa—and she was scheduled to pick it up today.

The Pattersons were moving. They'd liquidated almost everything, and they no longer had a truck or a horse to deliver it to Araby. She and Jasper planned to ride two of their horses over, hook them up to the sleigh and let the animals pull it back.

She stole ten minutes to grab a shower and put on fresh clothes, including her sturdiest boots. She arrived at the stables only a couple of minutes late.

But instead of finding Jasper, waiting impatiently with her tack in hand, she saw Nate, holding the reins of two fully saddled horses.

"Jasper's running a fever," Nate said, obviously reading her startled gaze correctly. "I'm afraid he's come down with the Joyland plague."

"Oh, no." She was ashamed that she thought first of the logistical problems. But she quickly remembered that this flu was tough, and Jasper wasn't young. "How bad is it? Has he seen Doc Wickerly?"

"Paul's driving him over there right now." Nate smiled. "I wouldn't worry about Jasper too much. Halfway down the drive, he was still sticking his head out the back window, shouting orders to me about which horses we should take to pull the sleigh."

She chuckled. Sounded like Jasper. He and Duke were of the generation that didn't believe in delegating. After the fall, Duke had run Joyland from his hospital bed. Until the pneumonia dragged him under.

She glanced at the horses. Sky King and Jasmine. Good choices. Sure-footed in the snow, which drifted lazily around them now, but might get worse as the day wore on. The sky pressed low, heavy with a dozen shades of silver, pewter and ivory.

The Patterson farm lay in a cozy nook at the bottom of the nearby foothills, a few miles from Araby. Nate led the way, automatically taking the back roads. Annie was surprised at first, seeing how familiar he was with the secret, twisting bridle paths. But he'd lived here for years. He was clearly a natural on a horse, so he probably had spent hours exploring these very trails.

They reached the farm easily, and the negotiations over the sleigh were quick, since Mr. Patterson wasn't the talkative sort, and price had been established beforehand.

She hadn't seen it before, though, and she was delighted to find that it was still in pristine condition, beautifully maintained. It was a piano-box sleigh from the late 1800s, cherry red with red upholstery, glossy white runners that blended into the snow and a charming folk-art scene painted on the back—a snowy woods full of fantasy deer, chipmunk and rabbits.

When Annie and Nate climbed into the sleigh, and he settled the white fake-fur lap blanket over her to keep out the cold, she felt positively Victorian. The horses seemed happy to break into a canter, and they skimmed across the snow briskly, the wind tingling against her cheeks.

After a few minutes, Nate pulled them back to a trot, probably unwilling to wear the horses out. The animals still had to draw sleighs full of tourists around the paddocks at Joyland tonight.

Unfortunately, the slower pace gave her far too much time to stare at Nate's elegant profile, and the way snowflakes spangled his dark hair.

He seemed more relaxed today, she thought, in spite of how tired he must be. His jaw would always be square and masculine, but the angles didn't seem as steely. She saw no rigidity in his shoulders.

As though he sensed her scrutiny, he glanced over and tossed her a smile. "Cold?"

She shook her head. The day was soft, in spite of the temperature. The wind was crisp, but not vicious.

"I love winter," she said. "I read too many fairy tales when I was a kid. I still believe every snowflake is a tiny fairy in a beautiful lace dress."

He arched an eyebrow. "I thought you didn't like fairy tales."

"I pretended not to like them. That's completely different."

He laughed. "Yeah, well, I must have read different stories. I still think there's an ice monster hiding in every tree, tossing daggers down to impale you. Duke wanted to be sure we both had a healthy respect for weather, and its secret agenda to kick your ass."

She kept her eyes forward, afraid to do anything that would make him lapse into silence. She wanted to hear about his relationship with Duke.

It was so mysterious to her. The grandfather who had made his life hell didn't seem to be even remotely related to the Duke she knew.

"*Both* meaning…you and your brother?"

"Yes. Garth. Duke thought the two of us were citified babies, and he considered it his duty to toughen us up."

She risked a look at him. He wore a half smile, but she sensed that the topic was fraught with unresolved emotion. How could it not be?

"Toughen you up? Sounds as if that plan might have had an unpleasant side."

His fingers tightened on the reins. "That's an understatement, I'm afraid. When my mother left us at the ranch, I was only twelve, so intimidating me wasn't very hard. Garth was fifteen, though, and he fought Duke tooth and nail."

"I guess that's fairly normal. Fifteen's not a very cooperative age. And a man like Duke, who finds it so hard to express emotion… Why did you go to live with him in the first place?"

"It was supposed to be a short vacation. My dad had just died, and my mother said she needed a little time to…I think her word was 'regroup.' Turned out she needed more than a little. That was eighteen years ago, and she hasn't come back yet."

"Oh, my God." Annie felt a cool trickle of horror, thinking what that must have been like for the boys. She'd been rejected plenty in her life, but never by her own flesh and blood. She'd always been allowed to nurse the dream that, if her real mom had been alive, Annie would have been cherished and adored. Nate and Garth couldn't even cling to that illusion.

Nate jiggled the reins and clicked to get Sky King's attention. The pace picked up a bit. "I take it Duke never mentioned that?"

"No. I don't remember asking, though. I guess I assumed both your parents had died."

He shrugged. "They might as well have. But being abandoned made Garth bitter, and it made him fight harder. I kept hoping Duke would back down. I kept wishing he'd realize that Garth needed affection more than he needed toughening up, but he never seemed to catch on. They fought like wild animals, until Garth couldn't take it anymore and joined the army."

This part she did know. "He died not long after he enlisted, didn't he?"

Nate ducked to avoid a snow-laden branch, then guided the horses to the right, away from the trees. "Right. An accident in tech school, right after basic training."

She wanted to touch his arm, and she was close enough to do it. Close enough physically, anyhow.

"What terrible luck. I can imagine that, at least on some level, you must have blamed Duke for his death."

Nate made a low sound. He looked over at Annie, then, with a short tug on the reins, he drew Sky King up abruptly. Jasmine, a sensitive horse, followed suit immediately. The wind stopped, and the sleigh settled into the powdery snow.

"Not *on some level,*" Nate said flatly. His breath made harsh clouds in the air. "On all levels. He sent my brother away to die, purely because Garth wouldn't submit. Because he wouldn't get down on his knees when Duke said *crawl.*"

She protested instinctively, an inarticulate noise of denial.

"Look, I get it that you don't see Duke that way," he said. "Clearly, a lot of people love him. Hell, in some miserable, leftover part of my heart, I probably even still love him, too."

Of course he did, she wanted to say. Didn't he know that was why he'd come home? She'd seen it, as clear as a neon marquee, when he finally looked at his grandfather's wasting body last night. Nate had come home hoping against hope that they could set things right.

She did reach out then. She let her gloved hand rest atop his. She left it there several seconds, until finally his body warmth rose to meet hers. He turned, and his face was only inches away.

For a minute she thought he might be going to kiss her. It was insane—he still had the tension of anger and pain on his face, and he clearly wasn't thinking soft thoughts. But something flared briefly behind his eyes, and his gaze dropped to her lips.

"Nate," she said. "Of course you love him. And he loves you, truly he does—"

"Please," he broke in harshly. He shifted his hand, ostensibly to adjust the reins, but she knew he also wanted to break the contact between them. He snicked to the horses, and they resumed their trot.

"I know you don't believe it," she said, "but—"

"Whether he loves me or not isn't the issue." Nate let out another deep, visible breath. "Love is just a word. I'm not even sure what it means. What I'm trying to say is that, as hard as it may be for you to believe, Duke was different with us."

She waited, her hands folded on top of the fur blanket.

"I don't know why," Nate continued after a short pause. "Maybe he was hurting because his own son had died. Maybe we reminded him of our dad, and he could hardly stand to look at us. If that's so, I'm sorry. But the bottom line is Duke was all we had. He was harsh when we needed comfort. He was judgmental when we needed mercy. We were starving for love, and he gave us puny rations of cold, grim duty."

They were almost back at Araby. The trees had thinned out, and before them stretched a pasture of unbroken white. The sun had fought through, and tiny crystals of new snow glittered like diamond dust against the soft velvet of the old.

The house rose from the edge of the pasture, looking like something out of a Christmas card. She'd turned on the lights before she left, so the colored strands twinkled along the roofline, and the windows gleamed with a welcoming, honeyed warmth.

She wondered what Nate saw when he looked at it. Did he see anything that could ever be called a "home"? Or did he still see only the prison he'd been so determined to escape?

"Duke has changed," she said impulsively. "Maybe it took losing both of you to teach him how to show love properly. But you should know. He really, truly has changed."

He nodded without looking at her.

"You may be right," he said, tugging the reins, guiding the horses toward the waiting stables. "Kind of ironic, isn't it? Because it doesn't really matter anymore. In so many ways, it's far too late for love."

WHAT THE HELL was the matter with him?

He had been within an idiot's inch of kissing Annie.

Yeah, she was gorgeous. But gorgeous women weren't exactly an endangered species. And yes, she was strangely fascinating, with her uninhibited mix of innocence, intelligence and pure grit.

Fascinating women were a lot harder to find.

But it was the innocence part that caused all the problems.

Well, that and the fact that she was Duke Araby's guardian angel. Nobody seduced a guardian angel and got away with it.

Even *considering* kissing her was insane. Dangerous.

And definitely not to be repeated.

Luckily, Joyland attracted crowds big enough to lose himself in, and he was able to spend the next twenty-four hours without more than an occasional glimpse of Annie in the distance.

Staying busy was good, because, between Duke and Annie, Nate's thoughts were a mess. He accepted every job that came his way, from shoveling snow to climbing scaffolds, from hammering nails to sanding floors. He even led a group of snot-nosed toddlers through Santa's Workshop and lifted every single one up to choose a toy from Santa's sleigh.

Turned out, kids were much heavier than roof beams. By the next afternoon, his muscles were complaining enough that he had to face the truth. Over the past few years, he'd become a desk jockey, and he had lost touch with the part of his business he loved. Working outdoors. Building things. He'd forgotten how to sweat and push his body, and reap the rewards of exhaustion at the end of a day.

Still, when Jasper asked him to cut firewood for the night's bonfire, Nate couldn't turn him down. The old guy didn't have the flu, thank goodness, but Doc Wickerly had told him to take it easy for a day or two, anyhow.

The stockpile was kept behind the old barn, which

now housed Annie's antique store, but he knew she wasn't there. Volunteers continued to call in sick, and she couldn't move from task to task fast enough.

He'd seen her ten minutes ago, buttoning up an elf suit, heading toward Santa's Workshop.

It was quieter over by the antique store than anywhere else. He heard the distant echo of someone singing "I'll Be Home For Christmas," and the wind soughing in the snowy branches, but that was all. He soon settled into a comfortable, mindless rhythm.

But he hadn't split more than a dozen logs when a pair of young voices broke in, coming from somewhere in the trees.

He listened a minute. It was two boys, and, from the sound of it, they were mad as hell and ready to kill each other. He started to put down the axe, then decided it might make a good visual effect, in case he had to referee anything really hot.

He recognized the two immediately. The first was the kid who worked for Annie after school—the little freckle-faced overachiever who was Mick's son. Jimmy, wasn't it?

The boy held an empty straw basket in his hand as if it were a weapon, and he was pointing it at Vance, the cocky kid who had almost crushed himself in the stage the other day.

They were only about ten, but the hostility had risen to grown-up levels. Red faces, narrowed eyes, heaving chests. On the ground around them lay about fifty brown pinecones, which Nate assumed had been inside that basket a few minutes ago.

"Hey," he said pleasantly as he broke into the shadows

of the trees. He rested the axe over his shoulder, visible but unthreatening. "Everything okay here?"

"No." Jimmy looked as if his fuse had burned down to the last inch. His shoulders hunched, and his knees were flexed, ready to pounce. "That shithead needs to shut the hell up, or I'm going to break his face off."

Wow. The kid had guts—and, even without knowing the details, Nate's sympathy instinctively leaned toward anyone who wanted to take Vance down a peg. The kid thought he was God's gift, just as his dad always had. He'd really gotten on Nate's nerves the other day.

"Break my face?" Vance screwed up his mouth scornfully. "Try it, pipsqueak. You're the one who needs to shut up. If I hear you sing that sappy Christmas song one more time, with every goddamn note going flat—"

"I said shut up."

Jimmy's intensity was unmistakable. Nate had to hold back a smile when he saw Vance blanch. This was the classic geek-versus-jock showdown, only in this case the geek apparently didn't know he was supposed to be cowed.

"The hell I will," Vance said, rallying. He sneered, the effect somewhat lessened by his pale cheeks. "I mean, really, Torrey, you sing as bad as your retarded sister, and I can't stand another—"

It happened so fast Nate didn't see it coming—and he'd been watching for it. Jimmy exploded from his crouch, and landed on Vance like a tiger on dinner. His arms were swinging so wildly they couldn't have done much damage, but Vance couldn't have screamed any louder if someone had been eating off his ears.

Nate dropped the axe and moved quickly. He peeled

Jimmy from the other boy and held the two apart by grabbing fists full of their shirts.

"Cool it," he said flatly. "Vance, stop squealing. Jimmy, get a grip."

It was like trying to hold a couple of bags of snakes. They both kept writhing and flailing out at each other, but luckily Nate's arms were long enough to prevent contact.

He didn't try to say anything else over the chaos. Better to let them siphon off the steam. Eventually, they'd get tired, or one of them would wake up to how ridiculous they looked.

Unfortunately, before that happened, Mick and Paul appeared at the edge of the trees, obviously drawn by the bellowing, which must have been loud enough to reach the Candy Cane fields, where both men had been working. Behind them, several other Joyland workers loped toward the scene, too.

"Damn it! Vance! What the hell?" Paul grabbed his son's collar and yanked him free of the fray. Now that he could get a good look, Nate saw that the boy was going to have a black eye.

"Jimmy!" Mick rushed forward and clutched his son, too. But anxiety was uppermost in this father's emotions, and he pressed the boy to his chest. "Jimmy, are you okay?"

"No, he's not okay!" Vance scowled fiercely, though he was still being gripped by the collar, practically dangling from his tall father's hand like a naughty kitten. "He's crazy. He was trying to kill me, Dad. He's out of his mind."

"Jimmy?" Mick sounded horrified and a little frightened. "Jimmy, did you hit Vance?"

Jimmy's anger had clearly drained away, leaving him weary. His face looked oddly adult, and fully aware that nothing good could come of this. "I did. But if you'd heard the things he said, Dad..." He seemed to run out of energy midsentence.

"I didn't say anything." Vance's voice was high, whining. "I was sick of listening to him sing his stupid song, and I said so, that's all."

"That's not all," Jimmy said, low and fierce. "And you know it."

Suddenly, Annie was there, too, and everyone seemed to assume that she was in charge. She still wore her elf suit, but her eyes were tight and worried. She went to Vance and put her hand on his chin, so that she could get a good look at his injuries.

"Let me get something to put on that."

She moved to Jimmy, and checked his face, too. But he was untouched, which of course made him look guilty. His face reddened under her gaze.

Then she turned to Nate. "Did you see it happen?"

Oh, hell.

He didn't want to get involved with this. Both of the kids were dimwits, and they both ought to be put on bread and water for a week.

"It had already started by the time I got here," he said. That was true, as far as it went. He'd heard Vance insult Jimmy's sister, but God only knew what Jimmy had said before Nate showed up.

Her eyes searched his face, as if his part in the episode could be read there, too. Under that knowing scrutiny, he felt strange—somewhere between wanting to laugh out loud, and wanting to blush like one of the kids.

Then she stepped back, and she began to herd everyone into the antique store, where they could sort things out and find some ice for Vance's eye.

As Nate watched them walk away, he had the oddest feeling she might be disappointed in him. The feeling that, somehow, she'd lost a little respect for him.

He thought about following them, then decided against it. He retrieved the axe and went back to the woodpile.

No. Let it be. If she decided she didn't like him, maybe that was the best possible outcome.

That way, if he couldn't stop himself from trying to kiss her one night, she'd punch him, just as Jimmy had punched Vance.

And maybe that would save him from himself.

SOMETIME IN THE WEE HOURS of that night, Annie awoke from a terrible dream in which she'd been hung and forgotten in a cold-storage vault. In the dream, she'd dangled helplessly, teeth chattering, trying to make conversation with a conceited mink stole and a haughty sable cape.

Her first thought was that the dream might be a comment on her nonexistent love life, but she quickly realized her apartment really was as cold as a meat locker.

The heat had gone out.

It wasn't the first time the system had given her trouble. The renovations on the barn had been done professionally, but they'd been completed at least ten years ago, and nothing lasted forever. Annie had been babying the exhausted central heater along for two winters now, praying it wouldn't give out entirely.

Looked as if her luck had run out. This wasn't the familiar bang-and-grind of an exhausted heater kicking out inadequate warmth. This was the stony silence of a unit that had admitted defeat and given up the ghost entirely.

Her bedside clock read 2:30 a.m. Great. Worst case scenario. She wouldn't dream of dragging any poor, sleepy soul out of bed to help her now, and it would be hours before the sun showed up to pitch in, either.

There was only one option. She'd slip quietly into the big house and snatch a few hours' rest on Duke's couch. She might even grab a snifter of the old man's brandy, to unfreeze her internal organs.

With any kind of luck, Nate was a sound sleeper and would never know she'd been there.

She put on an extra pair of socks, then slid her feet into her boots. She layered a heavy workout suit over her pajamas, and an ankle-length down parka over the suit. Even under all that, her skin prickled with goose bumps.

She topped things off with a checked, fur-lined trapper hat, a pair of gloves and a muffler. It was only about a hundred yards to the main house, but she'd rather look supremely ridiculous than lose her nose and fingers to the cold.

Still, when she glanced in the mirror on the way out, she had to laugh. If Nate was awake, he'd probably think he was being invaded by some psycho version of Gentle Ben. She'd be lucky if he didn't shoot her.

All the more reason to hope he was asleep.

The moon rocked, full and silver, in a sky as clear as a big bowl of black glass. The stars looked sharp, as if someone had been collecting the shards of a thousand shattered crystals. An owl hooted softly as she moved across the path, which had been cleared yesterday afternoon but already crunched underfoot with new fallen snow.

By the time she reached the house, her fingers were numb, and she fumbled with the key, hoping she could avoid making a racket.

But she needn't have bothered. The first thing she saw, when she eased open the door, was Nate.

Fully dressed, he sat in his grandfather's leather wingback chair. One arm was crooked, elbow bent above his head, his temple resting against his knuckles as he stared into the blazing living room hearth.

He looked utterly lost in thought, his expression frozen, although the play of the firelight danced over his features with the illusion of motion. He obviously didn't hear her open the door, or feel the rush of frigid air.

She hurried to remove the trapper hat, more from self-preservation than vanity. She wouldn't look much better without it, given that she hadn't even stopped to brush her hair, but at least she'd be recognizable.

"Nate?" She cleared her throat. "It's me. The heat's out at my place. I'm sorry I didn't knock. I thought you'd be asleep, and I didn't want to wake you."

It seemed to take him a minute to return from whatever faraway places his mind had taken him. But as soon as he saw her, he stood, manners obviously drilled in him to the point of instinct, and came over to take her coat.

"You must be freezing." He hung the puffy coat on the wooden tree, then added her hat and muffler. "Come on in."

It was always a welcoming room, large, with pecan paneling and curtained window seats now garlanded with pine, but it seemed especially so now. The temperature was blessedly warm, and she rubbed her nose as it began to tingle and thaw. She still couldn't feel her fingers, so she moved to the mantle and held them close to the fire.

"Let me help." He reached out and took her cold hands between his large, warm ones. The contrast stung, and she almost pulled back. But then, as he rubbed and chafed gently, the blood began to circulate again.

Methodically, he folded his hand around each finger individually. She shut her eyes and made a small purring sound. It felt heavenly, like coming back to life.

Then, gradually, as their temperatures began to match, his fingers slowed. His warmth had passed into her, and they were no longer ice against fire, but skin against skin. And that felt even better.

She opened her eyes, and found him staring at her. The caramel-colored flecks in his eyes seemed like captured firelight. His wonderful warmth seemed to be pooling in her midsection, and she recognized, not for the first time, how lovely it would be if he kissed her.

As if she'd spoken the words out loud, he let go of her hands.

"Better?" he asked politely.

"Much. Thanks." She looked away, feeling silly, especially when she caught a glimpse of herself in the convex early-American mirror over the wing chair and realized how decidedly un-sexy she looked. Tangled hair everywhere, no makeup, tired eyes and snow-stung nose.

Lumpy, faded sweats over flannel little-girl pajamas. Combat boots.

He would be as likely to kiss someone's dotty, oatmeal-stained grandmother.

He took one step to the side, gesturing toward the kitchen. "Do you want something warm to eat? Maybe some hot milk?"

"No, no, I'm fine. Tomorrow's another tough day. Probably I should try to get some sleep, if you don't mind my crashing on the sofa."

"Wouldn't you be more comfortable in one of the bedrooms? I'm camped in the guest room, but I can easily move down here—"

"No. Honestly. I don't often sleep over here, unless Duke's not feeling well. But I always bunk on the sofa. I'll be up at dawn to call the heating guy, anyhow. I truly thought you'd already be asleep."

"I should be. Every muscle I own hurts, and Jasper undoubtedly has another day of torture planned for me tomorrow." He smiled. "At least let me get you a pillow and some blankets. If I can find them, that is."

"Thanks. That would be great." She knew exactly where all those things were stored, but the situation was delicate. She had more years spent at Araby recently, but he was family. This had once been his home.

And would be again someday. Annie had seen Duke's will.

While she waited, she pulled the sweatshirt over her head, unlaced the boots and stepped out of the pants. She even ran her fingers through her hair, trying to tame the tangles, all the while telling herself it didn't matter how she looked.

She wasn't trying to attract Nate Araby. He might be handsome, and interesting, but long ago she'd developed a no-touch list. Her years in foster care, watching the ways in which vulnerable people—like women and children—could get hurt, had taught her what kind of man to avoid. Two kinds, really.

Bullies. And bolters.

Nate Araby was a bolter. She didn't blame him entirely for that. There was plenty of guilt to go around—to Nate's mother, for being a selfish bitch, to Duke, for being too tough, and even, in Annie's opinion, to the brother, Garth, who sounded like an unforgiving troublemaker.

Yeah, Nate undoubtedly had his reasons for fearing commitment, but the bottom line was he did. He might learn his lesson someday, as Duke finally had. But she wasn't interested in being the one he practiced on.

So why did her hands still tingle slightly, remembering his touch? Why did the idea of sleeping under the same roof seem...risky?

She walked around the room, settling her nerves. She'd dusted the room every week since Duke went into the hospital, but a faint haze already lay over some of the wooden tables. She ran her palm over it, restoring the gloss, then fluffed a couple of throw pillows on the sofa.

On the end table next to the wing chair, she noticed a piece of paper beside Nate's coffee mug. It hadn't been there last week. Nate must have been looking at it before he sank into that reverie.

She was close enough to see, and she couldn't help herself. She picked it up.

It was a photograph of Duke and two teenage boys, all three on horses. She recognized Nate immediately, and it wasn't a leap to assume that the handsome, cocky-faced older boy was Garth.

"I found that in Duke's desk," Nate said as he returned, blankets under one arm, a pillow under the other. He glanced at the photograph as he passed on his way to the sofa. "I was looking for a list of last year's donors, to see if we could find someone to fill in for Greenwood Florist. You knew they backed out, right?"

She nodded, trying not to feel awkward that he'd caught her looking at it. "Jasper told me. He said you were going to try to get a replacement. I appreciate that. I want him to rest as much as he can…not that he will, of course."

Nate began spreading out the blanket, covering the old-fashioned plaid of the sofa. "I couldn't find Duke's list, so I called the florist I use in Roanoke. They said yes, so at least we don't have to worry about that. But while I was looking, I came across this picture."

"It's a nice one." She studied it another minute. Both boys, even the cocky Garth, looked reasonably happy. You wouldn't have predicted, judging from this photo, that this family would disintegrate within a couple of years.

"Yes." Nate had the "bed" set up. He gestured for Annie to try it. She did, perching on the edge, but she brought the picture with her. She couldn't seem to stop looking at it. The scene felt like something from an alternate universe, like something that could have been, should have been…but wasn't.

After a minute, Nate sat beside her. He tilted his head

to look at the picture, too. "We rode for hours, just the three of us. It was one of our few good days. No fights. No trouble." His eyes were dark. "In fact, it probably was the only good day. It was definitely the last."

"How wonderful, then, that this picture has survived."

His body was very still. "I'd never seen it. I have to admit, I was surprised to find it in his desk, right at the top. I wouldn't have thought he'd be the type to keep it."

She didn't bother to disagree. She'd observed early on that Duke didn't fill his house with memorabilia like pictures and scrapbooks. The night she met him, he'd told her that hanging on to the past was like trying to swim backward carrying a pocketful of rocks. She'd been self-centered enough to think he was mostly trying to send her a message about letting go of her own unhappy memories.

Absently, she traced the faces in the picture with her fingertip. "There's so much people don't know about one another, isn't there?"

"Yes," Nate said. "Or about what's coming in the future. A few months after this, Garth was gone."

"It's hard to believe, looking at him." She heard her voice catch, thinking about the terrible waste. The boy was so young, so vital. It should be harder, she thought, to extinguish such a potent life force. "And now Duke, too, may be..."

Her fingers trembled, and Nate gently took the picture out of them. He put it on the other edge of the sofa. "Annie," he said, his voice low. "Don't."

"I know. I know I shouldn't let myself even think it. But sometimes—" She bent her head, ashamed to show such weakness. "He's been the only constant in my life for a long time. I just don't know what I'd do without him."

"You'd go on." He put his hands over hers, as he'd done when she entered. "You'd be fine, eventually. Because you're strong. You're one of the strongest women I've ever met."

But she wasn't. She wanted to cry out the words. Deep inside, she was still lonely Annie Browning, obnoxious little foster kid nobody wanted. She hadn't really changed that much. She still drove people away—mostly any man who wanted a way into her life. She found excuses, judged them lacking. She simply wouldn't take the risk.

She still didn't know how to trust anybody but Duke.

"Annie." In an instant, Nate's voice had changed, and the pressure of his hands on hers was hot.

She looked up, her eyes stinging with unshed tears. The firelight drew shadows on his face, and his eyes were burning.

"Damn it. I—" He took a ragged breath. "I can't..."

She didn't know whether he meant he couldn't let himself do this...or he couldn't stop himself. But it didn't really matter, because she could feel the change in the atmosphere.

He was going to kiss her.

And she wanted him to. She wanted it so much. She was so tired. She was especially tired of brooding about failure and fear and death. She wanted to stop thinking completely, and simply be alive.

She put her hands up and touched his elegant cheekbones. The bones were hard and high, but the skin was silky and warm. She brought his face toward hers, showing him that it was all right.

So much more than all right.

By the time he kissed her, she was trembling as if she were in the snow, naked under the hard white moon. His lips were so strong, and their heat tasted like boiling honey. She opened her mouth, and moaned as he drove in deeper.

For a long minute, nothing else existed but this kiss. His arms folded around her, and she pressed herself against his chest, absorbing the glorious life-fire. He eased back onto the outstretched blanket, bringing her with him, until she was above him, connected from lips to thighs, and burning everywhere.

She felt how much he wanted her, and that, too, seemed like an affirmation. Like a promise that the world held passion and shivering bliss, and, in rare and magical moments, the chance to lose yourself in joy.

A promise that sometimes it was enough to be a woman, and alive.

She moved, and she heard him groan. His hands tightened on her hips, tilting her into him.

"Annie," he said against her lips.

And in the word there was a tone.

A tone that belonged in the real world, the world she had been trying to leave behind.

His lips stilled, and, with a tension she could almost feel, he used the heels of his hands to push her from him, creating an inch of sanity between them.

It was enough. She felt the madness ebbing. Not dying, but banking enough to allow her to think again.

She looked into his serious gaze. She brushed the tangled, damp hair from her face.

She took a deep breath. Then she sat up, wondering how one kiss could leave her hollowed out inside.

He swung his feet to the floor, and pulled himself up. He looked at the ceiling. He waited a few minutes, until his breath came more evenly. Then he stood, moved to the wing chair and dropped the picture on the end table.

"Annie." He squared his shoulders, then turned back with a gentle smile.

"Yes."

"It would have been a mistake," he said softly.

She nodded. "I know."

"I'll be gone in a week."

"I know."

"I don't want to leave behind…regrets."

"No. You're right. I understand."

Then, though her body protested that it couldn't be true, he disappeared up the stairs, and she was once again alone.

"MR. ARABY, I'M GLAD you're here!" The nurse at the third-floor station smiled as Nate stepped out of the elevator. "I was about to call Annie. Is she with you?"

Nate had a momentary tightening in his chest. But why would the woman—he thought her name was Imogene—be smiling if the news was bad?

"Annie's working right now." He knew that was true. When he got up this morning, she was already gone. He'd seen a Hallam Electric van outside the Gray Horse this morning, then around lunchtime he'd spotted Annie in the arena, helping the finale choir set up for rehearsal on the new stage. They'd just finished it yesterday.

"Oh, well, that's all right," Imogene said. "It's just that Duke's fever is down some today, and he's actually been speaking a little. I thought she might want to know."

Nate's chest eased, but almost immediately another odd sensation appeared. He had driven to the hospital impulsively. He hadn't even quite sorted his mind about his reason for coming. He hadn't thought he needed to. He hadn't expected Duke to be awake.

"He's talking?"

Imogene's enthusiasm dampened a bit. "Well, it's not exactly conversation. More like a mumbling. He's in and out. But, given how grave his condition has been for more than a week now, it's actually quite remarkable."

Nate nodded. "Great. Thanks. I'll be careful not to tire him out."

Though it was a bright, cold midafternoon outside, the room swam in its usual cloistered twilight. He shut the door behind him and moved to the bed slowly, trying to gauge Duke's level of awareness.

"Duke?" He spoke quietly, loud enough to alert someone merely drowsing. "Duke, it's Nate."

His grandfather didn't stir. Though his color was a little better this morning, he didn't look substantially different. Whether it was fever, a coma or a sound sleep, he was as remote as ever.

And, in the presence of that stern-faced indifference, Nate wasn't sure what to do next. He stood, his hands on the cool aluminum rails, feeling absurd. Even when

Duke had been fit and well, he hadn't been much of a talker. The old man had clearly believed words were weak substitutes for action.

One pair of words he'd never used, or accepted from anyone else, was "I'm sorry." Once or twice, in the early years, when Nate had tried to apologize for some trivial mistake, Duke had cut him off. "A sorry mouth doesn't impress me much, son. If you've got sorry hands, show me by mucking out those stalls."

So that obviously wasn't the place to begin now.

"Joyland's going along great, Duke," he said. "The whole town's turned out to make sure everything stays on track."

His voice sounded odd in the echo chamber of linoleum, tile and stainless steel. In spite of the miniature Christmas tree someone—probably Annie—had propped on the windowsill, this sterile room seemed worlds apart from the colorful chaos of the festival.

"Annie is the one to thank," he went on. "She's been working like a one-woman army, night and day. You're mighty lucky to have her in your corner."

Nate heard the sudden energy in his voice and realized he was in danger of revealing how deep his admiration for her went. Better be careful. He didn't want Duke's subconscious to pick up hints of how close Nate and Annie had come last night to making love on Duke's sofa.

Or how bitter Nate's struggle had been, the rest of the night, to stick to his ridiculously noble decision.

"Anyhow, I'm staying at the ranch, too, and I'm helping as I can. But she's the glue that holds it all together. She's one amazing lady."

Duke's mouth twitched, and Nate stopped, wondering if it was possible the old man really heard him. It made him feel strange. It made him feel like taking chances.

"Duke, I—" He tried to choose the perfect words. "I found the picture you saved. The one from when the three of us rode to Henley's Creek."

Was he imagining it, or did Duke's face change again? Nate waited a while, but not even a twitching muscle revealed any awareness. Must have been wishful thinking.

"That was a good day. All three of us were happy that day, weren't we, Duke? Even Garth." Nate was annoyed to hear his throat thicken. If he was going to get maudlin, he might as well shut up. Even from the ethers of profound coma, Duke would be disgusted.

Another subject, then. He cast about, trying to think of one. But what else mattered at a moment like this? The weather?

It was quite possible, in spite of Imogene's fragile optimism about the easing of the fever, that Nate would never see Duke again.

Even if Duke lived—and that was far from likely—the hourglass had just about run out. It was December twenty-second, only two days from the finale, the closing of Joyland for the season...and Nate's return to Roanoke.

This could be his last chance.

Standing there, thinking of returning home, Nate finally realized an uncomfortable truth. Against all odds, the dream of reconciliation had remained alive, buried deep in his heart all these years. Buried under the anger and the pain, under the blame and the recriminations. Under the ice, too. The determination to be completely self-sufficient, to never need another human being. To show he'd learned the Duke Araby lesson by going it alone.

It had all been a lie he told himself. Deep inside, he'd desperately hoped that someday Duke could find the words to explain. The words that would make Nate understand and forgive.

With the realization came a sense of vulnerability, worse than anything he'd felt since the day he realized his mother wasn't coming back for him. He hated the sensation. It scared the hell out of him. He had to fight not to wrap himself back up in the lies.

"I was wrong to leave you without saying goodbye," he said, suddenly reckless. "I know you don't like rehashing old mistakes, but I need to tell you this before it's too late. I never stopped caring about you, or wishing you cared about me. But I was just so…so angry. I blamed you for Garth's death."

He shook his head, frustrated that there could be no dialogue, only this limping, lopsided soliloquy.

"I'm still struggling with that, Duke. I know he was difficult. He was a lot like you, really. But I guess…I wish you'd been able to find a way to help him through it, instead of sending him away."

Nate stopped. Where to go from here?

And, as he paused, Duke's eyes fluttered open.

For a minute, Nate couldn't catch his breath. Instinctively, he put out his hand and touched his grandfather's arm. "Duke?"

The blue gaze was clouded, confused—he seemed to stare right into Nate's eyes, but something was wrong.

Nate's heart twisted weirdly. "Duke? Can you hear me?"

"Goddamn it, Garth." The words fell like sharp, clear bell tones, each word distinct and audible.

"It's not Garth, Duke." Nate's throat was thick again, almost useless. "It's Nate."

"Garth," Duke said again. He tossed his head in a brief agitation. Then he shut his eyes.

He said something else, but much lower, and Nate couldn't understand it. Nate lowered his head, to be closer to the thin, tight lips. Duke spoke one more time, even more incoherent and indistinct.

Nate couldn't be sure, but he thought it sounded a little as if he'd said…

Garth always wanted…

The bells? The bess—the best, perhaps?

Garth always wanted the best.

Nate straightened, a cold sensation trickling down his spine. He knew those words. It was an accusation Duke had made a hundred times. Garth was vain, materialistic, greedy, everything guaranteed to offend a gruff, plain-living horse trainer. The boy wanted brand-name jeans, cooler kicks, faster internet. A car.

Garth knew Duke wasn't exactly poor, and he hated living as if he were. If he were in Washington, he always began scornfully, instead of this hellhole…

Nate cringed, but no matter how hard Garth struck out, Duke always had an answering thrust, like a dagger he kept ready in his pocket. "Well, your mother seems to have dropped you in this hellhole, and until she comes back to claim you, you'll live by the devil's rules."

The devil's rules.

Nate stared down at the old man, who had subsided, no longer restlessly shaking his head. Duke's thin lips moved, but no sound came out.

But Nate didn't need to hear it. He knew, now, what themes ran through his grandfather's dying dreams. Duke wasn't thinking of Nate at all. He was still fighting those same brutal battles, even though Duke had won the war long ago, and the cemetery in Hallam Fork had the headstone to prove it.

Nate slung his coat over his arm and left, one more time, without even saying goodbye.

THE CHOIR SOUNDED WONDERFUL. Annie sat to the side of the stage, working on her origami angels, and offering suggestions as the singers ran through each of the carols they planned to use for the finale tableaux.

And trying not to think about Nate. Or last night.

It was ridiculous, how often her thoughts turned to him. She'd known him just over a week, and somehow he'd burrowed into her consciousness and taken root there. This afternoon, she'd caught herself imagining how nice it would be if he stayed, if he lived with Duke, at least for a while. If they could get to know each other better, in a more peaceful time. If they could explore what these feelings—like the ones that had put them in each other's arms—really meant.

But that was it. The feelings didn't mean anything.

And he wasn't staying.

She needed to stop being an idiot. Nate was nobody to her, and if he could really abandon his grandfather again, he was a nobody she didn't even really like very much. She should be thankful he hadn't taken advantage of her strange mood last night. Now he could leave the ranch, go whenever he wanted, and it wouldn't matter one bit to her, except in how it might hurt Duke.

Right. A nobody.

And yet, her mind wouldn't stay away from him.

Luckily, the problems that always cropped up right before the big finale kept her busy. Every few minutes she was called over to the other end of the arena to arbitrate something about the sets. At least a dozen hot-headed creative types were still painting and creating the backdrops for the tableaux.

The first song, "I Heard the Bells on Christmas Day," would feature a fake steeple, with two elves swinging on either side of a huge bell. Apparently debate still raged over what bell material best balanced safety and illusion.

The second tableau would be a lighthearted version of "Winter Wonderland." It was a crowd favorite, partly because the high school drama club always provided the actors and sets. This year, the theme would be an enchanted forest, and Annie had already seen the clever costumes of snowy owls, crimson cardinals, long-legged fawns and flop-eared bunnies. The kids in the audience would go crazy.

The third was a traditional nativity scene, set to "Away in a Manger."

The fourth and last was always kept a secret as long as possible, and the most effort went into its creation. This year, Duke had chosen "I'll Be Home For Christmas." In this number, if everything went according to plan, Jimmy would be the star. He had a beautiful, crystalline voice with a naturally wistful quality. When he sang the last lines of the song, about coming home in his dreams, everyone lost it, even in rehearsals.

The set was simple, but elegant. Jimmy would stand in a glimmering silver, blue and white landscape, a true midnight clear. He'd sing alone, giving the song an almost unbearable poignancy.

In the final performance, the one that ended at midnight as Christmas Eve turned to Christmas Day, as he sang the last line Annie's origami angels would fall from the roof beams, twinkling and shimmering around him. They'd tested it out once, though Annie was still folding more every day. But, even without a full complement of angels, the effect was shivery good.

She'd already arranged for a videographer. That way, she told herself, when Duke was better, he could watch it.

She listened to the choir director give notes to his "Away in a Manger" soprano, and watched Jimmy standing in the corner, shaking his arms to loosen up his nerves. He always looked as if he might have a heart attack from fear, but the minute he hit the stage he came to life. He was meant for this.

Today, though, he looked more uncomfortable than usual. She set down her paper, which would be a feather-winged, trumpet-blowing silver angel if she could get it right, and went over to him.

"Everything okay?"

He looked grim-faced, pale under his freckles. Not a sign of his usual buoyant energy. "I hope so."

"What do you mean?"

"My dad. He's really mad at me. About the other day. With Vance."

She nodded. She knew that. She knew that there had even been talk about pulling Jimmy from the show. She had hoped that his arrival today meant Mick had relented.

"Doesn't he know you're here?"

"He does now." Jimmy stared toward the doors, unblinking and rigid. "He just came in."

Annie turned and saw someone striding in, but backlit as he was by the sunlight reflecting off the snow, she wouldn't have been able to identify him. Clearly, though, Jimmy saw something he recognized.

And sure enough, in a few seconds, Mick was close enough for both of them to be sure. His round face, unnaturally tight with fury, said it all.

He didn't even seem to notice Annie. His eyes were locked on his son. "I'm disappointed in you, Jimmy. You know I said we had to talk about this."

Jimmy glanced at Annie, clearly begging for help. But she knew better than to interfere.

"Well, you weren't home," Jimmy said in a small voice. "And rehearsal was starting."

"I need you to get in the car."

"I can't." His voice rose. "I've got rehearsal in, like... two minutes."

"No. You don't have rehearsals at all. You're done."

"Dad!"

Mick put up a hand.

Jimmy turned to her, bent with misery. "Annie!"

"Mick," she began diffidently. "He's really done so much work—"

"No. His mother says no. They've been fighting over this for two days now, and it's making her sicker. Jimmy hasn't spoken respectfully—"

"I have! I've been very respectful. I just said she didn't understand. I said she didn't know how important my role is, and—"

"Get in the car."

The tone was final, and Jimmy heard it. His eyes blazed with tears, and his mouth was so twisted from trying to hold back that he looked as if he might explode. The look he turned on his father was fierce, and for a minute Annie wondered whether he might lash out at his dad as he'd done at Vance.

She wondered how much stress there was in the Torrey household right now, with Elaine confined to her bed, and Carly in a serious situation. Jimmy was obviously not himself, and, now that she looked at him carefully, Annie saw that Mick looked pretty done in, too.

Thankfully, Jimmy got hold of his temper. He satisfied himself with kicking away a small screwdriver that lay on the floor near his feet, then, with one inarticulate growl of despair, he raced out of the arena.

Mick rubbed his hand over his face. "I'm sorry, Annie. I know it's short notice."

She tried to smile. "That part's not a big problem. He's the best, and I'm sorry to lose his voice, but we have other singers. It's just that—"

"I can't go against Elaine. She said no, and she meant it."

"I know. It's just that it's so important to Jimmy, Mick. He loves it so much, and he's good at it. It's one thing that the boys like Vance..."

She didn't finish. She knew Mick understood. He'd been a victim of the Vances of the world himself, and he had to know what a comfort it was to Jimmy to have a talent, a moment in the spotlight that a hundred Vances couldn't buy, or steal, or diminish.

He shrugged helplessly. "I know. But I can't fix this. He shouldn't have talked to his mother like that, and he knows it."

"What if I talk to her?"

He shook his head. She tried to think of something else to say, but out of the corner of her eye she saw a man arriving through the arena doors. Suddenly she understood how Jimmy had recognized his dad. Though this figure was just a broad-shouldered silhouette, she knew in an instant that it was Nate.

When Nate reached them, under cover of the polite greetings, Mick ducked out. She watched his hunched-over, departing figure and tried to hold back a sigh.

But Nate apparently was good at reading vibes.

"Trouble in the Torrey house?" he asked absently, as though his mind were really somewhere else. "Fallout from the episode with Vance?"

She nodded. "They won't let Jimmy sing in the show."

"Really? Over that little scrape?"

"It doesn't seem like a little scrape to his mom." The Torreys were good people, rule followers, gentle and generous and kind. They didn't approve of fighting for any reason. "But the poor kid. He's such a good guy, and he's heartbroken."

Nate's eyebrows drew together. "That's ridiculous. What did they expect him to do? Let Vance be an ass, and walk all over him?"

Then she remembered that Nate had been there. She'd always suspected he had heard what Vance had said to set Jimmy off.

"Nate," she said eagerly. "Do you think you might talk to Mick and Elaine?"

His eyes widened. "Why on earth would I do that?"

"Because you might be able to help Jimmy. You heard what Vance said, didn't you? You might be able to make them understand that Jimmy wasn't really to blame."

"I doubt it."

She saw the tension in his jaw, but she was too in love with her idea to catch on, really, to what it meant. "I think you could! After all, Mick clearly respects you. Maybe you knew Elaine, too, when you were in high school? If you did, you could go visit, as if it were old friends—"

"No, I couldn't," he said flatly. "I'm leaving in two days. I shouldn't have come back in the first place. I'm not a part of this community, and I'm not friends with Mick, or Elaine, or anyone else in Hallam Fork. I'm just some runaway they dimly remember gossiping about, way back in another lifetime."

"That's ridiculous. How can you think—"

"I don't *think*. I know."

She couldn't believe how flat his eyes were. She wondered what had happened to turn him back into this stranger.

She fought a weird instinct to simply get away. His expression made her shiver.

But for Jimmy's sake she had to try one more time.

"I wish you'd at least consider—"

"Listen, Annie." His stranger's voice had a sharp undertone of anger. "You're mistaken if you think they'd give a damn what I say about anything. Even if they did, I'm not going to do it. If I've learned anything from this ill-advised trip down memory lane, it's not to stick my nose in where it doesn't belong."

OUT BEHIND the Gingerbread Village, Nate had just spent an hour attaching fragile bits of fishing wire to the beams that would become the "sky" full of angels in tomorrow night's finale.

His shoulder was killing him. As he looked back over his work, he noticed he'd been hammering the nails so hard the heads sank beneath the wood.

Time-out needed.

He took a breath, put down the hammer and stood. He watched the families parading through the village, laughing and singing and marveling at the gingerbread houses. He smiled, so that he didn't spoil the holiday spirit for anyone, but his subconscious was counting the minutes until midnight Christmas Eve.

One way or another, he was going to see this thing through. He wasn't leaving until the last note of the finale was sung, the last paper angel had dropped out of the sky and the last guest had headed home in the cold Christmas snow.

But, boy, was he leaving then.

What a laugh, to think that last night he'd been worried about seducing Annie. The only person at risk here was Nate himself. He had come within a razor's edge of falling for every hokey, sugary fantasy of Christmastime in Joyland.

The fantasy of home, of forgiveness and redemption, of rebirth.

And angels with blue eyes and golden hair who could teach you not to be afraid of love.

What a joke. He picked up the hammer, and reeled off five feet of fishing wire.

"Nate? Nate Araby?"

He didn't recognize the voice, and he didn't recognize the woman, either. She was probably a little younger than he was, not yet thirty, and pretty in a Jessica Rabbit sort of way. Friendly eyes that looked smarter than the rest of her. Red hair that got a lot of help from a bottle, but an expensive bottle. A cinched waist, and a bustline that had also had help, either from a doctor or from God.

She wasn't his type—if he even had a type anymore.

Besides, she had two children with her, a boy about seven or eight, and a girl young enough to still be on a tether. Undoubtedly, there was a husband trailing somewhere.

"Yeah," he admitted, trotting out the smile again. "I'm Nate."

He waited for her to make the introductions. He remembered most of his high school's girls, some of whom had been dumb, athletic and fast. But he really didn't know this one.

She smiled nervously, and the wistful expression that flitted over her face took him by surprise. "Well, this makes it a little harder. I guess I really was a deep, dark secret. I'm Betsy Dawson. That is, I am Betsy Dawson now. I used to be Betsy Lasher..."

She trailed off self-consciously. "I'm making this too complicated. What I'm trying to say is that I used to know Garth."

He put down the hammer. "Really?"

"Yes." She glanced toward her son, who had wandered off to look at a gingerbread log cabin. He'd joined a man there who was probably Mr. Dawson. Nate sized him up and decided that writing the check for the redhead-making bottle would be no problem for this guy. He oozed money and confidence.

Apparently satisfied that no one old enough to care could hear, she went on. "Once upon a time, I was your brother's girlfriend. It was supposed to be a secret, but I was never sure he actually hid it from you, too. I guess, judging from your expression, he did."

"I guess so," Nate said. Now that he'd heard the name Lasher, he wasn't sure how to feel about this. Garth had always been what Hallam Fork called "bad." He smoked, dressed in black, drove too fast, smart-mouthed the teachers and didn't get daughters home on time.

But not any of the Lasher girls. Their dad was a congressman, and they lived in the proverbial mansion on a hill. They had servants and BMWs and vacations in Florence. They attended private schools for the solitary purpose of preventing them from rubbing shoulders—or any other body parts—with boys like Garth.

"Anyhow, you're going to think this is crazy, but I come here every year, hoping to run into you. Duke always says he doesn't think you'll come, but..."

Nate frowned. This did sound a little nuts. Or a little scary.

"It's just that—it's always weighed so heavily on my conscience. I thought I might feel better if I got a chance to...to apologize to you for what happened."

He tried to keep his face blank. "Why? What happened?"

Her eyes, which were greener than anything but contact lenses could create, glistened, and he saw that she had already made herself tear up.

What the hell?

"What happened?" he repeated, though he maintained a pleasant tone.

"I—I think probably I'm the reason he had to join the army." She had absently wrapped her daughter's tether around her hand so many times the little girl was practically glued to her leg. "I can't tell you how guilty I've always felt about it. Especially when I heard…heard about the accident."

"Mommy! That hurts! I want to look at Cinderella's castle."

"In a minute," she said, smoothing her hand over the little girl's auburn curls. She unwound the tether, and within seconds the child had moved off as far as the leash would allow.

"I can't believe you really didn't know any of this, Nate. It seems so strange that no one told you, not even Duke—"

"Not as strange as you think," he said. "But maybe you'd be willing to fill me in now?"

"Yes. Yes, that's what I wanted. You see, Garth and I…"

He bit back his impatience. He didn't want to spook her, but if she was going to break off every single sentence, this was going to take forever. And he'd already seen Mr. Checkbook glance curiously over at them. It wouldn't be long before the guy came over to claim his wife.

"Garth and I became lovers. I thought—I thought we were really in love." She smiled ruefully, as if inviting him to share in the sad little joke. "I was, anyhow. But I was only fifteen. And of course, I wasn't very smart about boys, or love…or any of it."

Any of it meaning sex, of course. She'd been a virgin, inexperienced, easily seduced. Translation: it was all Garth's fault.

Well, maybe it had been. If it happened shortly before Garth joined the army, he would have been nineteen—a grown-up god to a fifteen-year-old girl. He could have talked her into any reckless, stupid thing he wanted.

Reckless sex…

His heart thumping, Nate wondered suddenly whether Betsy Lasher Dawson might have a third child somewhere…an older child, a child who didn't have a proper father.

The lurch of hope that followed the thought shocked him. Garth's baby? It would be, what…ten…no, at least eleven, now.

His mouth felt dry. Could there be something left on this earth of his brother after all?

"Was there a child?"

Her mouth fell open. "What? Oh, no." She shuddered. "God, no."

Disappointment fell like lead. Together with the shudder, it hardened his heart a little bit. This woman had *loved* Garth? And yet the thought of carrying his child made her shiver and recoil.

He shoved the disappointment away. It had been a dumb idea, anyhow. The Lashers would have taken care of the pregnancy the same way they took care of her unwanted glasses. They would have made it go away.

"Okay. No child. So…*what?*"

"Well, I…"

Something in his gaze made her stumble on her answer. She was clearly having second thoughts about confessing. Perhaps she'd always thought of him as the naive little brother, kind of sweet and dumb, easy to fool. It wouldn't have been difficult to unburden her conscience to that boy, but the grown-up Nate was a different proposition altogether.

He had to give her credit, though. She blanched, but kept going.

"It didn't last long. When Garth got tired of me, when I could tell he was seeing other girls, I was devastated. I was so hurt. And I wanted to hurt back." She glanced one more time at her husband, then swallowed hard. "So I told my father."

"Ah." Nate had finally found his mental headlights, and with painful clarity he could see the rest of the nasty, dangerous road.

"You told your father. And your father came to Duke. He threatened to prosecute Garth for statutory rape. Unless he left town. Unless he joined the army and never came back to Hallam Fork again."

She nodded, as if grateful that he'd finished the story for her. She might not have been able to say the words.

"I didn't mean for anything like that to happen, Nate. Honestly, I didn't."

Good God. Could anyone really be that dumb?

Nate shook his head. "What did you think would happen? Did you want him to come on down to Araby and kill Garth himself?"

"No. No. I don't know. I have asked myself that a

million times, and I just don't know." Tears were rolling down her face, tears she would have trouble explaining to Mr. Dawson, who was strolling in their direction, making sure it didn't look as if he really cared.

"I loved him, Nate. I was young and spoiled and stupid, but I loved him. How could I have known it would end like that? How could I have known there'd be an accident, and—"

"Even without the accident, the army isn't exactly a luxury resort."

"I know." She bowed her head. "I know."

"All right. You've told me. Now what?"

This wasn't acting. Her face was melting with pain.

"Now I want you to forgive me."

As predicted, Mr. Dawson came up behind his wife, naturally at the worst possible moment. He put his hands around that cinched waist, a gesture of casual possession.

He smiled at Nate. Nate smiled back.

Betsy choked, and she tried to wipe her face dry. But through it all, her pleading gaze never left Nate.

"It was good to see you, Mrs. Dawson," he said politely. He picked up his tool box and directed one last, straight look into her agonized eyes. "And that thing you wanted me to do? For what it's worth, you can consider it done."

ANNIE COULDN'T REMEMBER a Joyland finale that had gone so well.

And she couldn't remember one in which she'd felt so miserable.

The crowds oohed and ahhed as each tableau was

revealed, and everyone agreed each of the four sets was a work of art. The audience rose to its feet and cheered the choir—through three long curtain calls. They sat in reverent silence for the nativity, hands folded in a joy that was its own kind of prayer.

Annie had decided to sing "I'll Be Home For Christmas" herself, rather than force Jimmy to endure letting another boy take his place.

The world seemed to want Joyland to end on a perfect note. The weather was crisp and slightly warmer. The flu seemed to have passed. Best of all, she'd received a call from Duke's doctor just before the first show. Duke had actually been awake for an hour tonight, and he'd been able to answer questions coherently.

The doctor, who had all along refused to encourage false hopes, was finally optimistic. He really believed Duke would pull through.

So Annie should have been ecstatic.

And yet, inexplicably, she had a heavy heart. She'd gone looking for Nate, not for personal reasons, but merely to tell him about his grandfather. But no one knew where he was. They said they remembered talking to him hours ago, long before it got dark. He'd been working at the shed behind the Gingerbread Village. But no one had seen him since.

She wondered whether, now that the work was done, he'd simply packed his suitcase and hit the road.

She tried to tell herself that the ache she felt was all on Duke's behalf, a piercing disappointment that grandfather would never reconcile with grandson. And yet she knew better. She ached because she had let herself start to care.

She had no reason to be angry. Nate didn't owe her anything, not even this one last night. He'd never pretended that he had any intention of staying in Hallam Fork. Heck, he hadn't even been willing to stick his neck out to help Jimmy's dream come true, for fear it might connect him to this town again.

She'd said it from the start, hadn't she? Nate was a bolter.

He'd disappeared on Christmas Eve twelve years ago, and it probably seemed like poetic justice for him to disappear into the darkness on this Christmas Eve, as well. Same time, same place, same disappointed hopes in his wake.

Oh, she'd been a fool to let her heart get involved.

Finally, the eleven-o'clock show started. It was the final one of the evening—the culmination of the entire six weeks of Joyland. The show would last about an hour, and it would end as the bells in every church of Hallam Fork started to ring, and the cold, snowy air was filled with the cascading sound.

Ordinarily, though Annie was always exhausted from the long ordeal of running Joyland, this was the moment of transcendent joy. This was the moment when her heart soared. When the miracle of Christmas hope was most real to her.

She wondered whether even a sky full of tolling bells and tumbling angels could help her find that feeling this year.

She put her costume back on, and stood in her marked spot, waiting for the set to rotate toward the waiting audience.

The stage manager raised his hand, and the set began

to turn. When the spotlights found her, standing against the shimmering silver-white-and-blue background, the audience broke out in applause.

It was mostly the effect of the gorgeous set. She wore a long white dress, with velvet at the cuffs and throat, and tiny silver sequins scattered near the hem, which trailed behind her.

The orchestra waited a few seconds, then the violins began the instrumental introduction.

The first notes were heartbreakingly sad. But she lifted her chin. For Duke's sake, she could do this. He wouldn't be home for Christmas, but he would be home, and that was everything.

If only Nate had stayed—

She couldn't think about that now. Already her throat was closing up, and she didn't know how she would manage to push the notes through. She closed her palm around the velvet cuff and pressed hard for strength.

Oh, Nate. He loves you. You could have made it work....

The saxophone joined the violin. When the flute came in, it would provide her cue.

But in the very last second before her solo was to start, someone joined her on the stage. She blinked, her vision poor after staring into the lights.

The figure came closer. Small. Bouncing step.

It was Jimmy.

Then, behind him—Nate.

And there it was. The soaring heart. The twinkling, sparkling bliss of hope reborn.

She smiled. She stepped back, out of the spotlight, in time for Jimmy to take her place. His freckled face beaming, he gave her a thumbs-up, turned to his surprised audience, and began to sing.

She couldn't help it. She had to turn to Nate, a hundred questions in her gaze. With three hundred guests watching, there wasn't much explaining Nate could do. But, oddly, in the end there was little explanation needed. His presence said enough—and the warmth of his hand as he clasped hers said the rest.

From that moment on, everything was magic. Jimmy's voice rang out like a blessing, and the audience listened, transfixed, silent tears streaming down their chilled cheeks.

Wives rested their heads on their husbands' shoulders. Children curled into their mothers' arms. Lovers kissed, and friends laced fingers. At this charmed moment, they were all at home now, one way or another. In their dreams or in their hearts.

Jimmy's last note died away slowly, lingering in the cold, clear air long enough to mingle with the first bell that called out from the steeples of Hallam Fork. And then, as the world filled with ringing, the audience gasped.

As if enchanted, the sky was suddenly alive with the glittering flight of a thousand tiny angels. The intricate, winged heralds danced and caught the light, the foil shimmering, the sequins gleaming.

No one noticed the human beings on stage now. Nate tugged on Annie's hand, drawing her into the relative privacy of a nook behind a blue-and-silver flecked hill.

He took her in his arms, and there were no words for how safe she felt there.

"You came back," she said softly.

He smiled. "I never left. It just took forever to talk Elaine Torrey into letting Jimmy sing."

"But you did it." It was such a little thing, and yet she knew it meant more than he would ever say. It meant that, after twelve years of running, he was willing to be a part of this world.

Her world.

"Nate." She put her hands on his chest. "Duke's better. Really better."

"I know. I went to the hospital first. I found out some things today—things he'd never told me. I needed to tell him I finally understood."

She didn't understand exactly what he meant, of course. But she didn't have to. This was just the beginning. She had a feeling they had all the time in the world to explain themselves to each other.

"Nate, that's wonderful."

He nodded. "It was still awkward, of course. After all these years, it's going to take more than—" He tucked in one corner of his mouth. "But still, you would have been proud. We made a start. I told him what I learned today, about why Garth really joined the army. I was so wrong about all that. Somehow, I actually managed to choke out the S word—"

She laughed. *"Sorry?"*

"Yes. And he said it, too. Amazingly, neither of us turned to stone." His smile deepened. "You were right. He's changed. And maybe I have, too."

"Of course you have. Everyone does, thank goodness." She smiled. "I'm so glad you went there. And so glad you came back here. To me."

"I had to. I'm hooked, Annie. Just like everyone else in Hallam Fork, I'm hooked on that angel magic in your smile." He tilted his head, a self-mocking expression in his wonderful eyes. "But it's not going to be easy, you know. Us, I mean. I'm no good…no good at any of this."

She had to laugh. Joy was tickling at her insides, and it had to find its way free. "Oh, I sincerely doubt that," she said.

The bells were dying out, and in a few minutes they would have to go back on stage and accept the applause of the audience.

But surely she had time for one very special Christmas gift to herself. She put both her hands on his face and pulled him down to her. It was too dark to see the flecks in his eyes that she'd already grown to love so much, but somehow she knew they were there, and burning.

"I'll bet you're very, very good at a great many things," she said.

He laughed softly. "I'm serious, Annie. I want to try. I want to stay. With you, if you'll have me. But I have been a loner for so long. I'm not sure how to…how to let other people in."

"Then it will be my very great pleasure to teach you, Mr. Araby." She shut her eyes and raised her lips. "Lesson number one. The Home-for-Christmas kiss."

* * * * *

Dear Reader,

The idea for *Kiss Me, Santa* came from a wonderful local street here in Auckland, New Zealand. On Franklin Road residents have been running a Christmas display for many years for the enjoyment of their fellow Aucklanders. Franklin Road's Christmas lights attract some 100,000 visitors a year and they really do have 2:00 a.m. traffic jams.

All the characters, on the other hand, come entirely from my imagination. I figured it would be a fun twist to have a Grinch living on Christmas Street and butting heads with a member of the organizing committee.

I hope you enjoy the story of Mike and Erica's battle of the tinsel, and I invite you to drop by my website, www.karinabliss.com, and say hello.

Merry Christmas to you and yours,

Karina Bliss

KISS ME, SANTA
Karina Bliss

To Barbara Drinkall, who manages to be
an inspiration all year.

CHAPTER ONE

BANG. BANG. BANG.

Mike woke on a jump start of adrenaline and stared uncomprehendingly at his surroundings. A bright sun yellowing the filmy curtains.

His wild pulse steadied. Suburban Auckland. New Zealand. December. Hideous curtains he kept meaning to replace. Three years, seven days since—

Repeated knocking interrupted the thought. The proficient rat-a-tat-tat of someone with no intention of going away. Rolling over, Mike glanced at the clock—noon. Four hours' sleep. "Son of a—"

Flinging off the sheet, he dragged himself out of bed and thundered downstairs. "What does a guy have to do to get some peace around here?" If it wasn't someone mowing their lawn, it was kids yelling. Or a real estate agent cold-calling. More likely one of his damn neighbors. *"I appreciate you work nights, Mike, so I won't keep you long but…"*

Muttering under his breath, "How'd you like *me* visiting at 4 a.m.," he hauled open the door and blinked into the sunlight. Erica Owens. The one damn neighbor who knew to leave him the hell alone. The only one he sometimes thought he wouldn't mind knowing better.

Her eyes widened as she took in his state of undress

and Mike had a sudden horrible thought. Glancing down he exhaled in relief. He *was* wearing underwear.

"Oh dear," she said in dismay, "and I planned this *so* carefully." *She wanted to see him naked?* Mike shook the last vestige of sleep from his brain. "I was sure it being Sunday you wouldn't have worked last night…."

Her gaze trailed over him again and he became aware of how he must look. Tangled dark hair, stubbled jaw, bloodshot green eyes and reeking of stale booze. Mike sighed, trying not to breathe fumes over her. "What's the brat done now?"

"Nothing!" Erica tried to be outraged but her eyes—a warm translucent brown—gave away her amusement. If you watched closely enough you could catch her thoughts, like the flick of a trout in a stream.

Mike wished he'd never noticed that.

In the eight months he'd lived in this place, bought over the internet when he was trawling for a rental for his two-year tech contract, they'd had four conversations.

The first, she'd brought "welcome to the neighborhood" cookies. Except he wasn't in New Zealand to make friends. He was here to work, make money…hide out. She'd got the message. It had taken a hell of a lot longer to hammer it home to the other neighbors.

His subsequent conversations with Erica Owens had been in the company of her eight-year-old son, Will, when she'd brought the kid over to apologize.

For clambering on Mike's roof to get a ball out of the gutter without permission.

For trampling Mike's shrubs climbing over the fence to retrieve his hang glider—not that Mike cared about shrubs.

For accidentally scratching the paintwork on Mike's BMW Z4 Coupé after losing control of his skateboard. Mike *had* cared about that one.

But he liked her brat and they both knew it. Liked Will's hurtling enthusiasm to test the laws of physics, particularly as they related to gravity and speed. In his previous life Mike had hoped for a kid just like him.

But this life was the one he'd ended up with.

"I'm here," Erica began, "in my official capacity as a member of the Lincoln Road Christmas Lights Committee."

"I'll get my wallet," he said in resignation. Only December 1 and already people had their hands out.

"No, it's nothing like that.... Look, can I come in for a couple minutes?"

Shutting the door behind him, Mike gestured to the wooden porch swing left behind by the previous owner. With the kitsch hearts carved in the back, he could understand why. Unfortunately the chains bolted to the overhead rafters required bolt cutters. Not worth buying and he wasn't going to borrow. Too personal.

Erica sat down, and he took the wooden porch railing opposite. It would be polite to put pants on over his boxers but making people uncomfortable kept conversations short.

The sun beat down on his naked back, exacerbating his hangover. He envied Erica the cool of the porch. Her shoulder-length dark hair in a ponytail, she wore denim shorts and a red T, and looked as fresh as a long cold drink of water. Under his scrutiny she crossed her long tanned legs and cleared her throat.

"Phil Mason—the committee chairman—said he

dropped a letter in your box explaining our street's tradition of Christmas lights when you arrived?"

Mike shrugged. "I don't remember, but I automatically trash junk mail."

"Oh." She straightened in the seat, sending it swinging a little. "Well, it was started twenty years ago by Burt Klausen, the old guy who owned your house. The whole street decorates their houses with Christmas lights… in fact, so many people do drive-bys we get midnight traffic jams. You could say we're world-famous in New Zealand." Her smile invited him to share the joke. Mike yawned. Her smile wavered. "Burt dressed up as Santa… he'd stand at his—*your*—gate and hand out lollipops donated by the supermarket."

"That explains the outfit I found in the spare wardrobe," said Mike. "I thought the previous owner had some kind of fetish."

She surprised him by laughing. "Oh, Burt would have loved hearing that. He fancied himself as a bit of a ladies' man."

"The perfect Santa," Mike sneered.

"He was." To his amazement, tears welled in Erica's eyes. "I'm sorry, we were close." She blinked them away. "But at least Burt got his wish of dying in his own—" Her gaze shot to his.

"Bed?" finished Mike. No wonder the real estate agent was so cagey about the previous owner. "Don't worry. I have no problem sleeping with ghosts."

It bothered him to be so aware of her, though. The tendrils of hair escaping from the ponytail, the stoicism under her smile, the smooth shapely legs.

"So, anyway," she continued, "the lights get turned

on December fourteenth, twelve days before Christmas and turned off on the twenty-sixth. You don't have to do it but—"

"Good." He stood up. Automatically she did, too. Otherwise she'd be eye level with his boxers.

"But you risk being ostracized if you don't," she joked.

"Promise?"

They were very close on the narrow deck so he saw the precise moment Erica realized he was serious. Tiny muscles contracted in her smooth face, like a gust of wind ruffling the surface of a lake. Then she sat down again. As a tactical move it was brilliant. Now Mike was the one acutely aware of his navy underwear.

"Burt's daughter said she'd left the Christmas lights for the new owner."

"I haven't found any," he lied.

"Well, you could buy some," she persisted. "Even a token gesture would be appreciated. Everyone spends what they can afford."

Mike smiled. "As you see, Erica, I can't even afford pajamas."

Her glance flicked down, she swallowed and stood up. Thank God. He couldn't have held his ground much longer. "Will and I have way too many lights. My ex-husband was an electrical engineer… He loved this stuff. We'll lend you some."

Despite his best efforts to remain an outsider, Mike still knew Jeff Owens had left his young family last year and was working in Dubai. Another reason to avoid his neighbors. Gossip.

"No point," he said. "I'm hopeless at all that home

handyman stuff. Your typical computer geek." She pointedly looked from his muscled torso to his arms and back to his face. He resisted the urge to fold his arms.

"I've read up on wiring Christmas lights this year. I could give you a hand." The woman obviously didn't have a life.

Shaking his head, Mike steered her toward the steps. "That's all very well but what about the carbon footprint? No, Erica, I don't think I could square it with my conscience."

"You could buy solar-powered," she suggested drily.

"Twice the price." The soft skin of her arm was silky warm under his fingertips. She smelled of lemon zest and cinnamon and baking. *Sugar and spice and all things—* Mike released her. "Virtue will have to be its own reward for me this year."

"HE DOESN'T WANT TO DO IT," Erica said. "That's the bad news. The good news is, I've got a yes from the three other new residents on the street."

Job done. She could tick it off and get back to the much more serious business of making ends meet while giving Will his best Christmas ever.

She smiled at him now—sitting cross-legged under the Christmas tree because chairs and couch were taken by committee members—and jerked her head toward the plate of mince pies she'd made to sweeten the disappointment.

Her towheaded son leaped to his feet and started passing them around.

Aurora Beasley helped herself to two. "Well, you tried," she said placidly. In her voluminous pink housedress, she looked like a melted marshmallow as she settled back on the two-seater couch, her plate on her lap. "That's all Burt would have asked, God rest his soul."

Late afternoon sun sharpened the shadows in her ample cleavage, dusted with fragrant talcum powder. A burlesque dancer in her youth, she'd once told Erica that she'd given up on men in her fifties, muscle tone in her sixties and moderation in her seventies. "Lord, it's hot for early December," she added, fanning herself with the meeting's agenda.

From his armchair where he was taking minutes, Phil Mason frowned at this misuse of official documents. A stalwart in local politics, he favored meetings, written agendas and an open bar. Erica had taken the precaution of half emptying the sherry bottle because she didn't trust him to leave the cupful she needed for the Christmas cake.

He straightened his glasses and shifted his frown to Erica. "How *hard* did you try?"

As hard as anyone tried on a lost cause. She'd known before she knocked on the door what Mike Ward's answer would be. His cynicism was harder to crack than a Christmas walnut. Though maybe he *was* short of money… Erica could relate to that.

When he'd opened the front door she'd glimpsed his living room. Just a couch and a coffee table in front of the exposed brick fireplace. No pictures, no knick-knacks. Beer bottles on the coffee table. A wine bottle. An upturned wineglass and spill of red across the golden kauri floorboards. Flies buzzing over a pizza carton. No wonder he didn't want to let her in.

And she'd only ever seen him in old jeans and faded T-shirts.

Until today.

Erica squirmed, uncomfortable with her total recall of every muscle and plane of that powerful body then refocused on Phil's ruddy face and realized the middle-aged chairman was waiting for an answer. "As hard as I could without alienating my closest neighbor," she admitted.

Their houses were twins—tiny two-story villas dating from the early 1900s built barely three feet apart. Burt's family had renovated his house before selling, knocking down internal walls to join kitchen and dining room, and opening the back with French doors to the garden.

All the things Erica and Jeff had planned for this place when they'd knocked off some of the mortgage. A lucrative three-month engineering contract in Dubai had seemed the perfect financial solution.

"I hope you're not giving up at the first hurdle," said Dorothy Griffin. Arthritis had whittled her down to a sharp stick of a woman, brittle-boned and brittle-tempered. She massaged her swollen knuckles and added tartly, "Jeff would've tried again." Erica's ex had been the committee chairman when Erica threw him out of the house three weeks before Christmas last year. Dorothy still hadn't forgiven her for the timing.

Erica still hadn't forgiven herself. She'd let her hurt, her anger, her…sense of betrayal…override her judgment. Ruined Christmas for her son.

She glanced at Will, caught him watching her anxiously and sent him a reassuring smile. "Okay, I'll ask again. I'd hate to let the side down."

He visibly relaxed. Will was intensely loyal to his dad

and she tried to keep any personal conflict with her ex separate from their role as parents.

"Which brings me to the next item on the agenda," Phil said, and Erica braced herself. She'd been expecting this. "Given your Christmas display has always been the street's showpiece I move that you get a professional electrician in."

"Seconded," said Dorothy. They'd obviously planned this.

"And who's paying for that?" Aurora reached for another mince pie. Silence. "Thought so. Ignore 'em, honey. I know you'll do just as good a job as that bas—" her glance fell on Will and she coughed delicately "—as Jeff did."

"Another fiasco like last year's and the power company will pull their sponsorship," Phil warned. The rebate on residents' electricity bills was the only commercial sponsorship residents accepted, and necessary for many to participate. "Burt had the special relationship with them. With him gone, we can't afford to put a bulb wrong."

Erica shifted in her chair. She'd blown it—literally—by using interior lights outside and stringing too many strands end to end. They'd overheated, causing a small electrical fire and left her and Will without power for three days.

At the time she'd given up on finding a holiday season electrician and phoned Jeff. To his credit he hadn't said a word—maybe because he'd been the one who'd dumped the light strands in the wrong bulb box. But it had taken him a week to rewire and repair the damage. "At least," he said, "you didn't burn the house down." Then he'd gone back to Dubai.

"Everything's under control," she reassured Phil. "Remember, I've done a course. Icicle lights, net lights, mini incandescent, LED, fiber optics...there's nothing I don't know about installing Christmas displays."

The phone rang, and Will's face brightened. "That'll be Dad!"

Erica beat him to the hall. "Listen, hon, I need a quick word with him first. Hand around the mince pies and I'll call you when I'm done."

She answered the phone upstairs, shutting her bedroom door. "Jeff...it's me. Listen, I haven't told Will yet so don't mention it, will you?"

"Erica, we have to sell."

She smoothed out a nonexistent crease in the quilt. "I'm still willing to put the house on the market in the New Year. But let's wait until after Christmas to tell Will."

"I've already referred a potential buyer to the agent. Friends of a guy I work with here."

She bit her lip. So soon?

"You have to tell him, Erica."

"Or you could." She did all the day-to-day parenting and worrying while "Fun Dad" sent toys and phoned twice a week.

"I think it's better coming from the parent he *lives* with."

Infidelity was the deal breaker in their marriage and yet Jeff had still expected forgiveness, then been angry when she'd refused it. But Erica had grown up with parents who'd stayed together for the sake of the kids. Knew what that felt like to a child.

Embittered, Jeff signed a second Dubai contract,

without thinking through the ramifications for Will. He effectively abandoned the son who adored him.

For a moment they trembled on the brink of more useless recriminations, then Erica took a deep breath. "Fine, I'll tell him," she said quietly.

"This week."

"Yes, this week. Listen, I'll put you on to Will." Opening the bedroom door, she headed for the stairs. "I'm in the middle of a Christmas lights meeting."

"You're on the committee?" His amusement grated her.

"What's that supposed to mean?"

"After last year..."

"I've done a course."

He laughed. "Good for you."

Her hand tightened around the balustrade. "And I've managed to get everyone in the street involved." He never had.

"Really?" Of course they were all supposed to fall apart without him. "Everyone?"

Erica crossed her fingers. "Everyone."

CHAPTER TWO

ERICA KNEW HER NEIGHBOR'S habits as well as her own.

Mike worked 2:00 a.m. until 7:00 a.m., then slept until one, jogged for an hour and was back at his desk by 2:30 in the afternoon, often working through until after seven at night. Sometimes he went out; mostly he stayed in with takeout or frozen dinners, books and the sports channel.

He never had visitors.

His office didn't have curtains and if she woke in the night she'd see his light filtering around her drapes. The sight had become as comforting as a night watchman.

Mike's was the first face Erica saw when she pulled back her curtains at six in the morning. Gaze fixed on the computer screen, hair tousled, and surrounded by coffee mugs.

Sometimes the movement captured his attention and he would nod a curt acknowledgment, but for the most part they avoided eye contact. Maybe it was because she wasn't fit to be seen in the morning, but Erica liked to think there was also courtesy in Mike's scrupulous respect for her privacy.

She finished lacing up her track shoes. And as soon

as she'd got his Christmas lights buy-in she'd go back to respecting his privacy.

Planting her palms against her gatepost, Erica stretched out her hamstrings. A surreptitious glance at her watch showed two minutes to one. Anytime now….

But it was another fifteen before she heard the slam of Mike's front door. Hamstrings cramping, she resisted the urge to snap, "You're late!" Instead she turned with a surprised smile. "Isn't this a coincidence?"

He wore a sleeveless T-shirt and his biceps bulged delightfully when he crossed his arms. "Don't you normally go running after you've dropped Will off at school?"

Erica's smiled faltered. Of course Mike knew her schedule, too. Houses three feet apart, windows mirroring each other, both of them working from home.

"I like to mix it up a little," she said. "Mind if I jog some of the way with you?"

"It's a free country." Mike started to run and Erica fell into stride beside him. His pace was faster than hers and by the time they'd reached the end of the street she forgot about softening him up with pleasantries. Better raise the subject while she could still talk.

"About the Christmas lights," she panted.

Mike sighed, his breathing deep and regular. "I knew it." Stopping to wait for a gap in the traffic at the T intersection, he shook his head. "One of the things I liked about you was that you left me in peace."

For a moment she wondered what else he liked about her then shook off the thought. "Hey, it's either me or Dorothy from Number Twenty or Phil from Number

Fifty-six." As her breathing eased, she remembered Mike's hope of being ostracized. "Or both."

After the traffic cleared, they crossed the road, jogging to the outskirts of the park. "Is that a threat?" he asked amicably.

By the pond, mothers and toddlers were feeding the ducks. Erica found her second wind. "Only if it works," she admitted.

He laughed, surprising her so much she stumbled.

His hand shot out to catch her elbow, his eyes gleamed. "Yes, Virginia, I do have a sense of humor." Mike released her arm. "But at the first sight of a delegation I'll add barbwire to the fence, get a guard dog and write rude slogans on my front door. And they won't be words you want kiddies to read."

They entered the park. Erica took a moment to appreciate the formal flowerbeds and wide green clearings. But then she had to sprint to catch up to Mike as he jogged down one of the paths that circled around the sprawling root systems of ancient oaks and maples. Still, out of the corner of her eye she took in the puriri and pohutukawa, the latter already in crimson bloom. Mike was headed for the summit of the volcano—inactive, thank God—at the center of the grounds.

Oh, hell. Up.

"Speaking of kiddies," Erica talked faster, "imagine the joy on hundreds of bright little faces..." she paused to suck in a breath "...when they see the displays...Mom and Dad...letting them stay up...hours past...their bedtime—"

"Because it doesn't get dark until after 9:30."

"You think we're nuts," she gasped. The day was

overcast but the northerly breeze carried the warmth of the Pacific Islands. It swayed the hairy green necks of a bed of orange poppies but did nothing to dry the sweat beading her brow. Mike didn't even look hot yet.

"When you're used to subzero temperatures and shoveling snowdrifts off the sidewalk it does seem odd that people blessed with a summer Christmas want to add fake snow and icicle lights to their houses."

"Maybe a little," she puffed. "But when in Rome..."

"A man's home is his castle."

The path spiraled up the hill. The muscles in her thighs began to scream. To her left, spiky purple asters rioted in flowerbeds edged with white gardenias. Her lungs felt like the bellows to a furnace—even her flared nostrils burned.

"How about I...do it for you?" she wheezed. "Everything...lending you lights...putting them up...taking them...down."

He glanced at her sideways. "Why does it matter so much?"

So many reasons too tangled with guilt and altruism for her to explain it coherently, even without oxygen deficit. She should have prepared for this. "This...is our...last Christmas...here." She pressed her hand into the stitch in her side.

Mike's pace slowed. "You're moving?"

"Don't mention it to Will... Doesn't...know...yet..." She indicated the drinking fountain fifty yards ahead.

He was silent as she bent double to catch her breath, then doused her face in the water and gulped back cold mouthfuls. Face dripping, she looked up hopefully.

"No deal," he said. "If I give in once, I'll be stuck doing

this next year." His expression was both apologetic and inflexible. "Start as you mean to go on."

Erica wiped her face with the corner of her T-shirt. "Why are you so set against it?" For all his prickly unsociability he struck her as a decent guy. Brusquely kind about Will's transgressions, he always put their unwieldy Wheelie Bin out with his own. She liked him because he put out her trash? Oh, she was a sad case.

Mike turned to look out over the park and the breeze ruffled his dark hair. "Living here means I finally get the chance to ignore Christmas. Step back from the consumerism, the stress and all the well-meaning relatives."

Well-meaning wasn't usually a derogatory term. "You don't like your relatives?"

"They're great...only there's far too many of them. You have no idea how much money I'm saving on gifts by being here." She'd noticed before that he used flippancy as a deflector. But deflecting from what?

Frustration got the better of her. "So you're a Scrooge as well as a Grinch."

His mouth softened. "The thing is, Erica, if you try and force people into participating then you compromise what Christmas is meant to be about. Goodwill to *all* men, not just the ones who want to hang fairy lights."

He resumed his jog up the hill. No way in hell could she follow.

"What about your goodwill?" she called.

Mike jogged backward to answer her. "When it comes to a conscience vote, the bad guy always wins. I just don't believe in this stuff anymore."

With a mocking salute he faced forward and picked up his pace. "But you did once?" Erica hollered, giving it one last shot. "Maybe deep down there's a good guy struggling to get out and do the right thing?"

"Yeah." His snort carried faintly on the breeze. "And Santa's real."

MIKE CAUGHT SIGHT OF WILL'S "store" as soon as he'd turned into the street. A makeshift trestle table covered by a billowing white tablecloth inexpertly weighted down against a gusty sou'wester with cardboard boxes of bagged plums on each corner. Where the wind blew hardest the eight-year-old had used his bike. What would Erica say about the grease on her white tablecloth? Shaking his head, Mike chuckled.

Serve her right. Over the previous four days she'd extended the rope lights decorating her picket fence onto his—a couple of feet each night.

"Haven't you heard of urban sprawl?" she'd said innocently when he'd confronted her this morning

Mike had looped the trespassing strands around her neck. "Nearly enough for a hangman's noose."

The kid hit him up as soon as he opened the door of his coupe. "Hi, Mike, wanna buy some plums?" Will Owens had fair hair, his mother's brown eyes and invariably a bandage covering something. This week a knee and an elbow.

The fruit tree dominated Erica's backyard and plenty fell into Mike's garden, but he put down his grocery bag and pulled his wallet out of his back pocket. "Sure."

You couldn't snub Will, though God knows he'd tried when he'd first moved into the street. Like his mother, the kid expected the best of people. Unlike his mother, he was too young to gauge when to give up on a lost cause.

His unrelenting friendliness probably came from growing up the same place he'd lived in since birth.

He'll miss living here when they move. Mike pushed the thought aside—not his concern he reminded himself for the twentieth time in four days—and eyed the plastic bags, each marked $2. "So, what are you going to do with the money you make?"

"I want to buy Mum a real good present this year since she's only getting one." Will took the two-dollar coin and dropped it into a glass jar, where it clunked forlornly against three others. The blustery overcast day must be keeping people indoors. "I mean, Granny and Gramps will send her a card but we're not going to the South Island this year. We can't afford it."

Did Erica have any idea how much Mike knew about her from the casual comments dropped by her son? He picked up another three bags, handed over six dollars. "I'm sure you'll have a great time at home."

"Yes," said Will, but his expression was doubtful. "I mean, Mum and I will have Christmas lunch and then I'll go have turkey dinner with my cousins but I'll just get dropped off. Auntie Jackie's still mad Mum didn't forgive and forget…something…" He shrugged his thin shoulders, signaling a boy's disinterest in that stuff.

Mike dumped four more bags of plums on top of his groceries and reopened his wallet. What the hell was it about these two that tugged at him? It would be good when they moved; he'd finally get some peace. "Well, at least you've got the Christmas lights to look forward to, no one goes overboard like this street, right?"

"Uh-huh."

He looked up from counting coins. "You don't sound all that excited about it."

Will started poking a hole in one of the plastic bags. "It would be cool if Dad was here, that's all."

"Yeah," Mike said. "I guess it would." There was no mitigating the simple truths.

Will glanced up. "I don't tell that to Mum," he confided, "because she's trying to make up for it...Dad leaving. And she feels bad because she blew out the lights last year and let the side down...well...that's what Mr. Mason and Mrs. Griffin said."

"Yeah, well, they're talking out of a hole in their—" Will's eyes widened and he changed tack "—head."

"I know what you were going to say."

Time for a change of subject. "I don't have enough cash on me. Okay if I owe you?"

Will nodded.

Pocketing his wallet, Mike motioned to the bike leaning against the tablecloth. "Your brake cable's coming loose."

"Don't tell Mum or she'll stop me riding it until she can get it fixed. Dad will do it when he comes home."

"When's that?"

"June."

Six months.

"I can fix it." Mike picked up the bike and the tablecloth billowed up. He rearranged the boxes to weight it down again. "I'll lean it against the fence when I'm done."

"Thanks!"

"It'll be later this afternoon, though, buddy. I need to catch up on some work first."

"Are you a spy?"

Mike chuckled. "Where'd you get that idea?"

"Mrs. Griffin says you act suspicious…working at night and all. She says you're either a spy or running from the law. Are you?" he finished hopefully.

"No, I'm an information architect." Will looked disappointed and Mike added, "But I guess I am kinda running away. Not from the law, though…" He dropped his voice to a conspirator's whisper. "From Christmas."

Will scratched the bandage on his elbow. "I guess you're too old to care about Santa now," he said finally, but it was clear he thought Mike was crazy.

Maybe he was.

Balancing the bike in one hand, Mike picked up his plum-laden grocery bag with the other. "So Santa's coming to your house?" he asked casually. He'd cottoned on to the truth when he was seven.

"I believe in him one night of the year." Will grinned. "Don't tell Mum."

"Cross my heart."

"Are you mailing your parents a present?" Mike's confession obviously still bothered the kid. He wished he hadn't said anything.

"I'll phone them Christmas morning." When Will frowned he added, "I guess that's kinda lame, huh?"

"People like presents," Will insisted. "Even old people."

"Okay, I'll send them something. But my brothers and sisters will have to settle for a card."

"How many do you have?

"Four…two sisters and two brothers."

"That's cool." The boy looked wistful but he was

bound to get another sibling one day. Women like Erica got snapped up. Still, that probably wasn't something Will wanted to hear. Oddly, Mike wasn't too thrilled at the idea, either.

"Nah, it sucks," he said instead. "I have to share my toys with them."

Will looked at him doubtfully, then grinned. "You can make jokes," he said on a note of discovery.

Mike lifted the broken bike. "You keep my secret and I'll keep yours."

CHAPTER THREE

BANG. BANG. BANG.

Groaning, Mike put a pillow over his head. This time, dammit, he wasn't going to answer it.

Bang. Bang. Bang. Faintly he heard a child's voice. "Help, Mike!"

Rolling out of bed, he hauled on his jeans. Tearing downstairs, he saw Will's face pressed against the glass, palms splayed. He jerked open the door. "What's wrong?"

"Mum's stuck on the roof. Can you come?"

"Let me get a T-shirt." In the laundry room he pulled a clean one from the bundle of clothes in the dryer.

Outside, an extendable ladder leaned against the side of Erica's two-story, rising to the sloping roof. Will led the way with a child's ghoulish glee. "It's not like it's hard," he confided. "But she won't let go of the chimney."

The brick flue was a feature of both houses, with hearths opening to the downstairs living room and upstairs master bedroom. As he followed Will up the ladder, Mike saw evidence of Erica's work over the previous week—a cascading waterfall of tiny red bulbs fell out of the upstairs bedroom, over the first story porch roof and down to the ground. She obviously knew what she was doing with lights.

"I got him, Mum!"

Mike's head cleared the roofline. Erica sat with both arms around the square, bulb-swathed chimney. Seeing him, she dropped one arm and tried to look casual.

"I got up here okay but I can't seem to get myself down again." She laughed, but her face was white.

Will climbed onto the roof. "But, Mum, it's easy, see?" He scrambled up and down the incline like a monkey.

Erica closed her eyes. "Get down," she said weakly. "I don't want you to fall."

"Hey, bud." Snagging the boy, Mike drew him back to the ladder. "Think you can take this down without dropping it?" With his free hand, he picked up the large star-shaped light balanced in the gutter beside them.

"'Course!"

They swapped places. Clutching the star, Will disappeared. Mike walked across the roof toward Erica and saw her grip tighten around the chimney. He sat down beside her, resting his arms on his knees and gazed around him. "Nice view from here."

The apple-green canopy of the plane trees lining the street softened the man-made angles of the surrounding rooftops. A week out from the official light-up ceremony, many roofs had sprouted decorative lights. In the far distance, the dark blue harbor sparkled in the sun.

"I know I'm being silly," she said. "I got up here fine, but when I turned around and saw the ground… Well, I got dizzy and had to sit down."

The thought of her falling made him clench his teeth. "What's a woman with vertigo doing on a roof?"

"I want to do the lights properly, like Je—like we've always had them."

Didn't she realize how precious life was, how fragile? Mike struggled to keep the anger out of his voice as he said, "So you risked your life to go one better than Jeff?"

She was momentarily diverted. "How'd you know my ex's name?"

"And you wonder why I don't do neighbors."

"Anyway, this isn't about going one better than Jeff. It's about reassuring Will that life goes on."

Down the street a sulky teenager was mowing his parents' yard. The mechanical whine of the lawnmower was as irritating as a dentist's drill. "By pretending nothing has changed?"

"By showing my son that even in the bad times, you can still believe in something. You can still make magic." Seeing his surprise, she pulled a face, embarrassed. "I'm only telling you this because I'm stuck on a roof and putting off going down."

Mike offered his hand. "As a first step, let go of the chimney." Maybe if he stuck to practicalities he could ignore how what she'd said had made him feel. Erica swallowed hard, then her fingers closed convulsively around his. He gave them a squeeze. "Relax, we won't move until you're ready."

She smiled faintly. "Then I hope you brought a sleeping bag."

Retaining her hand, Mike leaned against the chimney. "So tell me more about the magic in lightbulbs and electric Santas."

Another smile, this one less forced. The deathlike grip eased. "The magic lies in the way the Christmas lights bring the street together. January through November we squabble over curbside parking, loud music or a neighbor's tree shedding in our yard. But in December we become a community."

Will's head appeared over the roofline. "When are you coming down?"

"After I've showed your mom where your plum tree clogs my gutters," said Mike.

Erica laughed.

"Is that another joke, Mike?" Will asked.

"Certainly your mom's treating it as one." He frowned at Erica who was still chuckling. "And are those icicle lights hanging above my bay window?" Devious—he rarely walked down that side of the house.

She tried not to look guilty. "Must have blown up from Antarctica."

"Mum, I'm getting hungry," Will said.

Erica looked at the ground, then at her son. Squaring her shoulders, she set the alarm on her wristwatch. "I'll be down in exactly five minutes," she promised. "You can go on the PlayStation while you're waiting."

Will's head vanished.

"Five minutes," she repeated firmly, staring at the second hand. Her nails dug deeper into his palm. Mike needed to distract her or this wouldn't work.

"When did Will last see his dad?"

Erica dragged her eyes to his. "Almost a year ago." She misread his expression. "It's not all Jeff's fault. At the time our marriage ended, well, we both said and did things we regretted."

"Hey, it's none of my business." Who was he to judge family matters?

He was starting to lose sensation in his fingers. "Your son tells me you're a journalist?"

"Freelance." Her grip loosened slightly. "I write features for lifestyle magazines mostly but I also have a few PR clients." Her gaze started to drift to the ground and he gave her hand a little shake.

"It's polite to ask back, Erica."

"But I know what you do," she boasted. "You're an information architect."

"So the kid doesn't just relay news one way," he said. That got her attention. Now she was wondering what Will had told him. Maybe that she had an addiction to *The Young and the Restless,* or liked to dance with the vacuum cleaner, or did an oatmeal mask on Sundays and called it Fright Night.

"I figured," he continued, "information architect sounded more interesting than throwing around words like *hierarchies* and *interaction flows analysis.*" He thought of Will's disappointment. "So much for that." His hand had pins and needles now, a good sign. Returning blood flow meant she was reducing the pressure.

"It *is* interesting to an adult," she said. "But to be clear, you design and build…?"

Mike laughed. "The navigation system for digital worlds—websites or intranets, mostly. I've got a contract with one of your government departments." Defense, but that was confidential. "But I also still have two U.S.-based clients, which means I need to be awake some of the time they are."

The alarm beeped on her watch. Erica looked at him helplessly. "Yikes."

There was no advantage in putting this off any longer.

"Here's what we're going to do," he said quietly. "I'll go stand on the ladder, then you'll slide down toward me. Don't try to stand up."

"I'm sorry." Her mouth twisted. "You must think I'm an idiot."

"No, I think you're an incredibly gutsy woman."

Erica blinked. "Well, then—" she swallowed "—I guess I have a reputation to maintain—unless you want to revise your opinion to screaming hysteric?"

Mike shook his head.

"It was worth a try." Sucking in oxygen, Erica released his hand.

"Let's do this." Walking back to the ladder, he climbed down enough rungs to put him waist-high with the roof-line. Facing Erica, he stretched his arms wide to increase her sense of security. "Keep your eyes on me."

With a jerky nod, Erica started inching forward on her bottom. Her palms left damp patches on the roof.

Halfway down, she hit a smoother section and started to slide. Automatically she scrabbled for fingerholds. There were none. Erica whimpered, staring at the ground. "Look at me, Erica," Mike said sharply. Terrified, she obeyed, dug in her heels and slowed. "That's it," he encouraged her. "You're doing great."

Her hand touched his, fingertip to fingertip. She inched forward a little more and made a grab for it.

"Nearly there." He clamped his other hand on her shoulder. She was shaking. "I want you to turn around slowly and feel for the rung above the one I'm standing on. It's okay, I've got you. Perfect." He curled her fingers around the top prongs of the ladder, his chest against her back.

She was on the verge of hyperventilating and he put a supportive arm across her collarbone. Under his forearm her heart beat frantically. "Breathe with me."

For a full minute they stood there while Erica struggled to match the measured rise and fall of his rib cage. A plane flew overhead, its vapor trail a smear of white in a flawless sky. Birds chirped in the trees.

It was a peculiar intimacy, breathing in unison, his neighbor's warm body sheltered against his. Mike felt something he'd never thought to feel again—a strange and awful rightness.

Sweat broke out on his forehead. He wanted to release Erica, but he could only stand and suffer an emotional reawakening as painful as blood rushing back to a dead limb. Now he knew why he'd kept his distance all these months.

Erica's breathing slowed and her pulse settled. Her hair tickled his jawbone as she turned her head and said awkwardly, "Okay, you can let me go now."

It was what Mike wanted to do and yet his arm felt empty as he guided her down the ladder, one rung at a time.

At the bottom he turned straight for home. "See you, then."

"Th-th-thank y-you."

Shock. Reluctantly, he went back to her. "Let's get you inside first."

"I'm f-f-f-fine," she protested.

"You will be. Will…" Inside the boy turned from the PlayStation hooked up to the TV. "Go get a blanket for your mom, buddy."

The child scampered upstairs and returned with a

duvet covered with cartoon skateboarders. Mike wrapped it around Erica's shoulders and sat her down on the couch.

"Are you okay, Mum?"

"I'm-mm fi-ine."

"Give her a hug and warm her up, Will." The boy snuggled up to his mother. "Got any liquor?" Mike asked Erica. She pointed a trembling finger to the kitchen.

On the countertop he found a nearly empty sherry bottle and opened cupboards until he came up with a glass. The smell of roasting chicken wafted from the oven. Without French doors, the kitchen was dark and poky compared to Mike's. Still it had something his lacked.

His gaze swept over the child's colorful artwork on the walls, the rainbow magnets pinning timetables to the fridge and the fruit bowl of oranges and Granny Smiths. Hominess.

When he returned to the living room, Erica and Will were comparing hands. "See," she said, "mine's just as steady as yours now." She eyed the glass Mike carried. "Though it won't be if I drink that."

"No arguments."

She took it and pulled a face as she sipped, once. Twice. Then she stopped abruptly. "I need this for the Christmas cake."

He couldn't help but grin. "I'll buy you some more. Now drink it."

Erica emptied the glass and color returned to her face. She shrugged off the blanket. "Totally back to normal."

Mike bent and picked up her hand. She tried to pull away, but he held on. "Warm," he said brusquely.

"You'll do." He released her. "And I think the chicken's cooked."

"The chick— Oh!" Standing, she hurried past him to the kitchen.

He looked at the boy on the couch. "Tell your mom I had to go, okay? I'll take the ladder down on my way."

"So that means we don't have the star up this year?"

"Your mom can't go that high." When Will bit his lip and nodded, he added, "You got a relative who can do it?"

"My uncle Nate could—"

"Good." Mike headed for the door.

"—but he's gone over the hill."

Mike turned around. He knew the term through his work with New Zealand Ministry of Defense. The colloquialism was used by Special Forces to explain absences to friends and family. It covered everything from a local training exercise to active deployment overseas. "He's a soldier?"

"Uh-huh." From the coffee table, Will picked up the star he'd brought down from the roof and ran his grubby fingers reverently over it. "It doesn't matter."

Walk away, Mike, walk away now. "Give it here."

"Really? You'll do it, Mike?"

Erica came back from the kitchen. "Do what?"

"Put up the star," Mike growled.

She looked at him with astonishment, gratitude and—

"No," he said. "This *doesn't* mean I'm decorating my house. One star. On your chimney. That's it. And those icicles get taken off my tree."

"I was going to offer you lunch," she said with great dignity. "As a thank-you."

"I'm working."

"It's Sunday," she reminded him. "Which means you eat takeout in front of the sports channel then fall asleep on the couch." Her eyes gleamed. "You know you really need to do something about curtains."

"Thank God I left the old one in the bedroom." And fortunately the bathroom was on the garden side of the house. Though sometimes he walked naked from one room to the other. Mike looked at Erica who'd got busy folding the duvet. Her cheeks had flushed pink. He'd thought he was the only one fighting the temptation to look. "You seem to have your color back."

"Oven heat," she murmured.

No. He didn't want this.

"Look, I appreciate the offer but—"

"It's just lunch, Mike." Erica's blush deepened but she held his gaze with an awkward honesty that made him feel like an idiot.

"No," Will corrected. "It's a special Sunday roast." But Mike's mother had brought him up to be better mannered than this.

"Erica," he said humbly, "thank you for your invitation. I'd love a home-cooked meal."

CHAPTER FOUR

"SO," SAID ERICA, PASSING Mike the roasted potatoes. "We've had our first Christmas miracle."

Across the dining-room table, he eyed her with his customary mix of wariness and warmth. "How's that?"

"You said you were hopeless as a handyman yet you fixed the star in place and finished the wiring without once asking me for advice."

He grinned. "Busted. But I am telling the truth when I confess to lousy cooking skills. So thanks for the meal."

She didn't reply, still off balance from that roguish grin.

Erica realized she was staring. Flustered, she reached for the gravy. "You're welcome."

She hated the self-consciousness that came from being single again. And really hated that Mike had read her earlier blush as interest. She'd simply been embarrassed because she'd glimpsed him naked once or twice—and he'd guessed it.

Okay, maybe she'd stared a second or two longer than she should have, but Erica defied any woman to turn away from the sight of such a gorgeous male body. It didn't *have* to mean she was attracted to him.

After seeing that grin, though, she wasn't so sure.

Erica tapped Will's plate with her fork. "I want to see some green on your plate, mister." He pulled a face and she pulled one back, a mealtime ritual that steadied her. "And it's your turn to say grace."

Through the prayer, she glanced over her folded hands to Mike. *What happened to you?*

He caught her watching him again.

Mortified, Erica murmured, "Amen," then concentrated on her food. She had no idea what the rules were these days between consenting adults. No wonder she was putting off dating again.

So why, sitting across the table from Mike Ward, did she remember she hadn't had sex in sixteen months? Remember that she missed it. Not just sex, but a man's encompassing hugs, the simple warmth of him sleeping in her bed. The security... Okay, now she'd passed into fantasy. She speared a minted carrot medallion.

She'd never known security with Jeff, either financial or emotional. The qualities that made her fall for him at university—his daring, recklessness and spontaneity—hadn't translated very well into marriage.

Erica had soon learned that she was the only grown-up in their small family. And the only one who cared whether they could afford what they bought. Like this house.

The carrot stuck in her throat and she cleared it with a sip of water. Jeff's "keen" buyers were coming around tomorrow. And she still hadn't told Will. Fortunately he'd be at school. She was procrastinating, but how do you break news like that? "Hey, sweetie, you know how you had to watch Daddy leave? Well, say goodbye to your house and all your pals, as well. Mummy has to trade down."

To hell with Jeff. It could take months to sell in this flat market, why unsettle Will until I have to?

"My brakes work real well now," her son was saying to Mike between chews. "See?" Proudly, he lifted his chin to reveal a graze. "I went over the handlebars."

"What!" Erica said.

"You applied your brakes too fast," said Mike. "Next time, make sure you squeeze both handles together slowly."

"Okay." Will continued demolishing his chicken and potatoes. Three peas sat ignored on his plate.

Erica frowned. "You didn't tell me you went over the handlebars *or* that you were having trouble with your brakes."

Will stopped midchew. "Um...."

"I noticed they were a little loose," said Mike, "so I tightened them."

Will breathed a sigh of relief which Erica pretended not to notice. The hardest part of parenting solo was letting her boy *be* a boy and reining in her maternal paranoia. "That's kind, thank you," she said to Mike. "And for putting our Wheelie Bin out every week. You don't have to. I can manage."

"Of course you can." The glint in his eye told her he had seen that incident seven months ago when she'd been wheeling the five-foot bin down the path and tripped. Erica had ended up sprawled across a pile of garden waste. "And it's no trouble," he added. "I'm doing mine."

"Yes, I hear it rattling," she replied sweetly. His recycling usually consisted of empty glass Steinlager bottles.

Mike laughed again. She wished he'd stop doing that. It confused her.

"Hey, I got the wishbone." Delighted, Will pulled it free.

Erica feigned surprise. "Aren't you the lucky one."

"Wanna pull it with me, Mum?"

She looked at the greasy bone. "Why not let our visitor have a go. Mike?"

"I wouldn't want to deprive you of the pleasure," he said politely.

Erica wrapped a paper napkin around her end of the V. "You're such a girl, Mum." Will's hand fisted around the other end of the bone. "Have you got your wish?"

Her gaze met her guest's. "I wish that Mike puts up some Christmas lights."

"Mum, you can't use that now," Will explained patiently. "It doesn't come true if you say it aloud."

Mike grinned. "And you were so close."

She closed her eyes, blocking out his face and made the same wish she made every night Nate was in Afghanistan. The bone snapped. Will clutched the longer piece. As she congratulated him, Erica told herself it wasn't an omen. "So, who's ready for dessert?"

"Me," said Will. He ran to wash his greasy hands while Mike helped clear the table.

"Not many people go pale when they lose the wishbone," he commented as he found room for the plates on the crowded counter.

Erica opened the oven. Heat hit her face in a wave. Apple bubbled through the golden crumble like magma.

"My brother's in the armed forces. I wished for him to be safe." She smiled, trying to make light of it as she pulled on oven gloves. "Silly how much weight you give superstition when something really matters."

Mike cleared more dishes. "He's SAS, isn't he?"

She nearly dropped the hot dessert. "How on earth…?"

"Will said his uncle had gone over the hill." Mike made room for the dessert on the table.

An information architect with access to some highly classified information, then. Erica placed the crumble on a ceramic tile. "Yes," she admitted, "Nate's SAS."

"Then luck isn't something he relies on," said Mike. He smiled. "Or a sister wishing on a chicken bone."

Erica smiled back. "Double helpings for that reminder."

Will reappeared, wiping his damp hands on his board shorts. "What about me?" he protested. "I remind you of stuff all the time."

"Double helpings for everyone then."

After dessert, Will dragged Mike out to the backyard to show him where it would be great to hinge two boards in the fence. He'd got the idea from the cartoon network. "Then I can get my ball back from your garden without having to knock on your door all the time."

"Honey, Mike doesn't—"

"It's okay, Erica. I want to check for any loose boards that need nailing up to keep the brat out."

Will chuckled. "He's telling a joke, Mum."

"Isn't he lucky you're here to tell me that," she said.

Will dragged Mike out before he could make a rejoinder.

Erica watched them through the kitchen window as she began the dishes—her son's enthusiastic gestures, Mike's measured responses.

Why did she like him so much? He crouched down beside the fence, explaining something to Will. Because he's kind, she decided. Kind without being intrusive or patronizing. Over the past twelve months Erica had got heartily sick of having her emotional temperature taken by friends and neighbors. Of being pitied.

Mike might help her off the roof, fix Will's bike and put out her trash, but he never treated either of them like "poor things." She appreciated being called a gutsy woman by someone who didn't pull punches. Particularly when she was about to uproot Will from the house he'd been born in. Mike's view of her as capable was both reassuring and oddly sexy.

Whoa there! Erica scrubbed at the stubborn crumble baked hard on the pie dish. As a burned-out twenty-nine year-old solo mother her requirements were very different from the naive nineteen-year-old bride she'd once been.

And Mike didn't meet them.

Though he'd revealed a sense of humor, an important prerequisite for any future lover—not least because of her stretch marks—the guy was mostly unsociable and uncommunicative. And uninterested.

Giving up on the pie dish, she put it aside to soak and moved on to the equally crusty potato pan. And he was still single at thirty-something, which suggested a love 'em and leave 'em style.

Unless he was divorced. That would explain his Grinchiness. Erica picked up the dish brush and attacked the pan with vigor. Which meant he wasn't very good at marriage. Another strike against him.

Of course Mike could make that argument about her.

But her mistake had been one of spouse choice, not of commitment. Jeff had the monogamy problem. Erica glanced up at the kitchen clock. Her ex would phone soon. Whatever his failings he always called Will at the same time twice a week. It helped her forgive him.

Setting the potato pan to drain, she pulled the plug and watched the greasy water circle down the drain.

Her next husband would have a history of responsibility. Of constancy. In addition to loving kids he'd only have eyes for her and always put her needs first in bed.

A rogue carrot medallion got stuck in the drain hole. Erica laughed softly at herself as she fished it out. And a delight in drying dishes wouldn't hurt. She stepped on the pedal to open the trash can, dropped the carrot inside.

"A buck for them."

The lid slammed on the trash can. "What…?"

"Your thoughts." Mike picked up a tea towel.

Rattled, Erica rinsed her hands under the tap. "I was thinking about what I want for Christmas." She watched him dry a pot, added sharply, "You don't have to do that, you know."

He put down the tea towel. "Overstaying my welcome?"

Yes! "Not at all."

But he'd got the message. "It's time I was going anyway. Wonderful lunch, Erica." Through the window Mike waved goodbye to Will who was climbing a tree in the garden.

Erica's conscience pricked her as she showed him

to the door. Why was she punishing Mike because she found him attractive? "Thanks again for the rescue...I really appreciate it."

"No sweat."

Still overcompensating, she kissed his cheek, a light brush that burned. Their eyes met in a moment of mutual awareness, then they both stepped back. "Well," she said brightly. "Many thanks. For the rescue and putting up the star."

"Lunch was great." His expression was shuttered again, remote, but Erica couldn't count it a loss. When it came right down to it, she wasn't ready for another emotional risk.

As she closed the door behind Mike, she felt as if she'd had a narrow escape.

CHAPTER FIVE

MIKE WAS UNLOADING THE PROJECT meeting files and laptop out of his BMW when across the road he spotted Aurora Beasley struggling with two big bags of groceries. She was still about a hundred yards from her house.

He loosened his tie, dumped his jacket and headed across the road. "Need some help?"

"Lord, yes!" Face flushed, Aurora put down the bags, her enormous breasts rising and falling with each labored breath. "Time was, I wouldn't have had to walk half a mile before a good-looking man offered to help." She managed a wheezy chuckle. "But time was I could walk half a mile without relying on it."

Mike picked up her groceries in one hand, offered her his arm with the other. She took it gratefully. "Serves me right for divorcing three husbands.... So has Erica got past first base with you yet?" He stared down at her. "About putting up Christmas lights."

He was an idiot. "I'm afraid not," he said shortly. Since Sunday Mike had been avoiding his neighbor. Though Erica seemed equally dismayed by their attraction he was taking no chances.

"Well, I expect you've got your reasons." Aurora waited, but Mike didn't offer any. A smile curved her lips as she opened her gate and gestured him through.

He figured she must be color-blind because her lilac bungalow with its deep purple trim clashed with her riotous flower garden of yellow and orange.

"Outrageous," she said, guessing his thoughts, "like me. Dump the bags by the door, then give me a hand with these stairs."

One hand on his arm, the other on the balustrade, Aurora maneuvered the steps. "To think I could once kick my leg over my head. Now it's hard just bending my knees." She squeezed his braced arm approvingly. "Nice muscles. You work out?"

"Some." Mike started regretting his gallantry. It created an opening.

"And the strong, silent type. Mmm-mmm."

He laughed. "No wonder you had three husbands."

"Yeah, but it took me two to hit the jackpot." Her tone became sly as she said, "Like that sweet girl next door. Erica's first was a dud, too. But she's smart enough to get it right on the second I think."

He didn't make the mistake of looking at her. Aurora gave a low, throaty chuckle and squeezed his arm again. "Fine, I'll mind my own business. You know, she's been a good neighbor to me. I'll miss her and Will when they move. It's a damn shame she can't afford to buy Jeff out."

"She's not listing it until the New Year," he reassured her. "And it will probably take a while to sell in this market."

"Why, Mike, she's got buyers over there now. They arrived just before you did. And used their connection with Jeff to bulldoze their way into a viewing, even though they're supposed to come with the agent."

Aurora waited for some kind of response but it took him a moment to find one. "Would you like me to carry your shopping inside?"

"No, I can take it from here. The sad thing is, I don't know if our Christmas lights tradition will survive once Erica leaves. She's been our behind-the-scenes dynamo for years, though our chairman Phil—and Erica's ex before him—always gets the credit. We're all getting so old now, we need you young ones on the committee picking up the slack. Anyway, you get home and spy on those buyers for me…. Just teasing, I know you're not the nosy type. Thanks for your help."

His closed-up house was stuffy, with a faint stink of garbage. Mike could smell his life when he stepped inside…takeouts, loneliness and stale beer. Work ate up most of his time but there were still too many moments of regret and doubt, of guilt and grief. Dumping his gear, he flung open some windows to dispel the odor—*not* to spy on his neighbor—then carried the trash out back to the garbage can, resisting the impulse to glance into Erica's yard.

Even now she could be closing a sale.

Mike unloaded the bag and jammed the lid back on the trash can. If she moved he could stop worrying about her. Her faith had touched him—*Even in the bad times, you can still believe in something. You can still make magic.* Was she aware her precious Christmas lights tradition might be in jeopardy when she left? And why the hell did it bother him so much?

He heard Erica's back door open, then an unfamiliar female voice.

"What I *love* about your place is the potential. Tom, honey, we could turn this into something *fabulous*."

"Tom" answered in an apologetic tone. "Anyone could fix this up with fifty thou, Sue. Erica, didn't you and your ex have plans drawn up before he..." His voice trailed off.

Erica said faintly, "Did the estate agent tell you about my personal life?"

"Yes and it's very sad," said Sue. "Would those plans be included in the price? Don't nudge me, Tom, there's no harm in asking."

"So you intend to make an offer, then?" Erica didn't sound happy about it. Quietly, Mike stepped onto his deck so he could see her through the trees. She was biting her lip.

"Yes," said Tom. The big, middle-aged man and his diminutive blonde wife had their back to him.

"Now, honey." Playfully, Sue punched her husband's arm. "I need more information first. Erica, what's the makeup of this neighborhood?"

"Makeup?"

"Not that we don't enjoy diversity," Tom added. They were still unaware of Mike's presence. "Hell, we eat any kind of food going, Thai, Korean, Japanese, Polynesian, Mexican—"

"I can't do this," Erica said, quieter still.

"Can't do what?" said Sue. Even without seeing her face, Mike knew she'd be Botoxed and perfectly made up.

"Can't let you buy this house without...telling you about.... It's..." Erica's gaze darted around the property "...on a flood plane. Every ten years it's underwater."

"Why, Erica, you're misinformed," said Tom comfortably. "I have the survey map right here. Volcanic soil, free-draining. Sue particularly wanted free-draining—didn't you honey?—for her prize dahlias."

"I enter flower shows," Sue explained, "and your soil's perfect. All we have to do is pull down that plum tree for more sun."

"You can't do that." Stunned, Erica laid a protective hand on its trunk. "There's a…a protected species living in it."

She was the worst liar Mike had ever heard.

"How exciting," said Sue, "what is it?"

"A…a rare breed of weta." The native insect was like a long-horned grasshopper only big, brown and ugly. Most people hated the things.

"Wetas are my good luck talisman," Sue exclaimed. "See, I've got a silver one here on a chain. It's a sign, Tom."

Erica clutched the tree trunk. "Okay, I really didn't want to tell you this, but the house is falling apart…. It needs thousands of dollars put into it."

Tom looked at his wife. "Honey, I don't normally believe in your signs but this is downright spooky." A big grin split his face. "Erica, we didn't want to hurt your feelings but we intend gutting the place and rebuilding. Now we don't have to feel bad about it."

Okay, he couldn't stand this anymore. Mike waved, catching Erica's attention, then pointed to himself. For a moment she stared uncomprehending then said in a rush, "But I'm afraid the very worst thing is the neighbor next door."

Sue and Tom turned to see what she was looking at. Mike ducked.

"He's horrible!" Erica gathered steam. "Loud music all night, yet complains constantly about the noise my son makes playing in the garden... Strange habits... He...he wanders around naked without pulling his curtains."

"Oh?" Sue sounded more interested than revolted. "How old is he?"

Erica ignored that. "You must have noticed he hasn't put up any Christmas lights."

"Well, we did wonder," said Tom, "but—"

"And the worst thing? American."

"But we love Americans, don't we, honey?"

"Trust me, not this one." Erica warmed to her theme. "This one...um...chews tobacco and spits and...shoots at squirrels."

"But New Zealand doesn't have squirrels," said Sue.

"He imports them." Erica lowered her voice. "To eat."

"He can't have a firearm here," said Tom stolidly. "I'd call the police in a heartbeat—"

"I mean the gun you don't need a license for," Erica interrupted him.

"Air rifle?" Tom asked.

"That's it."

"An air rifle kills squirrels?" Sue asked.

"Eventually," said Erica darkly.

"You're making this up," Tom said in reproach.

On the other side of the fence, Mike slapped his forehead. *Ya think?* For all their patronage of foreign cuisine, it seemed Tom and Sue—*and* Erica—hadn't traveled much.

"Erica," Sue's voice was sharp, "are you trying to stop us making an offer?"

"Of course not," said Erica, with the classic liar's tell of looking guilty. "But I couldn't live with my conscience if I didn't warn you what you're in for." Her voice faded as she led them down the side of the house.

Thinking hard, Mike half filled his recycling bin with laundry then topped it up with every beer bottle he could find—full and empty—and went to his front door. Erica stood next to her mailbox with Tom and Sue, who were clearly reluctant to leave. Stripping down to his underpants and business socks, he retied his tie and slung the long end over one shoulder hoping it would suggest an interest in autoerotic asphyxiation.

"I *want* this house," Sue said to Tom. "And she's not going to put me off with ridiculous stories about the neighbor. No one's *that* bad."

Stumbling out to the curbside, Mike dropped the recycling bin so the bottles rattled. Sue and Tom jumped.

He glared at Erica. "If your goddamn cat takes a dump in my garden again, the next time you see Fluffy she'll be stuffed and mounted, you hear me, y'all?"

While the other three stared in stunned silence, he lurched back into the house and slammed the door.

Erica knocked ten minutes later. With a sheepish grin she handed him his recycling bin. Sitting on top was a large piece of Christmas cake in plastic wrap, tied with a red bow. "That's to buy your silence. If Jeff knew what I'd just done. . .or Vonnie the estate agent. . . Anyway, it worked, so thank you. I may have to move but I still want nice people living here."

"So do I," he said. Behind her usual sunny smile, Erica

looked tired. The past couple of nights her light had been on almost as late as his had. Mike suspected she was taking on extra writing assignments to cover seasonal expenses. "So where will you move to…when it sells?"

"Somewhere with cheap rent," she joked.

"Aurora's concerned the Christmas lights won't continue without you." Now, why the hell had he blurted that out?

Her expression clouded. "I can't do anything about that," she said lightly, but she pressed a hand to her nape and massaged it. "Still, good news for you, right?"

"Just because I don't celebrate Christmas doesn't mean I begrudge those who do."

"Of course not. I'm sorry…. Mike, why don't you celebrate Christmas? And don't give that story about consumerism and relatives because I don't believe it."

For a moment he almost told her the truth. Except as much as he'd like this woman's understanding he couldn't risk her pity, too.

"I was scared by Santa as a child."

Her eyes narrowed. "Fine," she said. "Keep your secrets. But you've done me a big favor so I'm not going to hassle you anymore. You'll be pleased to know I've given up on you."

"The perfect Christmas present," he said. "Peace at last."

As Mike closed the door, he felt a pang of something that could have been regret.

CHAPTER SIX

AT EIGHT-THIRTY THE NEXT NIGHT Erica opened the door to Vonnie Connors, the estate agent. Fortunately Will was already in bed.

"I know it's late to call," Vonnie apologized. She was an attractive brunette in her late thirties, charming and relentless. Without waiting for an invitation she stepped inside. "But if you counter-sign tonight the for-sale sign can go up first thing in the morning."

Erica kept standing at the open door. "But we're not actively selling until after January 5, remember? Sue and Tom Gordon were a one-off. And I've decided not to tell Will until after Christmas."

The other woman lifted salon-shaped brows. "Didn't Jeff talk to you?"

"Talk to me about what?" She'd been out most of the day.

Vonnie sighed. "Oh dear. I just assumed since he faxed the agents' contract through from Dubai that he'd got hold of you. I should wait until you two have had a chance to talk."

Erica looked at the document in the agent's hands. Even though she knew it killed cats, curiosity got the better of her. "Come in, Vonnie, and tell me what's going on."

Flashing a best-friends-forever smile, Vonnie was in

the lounge and seated on the couch before Erica could say "foreclosure." This agent had told the Gordons that Jeff had cheated on her. Erica didn't offer her any refreshments.

"It was only when I was talking to my kids about bringing them to Light-Up this Sunday that the penny dropped," Vonnie began. "I apologize for not thinking of it before."

Erica said cautiously, "Think of what? And what does this have to do with Jeff signing contracts?"

"Like I told your ex, you'll have *hundreds* of people—potential vendors—here for the street's Christmas lights. He agreed it would be *madness* not to take advantage of that and put up a for-sale sign."

Unfortunately, the estate agent was right. Still Jeff should have cleared it with her first. Come to think of it, *Vonnie* should have cleared it with her first. Instead of sneaking behind her back to the person most likely to say yes. The person with no home to lose.

Erica stood up, gesturing to the hall. "I'll phone you when I've talked to Jeff."

As Vonnie walked past she waved the contracts playfully. "Or you could sign now?"

"I don't think so." *Go home to your nice safe husband, your nice safe house and your probably neglected kids.* Erica went to open the door.

Vonnie put out a hand and stopped her. "Look, Erica," she said seriously. "I know this is hard for you. I recently got divorced myself." Seeing Erica's surprise she pulled a face. "Yeah, there are a lot of us. And telling your kids... well, I understand why you're putting it off. But this way, you'll get the very best price, and trust me, every penny counts. I'm not suggesting this to help Jeff, I'm suggesting it to help you."

For a moment the two women looked at each other, then Erica took the papers and signed them on the hall table.

"You're sure?" But there was relief in Vonnie's voice. It was Christmas. The agent probably needed this sale as much as she did.

"I'm sure." But that didn't stop Erica from ringing Jeff as soon as Vonnie left. She didn't bother with pleasantries. "Why didn't you talk to me before signing that agency agreement?"

"Didn't Will tell you I phoned earlier this evening? You were at Aurora's for some committee meeting."

"No." Erica returned to the kitchen where she'd been making Will's school lunch before Vonnie knocked. "He was already in bed when I got home, and the sitter didn't mention it." Putting Jeff on speakerphone she cut the ham-and-cheese sandwich into halves and wrapped it in cling wrap.

"I told him about selling the house," Jeff said. "Because you were right, Erica. It's time I stopped leaving the hard stuff to you."

She'd opened the fridge, now Erica forgot what she was looking for. She closed it and sat down at the kitchen table. "How did he take it?"

"He was...stoic. I told him he'd still be going to the same school and that cheered him up."

It would probably mean a commute but Erica had already mentally committed to that. Something in her son's life had to stay the same. Outside a movement caught her eye. On the street, Vonnie was chatting animatedly to Mike.

"I'll talk it through with him tomorrow," she said to Jeff. "But thanks for breaking the news first, I'd been dreading it." Why wasn't Mike doing his usual brush-off instead of encouraging Vonnie with his rare smile? Of course the agent was very attractive. Irritated, Erica got up and closed the curtains.

"I realize I've been an asshole this past year," said Jeff, taking her by surprise. "Getting all bitter and twisted when you wouldn't forgive me, then accepting a second contract in Dubai. I'm bloody sorry, Erica. Sorry for letting you both down so badly. I promise to do better by Will in future."

For a moment a lump in her throat stopped her from replying. Slowly, Erica sank back into her chair. How long had she waited for Jeff to admit culpability? She'd expected to feel triumph; instead there was only a terrible sadness. Because the ruins were still ruins. "What brought this on?"

"I've had some counseling and… Well, I've recently met someone who's helped give me new perspective."

He'd always needed a woman to teach him a value system. Erica was suddenly grateful they were no longer together. She didn't want to be his moral compass for the rest of her life. "Is it serious?"

"Too soon to say… Are you okay with me in another relationship?"

Was she? Desperate for security after an unhappy childhood she'd been smitten more by Jeff's self-confidence than the man himself. Their divorce had forced—and freed—her to become her own person. "Yes," she said. "I'm okay with that—as long as she's kind to Will."

"I want to thank you, Erica." There was rare humility in Jeff's voice. "You've never once bad-mouthed me to Will and God knows many times I would have deserved it."

"And many times I was tempted," she admitted. "But you're his dad, Jeff." *And before this year, a good one.* "Nothing changes that."

"My contract runs another six months." For some reason he sounded nervous. "It's a big favor…and I know I don't deserve it." His next words came in a rush. "I need to see Will before then. And more important, he needs to see me. Please, Erica, let me have him for Christmas."

THIRTY MINUTES LATER Erica was tiptoeing past Will's darkened room on her way to bed when her son's voice stopped her.

"Mum."

She stood in his doorway grateful for the hall light behind her and pitched her voice cheerfully. "What are you doing awake, mister? It's nearly ten-thirty."

"Did Dad talk to you? About me going over?"

She could hear his hope, palpable behind the casual enquiry. Erica went and sat on his bed, her fingers instinctively finding his face in the dark. She smoothed back his hair, squeaky-clean from the shower, breathed in the scent of shampoo, mint toothpaste and boy.

"Yeah, he did."

He caught her palm against his cheek. "It's okay," he said. "I already told him I can't go. Because you're trying to make Christmas special this year…with the lights and everything."

In the dark, Erica closed her eyes.

He was only eight, for God's sake. Eight years old and too sensitive to adult sensibilities, adult feelings. Like she'd been at his age. She opened her eyes. "I think you should go," she said. "Nana and Pop are heading over on Saturday and they've offered to buy your ticket and take you there and back. And you haven't seen your dad for such a long time and—"

"Really, you don't mind?" Will sprung to a sitting position and started bouncing up and down in bed. "Only there's this indoor snow place and you can do 4WD tours through the desert and watch camel races. Dad said Christmas decorations in some of the hotels and malls are even better than here."

Erica stiffened. So Jeff wasn't above using emotional blackmail. For a moment she was angry enough to want to say, "Screw your father." Except… She bit back the hot words. Their son needed his dad more than she needed the last word. "Bring me back the star," she said. "The one the three wise men followed."

He giggled, flopped on his back. "That's silly…how about some sand from the desert?"

That was pretty much the taste in her mouth right now. "Yeah, sand…lots of different colors. Give me a hug." Erica buried her face in Will's fine hair, breathed him in and then released him. Above all she wanted to raise a happy, well-adjusted child. One secure in the knowledge that at least one of his parents could always be relied on to put his interests first.

"Time for sleep, big guy." She tucked him in as calmly

as she always did. Tomorrow they'd discuss the house sale; tomorrow she'd spin it as their latest, greatest adventure. Not tonight. "Good night, sweetie."

He snuggled under the covers. "'Night, Mum."

Erica closed the door quietly, then rested her forehead against it. Reminded herself that it was the season of giving. Giving, even when it hurt.

CHAPTER SEVEN

THROUGH THE LIVING-ROOM WINDOW, Mike saw the courier's van pull up to the sidewalk. Dave jumped out, leaving the engine running. Rolling off the couch, Mike grabbed the software package and walked out to meet him.

"How's it going, mate?" Dave had the staccato delivery and bouncing gait of a man permanently in a hurry.

Mike gave the standard Kiwi bloke reply. "Good, mate."

Dave took a closer look at him as he accepted the parcel. "Jeez, you look knackered. Pulled another all-nighter for this one?"

"Up all night yeah...and beat." He'd worked eighteen-hour days since Wednesday to meet this deadline. "I can go to bed now you've picked up."

Dave gestured to the street. "It's looking pretty around here, eh?"

Mike refocused on his surroundings. While he'd been lost in the virtual world, his neighborhood had been transformed.

Houses, fences, trees...anything over three feet high seemed to have been light-nuked. He shaded his eyes against the glare of silver tinsel in the sun and winced. "Fairyland on steroids more like."

Dave laughed. "I'll be bringing the ankle-biters for Light-Up tomorrow night." Dave jogged around to the driver's door. "See ya then, mate." The van roared off in a cloud of diesel fumes.

No, you won't. Mike had booked himself into a hotel for two nights to avoid the festivities. A couple of hours' sleep then he'd throw some clothes together and be out of here. Across the road, Aurora waved. Two male helpers were hauling a dangling Santa and his sleigh up onto her bungalow's roof. "Left a bit, boys. Watch the antlers."

As he cleared his mailbox of Christmas junk mail, Erica's red Fiesta turned into the street. Mike moved the traffic cones that residents used to block off parking space outside their houses, conscious of his unshaven jaw and general dishevelment.

But Erica got out of the car looking equally exhausted. That was Christmas for you. "Thanks, Mike."

He handed her the traffic cones. "Any more offers on the house yet?"

"It's only been on the market four days. Give it a chance." She wore a sleeveless sheath dress the same rich brown as her eyes and higher heels than usual. "Are you that eager to get rid of us?"

"Only so I can avoid paying my debt to your brat," he said easily. "I owe Will eight bucks for plums."

She took a minute to answer, opening the trunk and restacking the cones next to two bags of shopping. "It'll have to wait two weeks. I just dropped him off at the airport."

Pulling out his wallet, Mike paused. "The airport?"

Erica kept her head down. "Will's spending Christmas in Dubai with Jeff."

Mike stared at her back. "You're kidding."

Shrugging, she removed the grocery bags, closed the trunk. "The opportunity came up. It seemed crazy not to take it."

"But you've been putting so much effort into making it a good Christmas for him."

"You're the *last* person I'd have expected to give weight to the trappings." Her eyes skipped past his like a pebble on a pond. Instinctively, he knew what this selflessness must have cost her.

"Let me carry those for you."

"They're not heavy."

Ignoring her protests, Mike took the grocery bags and walked Erica to her door. On her porch, an artificial Christmas tree stood half-assembled, and giving the impression of having been attacked by a chainsaw.

Erica moved it out of the way. "Will ran out of time to finish it before we had to leave." She unlocked the door, and then reached for her groceries. "Thanks. I can manage from here."

Somehow he couldn't walk away. "So what are you going to do instead? For Christmas."

"Follow your example," she said cheerfully. "Only instead of thrillers and beer I'll rent half a dozen romantic comedies and work my way through a box of chocolates."

Dammit, this felt all wrong. Mike jammed his hands in his jean pockets. No one who invested so much energy making Christmas special for others should have to spend it alone.

"It's just a day in the calendar same as any other," she added, smiling.

He wished she'd stop repeating his words back to him. "Does it sound that lame when I say it?" he asked irritably.

A real smile flashed in her eyes. "Lamer. But I'm fine about spending Christmas without Will. Really. Now go to bed, Mike. You look like you're practically falling over with exhaustion."

In the face of all that impenetrable pluckiness he was helpless. So Mike did what Erica was doing and pretended he was fine. He went home, showered, shaved and crawled into bed. And tossed and turned for half an hour.

ERICA SHUT THE DOOR ON MIKE and leaned against it. Why did one swift glance of understanding from the Grinch threaten to undo her?

She realized she was squeezing the bags too hard—that wouldn't be good for the bananas—swallowed her tears and went into the kitchen where she unpacked her groceries. The flurry of activity to get Will ready over the past few days had left the house a bomb site. Good. Cleaning would keep her busy.

Putting the kettle on for tea, she ate the last cookie in the tin. She could stop baking Christmas treats now, maybe even lose a couple of pounds.

Her gaze drifted to the kitchen clock as she dropped a teabag into her cup then poured in boiling water. Will would've been in the air three hours by now. Finished his meal, he'd be engrossed in an in-flight game or movie.

While her tea steeped, she went into the laundry room and put in a load of washing, holding Will's pajamas close for a moment. The only time he'd wavered was saying his final goodbye. "You're gonna have so much fun!" Erica had enthused. "Remember, I want lots of pictures of Nana on a camel."

Jeff's mother had looked at Will's wobbly lip, then at Erica, furiously blinking back tears. "Only if we can find one without a hump."

Will burst out laughing. "Nana, there's no such thing."

"Maybe I'm thinking of an elephant," said Nana. "Well, I won't be riding one of those, either."

"Naaana, there's no elephants in Dubai."

Deftly, the older woman had steered her grandson toward the departure gate. "Just as well I've got you to tell me how things work there."

"Bye, Mum. We'll phone when we get there."

Erica checked the time again on her wristwatch and did the math. Seventeen hours, thirty-nine minutes' flight time. Add two hours for customs and immigration and the drive to Jeff's and—

She caught herself. Obsessing.

She dumped Will's pajamas in the washing machine and turned it on. As she wandered back to the kitchen, her cell rang. And even though she'd just worked out she wouldn't hear from Will for another fourteen and a half hours, Erica's pulse skipped. *Idiot.*

Checking caller ID, she saw Vonnie's number and let call answer pick up. The house wasn't tidy enough for potential buyers and Erica wasn't in the mood for wheedling, however well intentioned. On second thought she wasn't in the mood for cleaning, either.

Instead she picked up her mug of tea and went upstairs to her bedroom where one corner had been set up as an office. She'd get ahead on a couple of freelance assignments, she decided as she sat down at her computer desk, including an article on making Christmas ornaments. Which reminded her of the half-erected tree on the porch. Erica stood up, then sat down again. For God's sake just settle to *something.*

She glanced over to Mike's office while she waited for her laptop to power up. *Now you're just being pathetic.* Forcing herself to concentrate, Erica lifted her fingers to the keyboard.

Christmas decorations don't have to be expensive. If you get the kids involved...

She paused to gulp tea and burned her tongue. Tears in her eyes—from the burn, nothing else—she resumed typing.

...in making decorations that will end up treasured mementos.

Erica worked through dinner, sustained by a bag of nacho chips that she ate at her desk. Her cell rang—Vonnie again—and she ignored it, caught in a flurry of nervous productivity. At nine she'd finished two articles. "See," she said aloud, "this isn't so hard."

Surreptitiously she checked her watch. Only five and a half hours before Will called to say he'd arrived safely. "I don't care that it's 3:30 a.m. here," she'd told Jeff's mother. "Phone anyway."

Feeling less fragile, Erica turned on her cell and cleared Vonnie's messages.

The estate agent's voice bubbled with excitement. "You're not going to believe this but you've had an offer... for the asking price! And there's more good news—"

Erica deleted the message.

This is good news, she chided herself. Great news. She forced herself to listen to Vonnie's second message. "Well, I guess I'll hear from you tomorrow and we'll celebrate the sale then." There was disappointment in the agent's tone. "Incidentally they *love* what you've done with your Christmas lights—particularly the waterfall from the top story—and absolutely *adore* the hominess of the place."

Erica rose from her desk and went to the window. By mutual consent, Lincoln Road residents didn't switch on their festive outside lights until tomorrow but you could still catch a glimpse of indoor Christmas trees, blinking red, green and silver, all tinsel and sparkle and magic.

Will away for Christmas and now they were moving.

CHAPTER EIGHT

MIKE'S DREAM ALWAYS STARTED the same. He was in bed with the flu, irritated by a continual pounding on the front door.

"Diana, you answering that?"

There was never a reply. Dragging himself out of his sickbed, he stumbled to the top of the stairs. Red lights flashed through the downstairs windows and pulsed on the white walls, as pretty as Christmas—until Mike realized what caused it.

Fear clawing at him, he slowly opened the door. A black silhouette turned against a snowy backdrop, badge glinting, police car behind him. "Mr. Ward?"

Mike jerked himself out of the dream and woke with pulse hammering and the sweaty sheets tangled around his body. His shout still reverberated in the dark bedroom. Kicking off the sheet, he swung his feet to the floor to ground himself.

Wiping sweat off his brow—the room was stifling—he caught sight of the luminous bedside clock and cursed: 9:20 p.m. The hotel had been expecting him to check in around three. Before calling them, he opened a window and let the coolness swathe his naked torso.

Erica's curtains were open. She sat on her bed, the lamp casting her shadow across the wall behind her. The grief from his dream was still so raw that for a moment Mike didn't see anything unusual about her posture—head bowed, arms hugging her knees. Then he sucked in a sharp breath.

She was crying.

He turned away. Heartache was private. And she'd already made her position clear. No sympathy. He'd always hated it, too. He rang hotel reception and reconfirmed his booking, and then showered, packed some clothes and left the house.

Don't look, he told himself as he walked past Erica's. Do. Not. Look. Mike looked but the angle was wrong. Nothing to see of her bedroom window but a sliver of light. He dumped his bag in the Z4.

She'd feel better tomorrow. Hell, she'd probably stopped crying by now anyway. He started the powerful engine, listened to the throaty purr of freedom. In half an hour he'd be a stranger among strangers—just how he liked it. So why couldn't he release the handbrake? Shit.

Mike cut the engine. Furious, he slammed out of the car, bounded up Erica's steps and jabbed her doorbell. Waited one minute, then two. He stepped back to check her bedroom window. She'd turned off the light. Even madder, he stabbed the doorbell again. "Erica!" he bellowed through the keyhole. "I know you're awake. Let me in."

"Go away."

Mike held the doorbell down.

Over the buzzer, he heard the thud of feet on the stairs. A light went on. Erica wrenched open the door. "What the hell do you want!" Brown eyes puffy, tearstains on her cheeks. A worn pink dressing gown clutched over that pretty brown dress.

Without a word Mike stepped inside, kicked the door closed and took her into his arms. Erica stiffened, then collapsed against him, a soft, sweet bundle of misery. "It's so hard," she wept. "It's all so hard."

"I know." Her arms tightened around his waist, she buried her face in his shoulder and cried and cried. *Oh, God, I know.*

"I *hate* doing the right thing," she wailed.

Mike rubbed her back and murmured consoling sounds. Because that's all this was. Comfort. After several minutes Erica pulled away and wiped her eyes dry with the back of her hand. "You were right to question my motives about the lights," she said bitterly. "I wasn't thinking about the greater good, I was just trying to impress my son."

She gave a choked laugh. "And now Will's not here, I don't give a damn about Christmas." Pulling a tissue out of the pocket of her dressing gown, she blew her nose hard. "I've been a hypocrite all along."

"You're not a hypocrite, you're a giver. And we both know you'll be back magic-making tomorrow. You can't help yourself." Her dark hair was tangled; Mike combed it back with his fingers, in a gesture too tender for her to ignore. Erica looked up, a question in her eyes—and an invitation.

Mike's hand tightened on her nape. Don't kiss her. Do. Not. Kiss. Her.

He lowered his head. Savored her warm lips, salty with tears. Erica quivered then wrapped her arms around his neck and kissed him back. And every defense he'd protected himself with for three long years crumbled away.

He needed to think but he could only feel. Her mouth, so sweet on his, the heat of her body. It had been so long. Gathering her closer, he pushed the dressing gown off her shoulders and deepened the kiss. Her hands slid under his T-shirt, played down his spine.

Mike groaned and stroked her bare arms. Her breasts pressed against him. Breaking the kiss, he rested his forehead against Erica's. They were both breathing hard. "I don't want to take advantage of you."

She laughed huskily and kissed the corner of his mouth. "I do."

He forced himself to pull back. "I have to tell you something first." *Before I do something we might both regret.*

"You're married," she joked. Then saw his expression and the teasing in her eyes faded. "Mike?"

"Sit down," he said. "Sit down, and let me tell you why I really hate Christmas."

NOT KNOWING WHAT TO THINK, Erica opened the door to the living room where the fragrant pine Christmas tree twinkled through its light-play patterns. She switched on a floor lamp. Its soft glow cast enough light to see, but not enough to expose either of them. Then she curled up on the couch and waited.

Mike remained standing. "My wife died December 4, three years ago," he said abruptly. "We were married ten years."

Everything Erica had surmised about his past—commitment-shy maverick—changed. The condolence sounded so paltry compared to the immense sympathy she felt for him. "I'm so sorry." She'd always sensed there was more to Mike than met the eye. What had always attracted her were the qualities of kindness and concern he couldn't quite hide from her and Will. This explained so much.

"I was in bed with the flu," he said, "and Diana insisted on going out to pick up supplies...lemons, cough medicine. Where I come from—Vermont—icy roads are standard in winter. Locals know how to drive according to the conditions. The Florida driver who hit her car didn't."

He seemed to realize his impassive tone didn't match his stance—hunched shoulders, hands jammed in pockets. Mike straightened and freed his hands, only to fold his arms. Erica could imagine the regrets he tortured himself with.

"I found out she was six weeks pregnant through the autopsy. She'd probably been saving the news as a present. We'd been trying awhile."

She thought of Mike's patient good humor over Will's pranks, of him quietly repairing her son's bike. Erica said slowly, "No wonder you avoid Christmas."

He sat beside her, fixing his gaze on the tree. The bulbs winked through their sequence—all the greens, all the golds, all the blues. In every color she saw the sadness etched on his face.

"I came to New Zealand because I was tired of pretending to friends and family I was getting over it." One corner of Mike's mouth twisted. "And they needed a break, too. I have a lot of relatives. Every other week there's a birth, engagement or wedding anniversary.

When I was around they reined in their celebrations. I didn't want them to feel guilty about being happy, but at the same time pretending I was over losing Diana and our baby felt like disloyalty."

Another piece fell into place. "Did you feel disloyal when you kissed me?"

Mike picked up her hand, holding it lightly. "When I date again it will be for sex and companionship, not love and commitment. That part of my life is over. And if I can't offer you at least the possibility of a future…" he raised her hand to his lips then returned it to Erica's lap "…then I shouldn't be here."

Lately, her life seemed to be about goodbyes. To her marriage, her home. And this morning, her son. Now Erica said goodbye to a hope she'd had for Mike that she hadn't acknowledged until now.

"Stay anyway," she said.

He blinked. "You don't mean that."

The house had sold; she and Will would be leaving soon. And Erica was so tired of doing the right thing, of putting everyone else's needs before her own. "You're lonely," she said. "So am I. We want each other. I only have one condition—no regrets tomorrow."

It was the vulnerability behind Erica's bravado that defeated Mike; that roused a dangerous tenderness. And when she swallowed convulsively, suggesting she was bracing herself for rejection, he was lost. Because once he'd been good at giving, too.

Leaning forward, he slid his fingers through the silky mass of Erica's hair to massage the nape of her neck. Her shoulders relaxed, she closed her eyes. With his other hand, Mike brushed his thumb across her mouth, tilted up at the corners. "Are you sure this is what you want?"

Erica opened her eyes. For once he couldn't read her. "Yes." She led him upstairs to her bed.

Seeing it, lust clashed uneasily with his guilt. He'd met Diana at college and she'd been the only one for him.

"You can change your mind," Erica said softly, perceptively.

But Diana wasn't the only reason for his hesitation. "I'm new to this."

"Me, too," Erica admitted.

A pulse throbbed at her throat; he pressed his lips to it. Fast, it beat too fast—she was nervous, too. The realization steadied him. He wasn't the only one taking a risk here.

Slowly, Mike began to undress her, pausing to kiss every silky inch he uncovered. "You're beautiful, Erica," he murmured. All that mattered right now was making her see herself the way he did—as special.

And she was so responsive, quivering under his caresses. Her hint of surprise at his unhurried exploration only intensified Mike's tenderness. Why hadn't her husband appreciated her like this...how could anyone walk away from her?

He stalled on the thought, conscious of the new danger she represented. Naked, Erica leaned forward, her long hair falling across her breasts. Closing his eyes on a groan, Mike lost his train of thought in the heavy throbbing need of his body, in the teasing flicks of her tongue as she played her way down his torso. It had been so long. So long since he'd been touched.

And so long since he'd laid with a woman in his arms,

skin to skin. Erica's breasts smooth and full with tight nipples brushed his chest.

In thrall, he sloped a hand down her ribs to the indent of her waist and lower across the feminine curve of her hips and rounded bottom, reveling in her arousal. Reveling in the way her back arched when he suckled her, in her sharp indrawn breath when he circled her inner thighs with light strokes that made her open for him.

For the first time in three years Mike forgot himself for someone else. And the more he gave her, the less empty he felt.

When he thrust into her, every boundary dissolved. For a moment he seemed to hang suspended. Then Erica lifted her hips to welcome him and life began again, rising in a joyous surge that swept them into orgasm.

Afterward they lay spent, every muscle relaxed, every tension gone. Mike didn't know what he felt, only that he wanted to surrender to this rare peace. But as he moved to draw Erica closer she sat up, a shadowy figure, hair tumbling over her shoulders. Her soft lips brushed his. "Thank you," she said. "That was lovely."

Lovely? It was incredible. Extraordinary.

"It's 3:30 and Will should be calling any time." She reached for her clothes and started dressing. "It's probably better if you're not here."

She was protecting herself. Like he'd told her to. "Erica, I—"

"Don't say anything." Touching a finger to his lips, she smiled. "Don't ruin it."

Nodding, he sat up and reached for his jeans. No, she was right. He already felt too much for her. They finished dressing in silence, and then Erica led him downstairs.

As he stepped out on the porch, he activated the outside light, making them both blink. Their eyes met.

Wordlessly, they embraced and he resisted the urge to bury his face in her hair. Her arms tightened briefly around his waist.

"I don't know if this will help reconcile you to Diana's death, but have you ever thought…" Releasing him, Erica shook her head. "It doesn't matter."

"Have I ever thought what?"

She took a deep breath. "How lucky you were to have loved and been loved like that." Standing on tiptoe she kissed his cheek, then went inside and closed the door.

Mike stood dumbstruck.

Lucky? Dazed, he started walking home, incredulity growing with every step. Was Erica crazy? He'd lost his wife, for God's sake, his unborn child. She obviously had no understanding what it was like to lose someone. He shoved open his gate. Dorothy's obnoxious tabby, Matilda, had taken possession of his porch and hissed as he approached. "Don't push it," he growled.

Matilda shot off the porch and up the fence with a scrabble of fat hind legs. Slamming the door behind him, Mike made himself a Scotch on the rocks then sprawled on his couch feeling scratchy and irritable and offended, just like that damn tabby.

"Oh yeah, I'm the luckiest guy in the world, all right!"

Through the family-room window, the star on Erica's roof was a black silhouette against the bright moon. Mike scowled and took another slug of his drink. "And there's no such thing as magic," he said. There was a thud outside. Could have been a dead fairy hitting the ground, more likely it was Matilda reclaiming the porch.

He shouldn't have slept with Erica. Sex with a woman other than his wife had only released the emotions he'd held at bay for three years. Anger, guilt, grief, confusion—and another emotion that scared the hell out of him.

Groaning, Mike leaned forward and dropped his head in his hands. No, he loved Diana; he couldn't feel like this about another woman. Suddenly he felt as if he'd cheated both of them—Diana *and* Erica.

A bitter laugh escaped him. He was no better than Erica's louse of an ex-husband.

Except that…

Mike suddenly saw the point Erica had been trying to make.

They were both coping with the end of a marriage—Mike through bereavement, Erica through divorce. But as devastating as his loss had been, he and Diana had been happy. He'd never had to suffer the slow painful loss of hopes and dreams. The loss of love.

And yet Erica still believed in love. He'd been the one to give up on it.

Emptying his Scotch down the sink Mike headed for the spare room, finding what he was looking for at the top of the wardrobe. Erica didn't deserve halfhearted and he couldn't offer her more.

But there was something he could do to make her happy.

CHAPTER NINE

ERICA TOOK ANOTHER SIP of her coffee, tightened the cord of her dressing gown and steeled herself to ask Vonnie the critical question. "So—" she sucked in a breath "—when do the new owners want to take possession?"

"What do you mean, take possession?" Vonnie drank coffee like she sold houses. Fast. "I explained all that on the voice mail."

The one Erica had deleted. "Tell me again." She refilled the agent's cup. The woman was impeccably dressed and made up, despite it being Sunday.

Vonnie added two sugars and stirred vigorously. "They want you to stay on as a tenant, at least for another year until they can move back to New Zealand."

Erica's spirits soared, then plummeted. She'd slept with Mike as a goodbye. Did she really want the daily torture of living next to a man she couldn't have?

"I thought you'd be thrilled."

Erica hid her face in her cup, breathed in the fragrant aroma of roasted coffee beans. *Hey, it was your choice to sleep with him. No regrets.* "That depends on the rent," she hedged.

Vonnie sat back and beamed. "A thousand a month."

Only half her current mortgage payment. Erica's cup

landed in the saucer with a clatter. She stared at the agent. "That's crazy."

"I *know,*" Vonnie said gleefully. "But they want someone who'll look after the place as if it was their own."

They obviously don't know the going rate. Erica's conscience kicked in. "Tell them I'll pay thirteen hundred."

It was Vonnie's turn to stare. "If they're happy, don't quibble." When Erica started to argue she held up a hand. "It's my job to look after your interests. Trust me, he's—the husband's—perfectly capable of looking after theirs."

"I could save money on that rent," Erica said slowly. She could barely imagine the security of that. On impulse she leaned forward and pressed the agent's hand. "Thanks, Vonnie."

The other woman cleared her throat. "Don't mention it." She gulped down her second coffee. "Anyway, I'd better go. My ex is dropping the kids off in an hour. But I'll be bringing them over for Light-Up tonight."

The reminder galvanized Erica. So much to do before then. As she walked Vonnie out she mentally ran through her checklist. Finish assembling the porch Christmas tree; pick up lollipops for Phil's Santa sack; help set up the hot-chocolate stall and sausage sizzle.

Vonnie paused at the hall mirror to check her appearance. "Mike's lights look great, incidentally."

"What?" Erica opened her front door and stalled. Her exterior Christmas tree was up. Astonished, she turned to Mike's house. All Burt's displays were up…icicle lights followed every roofline, electric Bambi ate grass in the front yard. And Mike sat on the swing seat stroking Dorothy's purring cat.

He glanced up and instinctively she looked away. No, no, *no!* They were supposed to act cool about this, no embarrassment, no regrets. Meeting his eyes, Erica smiled a casual hello, ignoring her hammering pulse.

"Wow, Mike!" Vonnie called. "What did Erica have to do in the end to persuade you?"

Heat swept across Erica's cheeks. Mike returned his attention to the cat. "I guess I just saw the light," he replied. But she'd already seen the truth.

The moment Vonnie left, she headed next door, not caring that she was still in her dressing gown. Mike smiled tentatively as she approached. More astute, Matilda leaped off his lap and disappeared under the house. "So." He gestured to the lights. "What do you think?"

Erica picked up a bundle of leftover bulbs on the path and threw them at him.

He caught them midair. "What the—?"

"Don't you dare make me regret last night." She ignored the fact that *she'd* been regretting it all morning.

Clutching the bundle of bulbs, he blinked. "What?"

"I don't need your pity, mate!"

"I'm trying to do something nice for you here."

"Bullshit." She contemplated wrapping the lights around his neck and strangling him with them. "You feel guilty in case you hurt me. If you want to regret last night, fine. But don't try and second-guess *my* reactions."

"Look—"

"No, *you* look. You made your position perfectly clear at the time. If I was still stupid enough to risk a broken heart that's my business. Got that?" Without waiting for an answer Erica spun on her heel. "Though guys with as much to offer as you do have no right giving up," she flung over her shoulder.

Mike stared after her. Okay, that wasn't the reaction he'd been expecting. He glanced down at the bulbs in his hands. He wanted to laugh. Erica had been so magnificently honest while he'd sat gaping like a goddamn goldfish. She loved him?

But mostly, he wanted to hide. Guess that wasn't an option anymore.

He went inside and walked around his empty house. Last night, after hanging the lights, he'd spring-cleaned the place, dumping all the alcohol he'd been using to anesthetize his grief. He was ready to move on. Maybe even invest in some new curtains.

Pausing at the window, he looked across to Erica's house and yard where he'd often watched her gardening or Will playing. It was so obvious now. He hadn't got curtains because observing their lives, their comings and goings, had given him a sense of connection to the outside world.

He'd thought that peace would come from isolation when what he really needed to do was reengage.

Mike pulled Diana's picture out of a chest of drawers, feeling the familiar cocktail of sadness, guilt and angry helplessness. He expected to get over his wife's death. Of course he did. He refused to be a victim. But asking him to love someone like he'd loved Diana was like asking a burn victim to walk across hot coals.

"The trouble is," he told his wife's smiling face, "Erica is too easy to love."

He searched her eyes for a response but she was frozen now in time and place, in memory. She was gone.

Until her death everything in Mike's life had come easy to him, even love. When Diana had offered to go to the store in bad weather for a cold remedy he hadn't even thought to stop her. Why hadn't he?

Because he'd been a man who took too much for granted—thoughtlessly selfish. His throat tightened. "I'm sorry, honey," he said. "I'm so sorry."

He touched Diana's face. It was time to stop holding on to his grief like a miser. "Erica was right," he murmured. "We were lucky." Gently, he returned her photograph to the drawer.

He was still lucky. Because life had not only miraculously given him another chance to be happy, it had given him a woman who deserved and needed the kind of commitment he was good at.

ERICA HAD HER RESPONSE prepared when an hour later Mike said quietly over the back fence, "We need to talk."

But she still had to fight the urge to wrap herself in the sheet she was hanging on the line. Unable to look at him, she pegged one corner. "I overreacted, I'm sorry." Another peg, another corner secured. "Hanging Burt's lights was a lovely gesture…thank you."

"Erica—"

"And maybe I am a little wobbly over last night but—" pulling a funny face, she grabbed a pillowcase "—I certainly didn't mean to imply that my feelings run deeper than friendship." She laughed and it sounded just like she wanted it to—wry, sophisticated, tolerant. Encouraged, she flapped the pillowcase to unfurl it. "And it *certainly* doesn't mean that..." Her panties flew across the yard.

The ones Mike had removed last night.

"Certainly doesn't mean that..." she repeated, eyeing the pink hearts and purple lace. Should she pick them up? Ignore them? Mike climbed the fence, retrieved her underwear and handed them to her.

"I love you," he said. "And I'm through fighting it."

The breeze caught the sheet, flapped it around her bare legs. "God, I am so sick of reluctance!" Erica shoved the panties in the pocket of her red skirt and returned to pegging the pillowcase.

"Excuse me?"

She picked up a tea towel and another two pegs. The hot pink plastic had faded to a prawn color, ugly against the orange cotton. "When Jeff proposed he said, 'I hadn't planned on getting married but I know it's the only way I'll keep you.' What is it with men that they have to be dragged kicking and screaming into loving me?"

Mike raked a hand through his hair. "I've put this badly but I didn't mean—"

"I've already carried one relationship," she said. "I'm not carrying another."

"I come with a good track record," he said.

Erica remembered how much he loved his late wife. "Mike, I ended up sharing Jeff with another woman. I can't do that again."

"You won't have to." His voice was gentle.

If there was only herself to consider she might have taken a risk on Mike's sudden change of heart, but she had Will. And he'd had enough upheaval in his young life.

"No, you were right the first time," she said. "Last night was a mistake."

She left him there, standing in her garden. Shut the back door on him. Grabbing her purse she walked straight through the house, out the front door and to her car. She'd drive to the supermarket, buy the lollipops for the Santa sack.

"Good job, Erica!" Phil hailed her as she fumbled to unlock her car door. He crossed the road with Dorothy, whose bony face bore an uncharacteristic smile. They were busy distributing stopwatches to ensure every resident switched their lights on at the same time. He slapped Erica on the back. "You whipped Mike Ward into line."

She frowned. "It's not about winning or losing, Phil."

"Of course not." Grinning, he exchanged a high five with Dorothy.

Erica drove away, dismayed. Mike would have known they'd react like this, yet he'd still put up his lights. For her.

She was so confused.

She stayed away as long as she could, sitting in her car in the supermarket parking lot and numbly watching the Sunday shoppers staggering past with bulging bags of turkeys and wine.

And if she cried a little at how badly she'd messed up, there was no one to see her.

CHAPTER TEN

"WE'RE IN TROUBLE," AURORA said as she dumped the candy-filled Santa sack beside the barbecue where Erica was cooking sausages.

The crowds had grown as twilight deepened and so had the buzz of anticipation. The aroma of sizzling meat and hot chocolate mingled pleasantly with the strains of "Hark the Herald Angels Sing" from the choristers outside Number Twenty-four.

"Phil put his back out hauling on his Santa boots." Aurora picked up a knife and began buttering more bread, adding slices to the diminished pile. "He says there's no way he can 'ho ho ho' tonight. Mike had to carry him to bed."

"Then we need to find a replacement quickly." Frazzled, Erica grabbed the tongs and moved the cooked onion rings to a cooler part of the grill and tried not to think of Mike. Or being carried to bed. Or anything that might make her break down and sob like a baby.

"I tried that— Yes, love?" Aurora addressed the first person in the queue for a sausage sizzle. "Two orders with onion, mustard and ketchup? That's four dollars, please." She turned back to Erica and said in a low voice, "I took Phil's Santa suit up and down the street like Cinderella's bloody glass slipper. The only Lincoln Road residents who fit it were boys or women."

"And the kids will see through that." Erica rolled the cooked sausages in bread and added the condiments, racking her brains for alternative Santas to fill Phil's specially made suit. Adding bulk was easy, but his short stature posed a problem.

Scanning the crowd for a five-foot-four male of the rotund variety, she picked out a muscular six-foot-two male with wide shoulders carrying a cooler and heading in their direction. She wiped suddenly sweaty palms on her apron.

"Thanks for carrying that for me, Mike," said Aurora. "You're always rescuing this damsel in distress. Erica, where do you want the extra supplies?"

"Um, over here would be great...behind the barbecue." Erica dared to glance at Mike's face but saw nothing in his impassive expression to suggest that he'd been rejected with panicky ineptitude only hours earlier.

"Don't worry," he muttered as he put down the cooler, "I'm not going to hassle you. I might be an insensitive ass but I'm not a jerk."

"Mike, I..." Erica stopped. She was a mass of contradictory impulses and right now she couldn't deal with any of them. "Thank you," she said awkwardly.

"No problem. Aurora." With a polite nod he left.

The smell of burning onion rings dragged Erica's attention back to the barbecue. "Okay," she croaked, shoveling them onto a plate. "We'll just have to do without Santa this year. I'll hand out the candy when we finish here."

Her cell rang. Digging it out of her apron, Erica checked caller ID and scrambled to answer it. "Will!"

"I want to count down to Light-Up with you."

"What a lovely idea." Erica's heavy heart lifted. "But we've still got ten minutes. Tell me what you did today."

"A camel spat at Nana," he said with satisfaction.

She laughed. They talked for ten minutes, while Erica turned the sausages and onions on the barbecue, and Aurora filled orders.

"I'm having a good time but I miss you, Mum. Do you miss me?"

Terribly. "You know I do…oh…the crowd's started countdown." Because she and Aurora were manning the sausage sizzle, other neighbors were switching on their lights. "Ten…nine…eight." Erica caught Aurora's hand. "Count with us, Will. Three…two…one…Light-Up!"

Every house in the street sparked into life in a twinkling 3-D spectacle of multicolored magic. The crowd aahed.

"Does it look pretty, Mum?"

"Beautiful, Will." Erica blinked away tears. *Even in the bad times you can still believe in something. You can still make magic.* At least, for other people. As one-handed, she hugged Aurora, a small child tugged on Erica's apron.

"One sausage, please. *No* yucky onions or mustard."

"Will, honey, I've got to go. I'll call you back later." Returning the cell to her apron, Erica filled the child's order. Beside her, Aurora suddenly stopped buttering bread and stared.

"Isn't that Burt's old Santa suit?"

Erica glanced up. Santa strode toward her, tall, round-bellied, but with an athleticism in his step that belied the fluffy white beard and matching eyebrows.

Her mouth fell open. As he came closer she saw the suit was short around the ankles and wrists, and straining across the shoulders.

"Give me the damn candy," said Mike, "and don't say a word." Stunned, she handed over the Santa sack. He swung it over his shoulder and headed off into the crowd, attracting kids like the Pied Piper.

Erica bent over the barbecue, hoping her streaming eyes would be attributed to the smoke and onions.

"If you don't take him, I will," said Aurora. "Some men you just don't pass up."

"I got over Jeff," Erica said thickly, wiping her eyes. "But I guess I'm not over what he did to my trust in men. All I could think when Mike said he had a great track record was, 'I don't want to be second-best to your late wife.'"

"The man's in a Santa suit for you. *After* you rejected him." Aurora took the tongs from Erica and turned over some sausages that were burning. "If that's not unconditional love, honey, I don't know what is."

Erica gave a watery laugh. "Can you hold the fort for ten minutes?"

"That's my girl."

Pulling off her apron, Erica walked through the crowds searching for Mike, her task more difficult because the brilliantly lit houses made the shadowy figures milling on the road harder to identify. Erica was so intent on finding Mike that she didn't notice Vonnie until the woman stopped right in front of her.

"Erica, I've said hello twice!"

"Hey," she replied, reining in her impatience. "You made it."

Vonnie drew two children forward. "These are my kids, Sasha and Simon. Guys, this is the lady who lives in the house with waterfall lights."

The kids looked at Erica with respect. "You are *so* lucky," Sasha said.

Erica smiled. "Sometimes you have to make your luck. Right, Vonnie?"

"You said it."

"Mum, there's Santa." Sasha tugged on her mother's jacket. "Can we go see him?"

Erica's pulse began to race. "Where?"

"Over by that hedge." Sasha pointed. "Can we, Mum?"

"Go ahead," Vonnie replied. "I'll be there in a minute. Since when did Santa get a makeover?" she asked Erica. Then her eyes widened. "Is that Mike?"

"Yes." Erica wavered. She couldn't declare her love for Santa in front of all these kids. They'd get confused. Worry about Mrs. Claus. She'd have to wait for the candy to run out.

Vonnie pulled out a camera and started snapping, reminding Erica of a question she'd been meaning to ask. "How did the people who bought my house know about my waterfall lights? They weren't in the pictures you posted on the agency's website."

"Weren't they?" Vonnie fumbled with the aperture. "You, know, I really can't remember."

The woman had a memory like a steel trap. Erica got suspicious. "Who bought my house?" A trust had been the other party to the contract. She couldn't recall the signature.

"I can't tell you. He...they made me promise not to. My kids are wandering off, I'd better go."

A fantastic suspicion entered Erica's mind. She caught the agent's arm. "Vonnie, please."

"Erica, I promised." Vonnie looked at her pleading face and relented. "Let's just say *Santa* came early this year." With a wink, she followed her children.

Sorry, Mrs. Claus, this can't wait. Erica pushed her way through the throng. "Excuse me...important message for Santa...from the North Pole. Coming through."

Breathless, she reached Mike. "Santa, come with me please. It's okay, kids, he'll be back soon. We just need to refill the candy sack." She dragged Santa through a hedge into Number Sixty-two's garden.

"When did you buy my house?" she demanded.

"Who said I bought it?"

"Mike!"

"After the Munsters visited. You made me realize how important it was to get good neighbors."

"But you're poor."

"No, I'm scruffy." Green eyes narrowed under white fluffy eyebrows. "And if you're going to fall into my arms from gratitude, don't. You're not the only one with pride issues."

She clutched his sleeves. "I was going to fall into your arms anyway."

"Uh-huh," he said skeptically.

Erica punched his pillow belly. "Look, you're not the only one with emotional history here. I might have got over Jeff but that doesn't mean I'm jumping for joy at falling in love with you. In fact, I'd say we're both terrified. Now shut up and kiss me, Santa."

He kissed her.

The beard tickled and they both ended up with cotton batting in their mouths. Neither cared.

EPILOGUE

Christmas Eve. A year later.

LATE-NIGHT TRAFFIC JAMS were one of the drawbacks of living on Lincoln Road during Christmas Light-Up. Which was why Erica really tried to be in bed well before that. On the other hand when you'd forgotten the cranberries for the turkey stuffing there wasn't much the cook could do but brave the tailgaters.

Her Ford Fiesta inched down the street, taking a full five minutes to pass Number Eight. It said a lot about how busy she'd been that Erica was grateful for this brief respite. Pumping up both the air-conditioning and the carol music she belted out "Good King Wenceslas," smiling as she came within sight of the house, still under renovation, with light cascades hanging off the scaffolding. Okay, they'd had to improvise this year.

A new section of two bedrooms over a double garage now joined her house with Mike's and made one spacious family home. And they needed it. Through the lit windows she could see the living room brimming with people—Mike's family, hers. All staying on after the wedding to celebrate Christmas.

At last Erica reached her driveway. Tooting to alert the hordes of pedestrians, she turned into the garage.

Mike came out of the house to help. "I knew you'd end up with more than cranberries," he said, taking the bag of groceries from the trunk. "What's in here, anyway?"

"Hey, no peeking until tomorrow," she ordered. Maybe she'd added a stocking filler or two.

Together, they walked out of the garage. A family group had stopped to take pictures of the house. "I just love what you've done with your lights," enthused the woman with a camera. "You must have twenty thousand bulbs at least."

"Thirty," said Mike resignedly, "at least."

Erica had talked him into it—and into helping her set them up.

"Oh, you're American." The woman nodded. "That explains it."

Erica burst out laughing.

"Yep." Keeping a straight face, her new husband put his arm around her. "And you know how we like to go overboard at Christmas."

* * * * *

Watch for HERE COMES THE GROOM
by Karina Bliss—
the first in a new series featuring SAS heros—
out January 2011.